Kuroda Josui

EIJI YOSHIKAWA

SHELLEY MARSHALL
(TRANSLATOR)

CONTENTS

CHAPTER ONE
THE BEEHIVE

1

IN THE SHADOW OF the drum tower's roof ridge, bees flew in like a soft intake of breath to hide and flew away with a droning hum.

The drum also seemed to have dwelled in this place for ages. One by one its rivets tarnished to a rusty red. The four thick, weathered pillars of the tower exposed a rough wood grain resembling the bones and the sinewy muscles of an old man. No doubt, the tower was erected when Gochaku Castle was built.

"Eyah! Is that a beehive?" asked Kanbei when he awoke. He slapped the scruff of his neck and turned up his red eyes to look at the underside of the eaves. He had not slept since the previous night and had been unable to steal time for a nap. But he managed to escape to this place, rest his back against the lower part of the pillar, and sleep a good sleep.

He could not be seen from the castle keep. The surrounding green foliage lusting for rays from the summer sunlight blocked any view of him. Also, this position was the highest on the castle grounds. A gentle breeze blew in from the ridges of the Chugoku Mountains as he fiddled with his side locks and his breast pocket. This was a splendid place to indulge in a short nap.

"This is no good. I'm being eaten alive.... I can't sleep around bees."

Kanbei smirked while constantly rubbing the nape of his neck and his eyelids.

Thus, the time he slept was brief. As he released a lengthy yawn, fatigue from the previous night washed down from his head through his entire body. He thought he would have to persevere without sleep again tonight.

However, he did not easily wake up. Hugging the knees of his *hakama* trousers, he leaned on the pillar and blankly looked up at the underside of the roof. The bee world seemed to be at war centered on the beehive. Reconnaissance bees flew off, and attacking bees were driven back. Kanbei didn't tire of watching, but his mind might have been absorbed in an entirely different matter.

Eventually, two vassals climbed up. These two samurai sub-captains were Muroki Saiha and Imadzu Gendayu. When they caught sight of Kanbei, both went to the trouble of announcing their unexpected arrival. One asked, "Chief Retainer, why have you come to this place? They're in an uproar down there. Some think you've returned to Himeji in a fit of rage. Others say, 'No, he's not so foolish as to leave without permission from the lord. He's somewhere around here. Make sure to search outside the castle …'"

Kanbei laughed and said, "Really? A search so vast?"

His expression looked like this was another man's affair. The bigger problem he faced was an eyelid that had been feasted on by a bee. The pads of his fingers never stopped stroking the flesh between his eyebrow and his eye.

2

A castle anywhere in the country always had a council room. However, examples of important plans actually resembling noteworthy policies rarely emerged from these rooms. Many were formalities, and many were theories. At other times, they merely echoed indifferent decisions, and first announced that the suitable time for adjournment was now.

Monju Bosatsu taught us that wisdom comes from the counsel of three. This occurs if at least one and one come together. A meeting of zero and zero is no more than zero even if one hundred people are gathered. Only eyes unable to see the coming of a new age will be unable to forecast the next age at a place where one thousand people are present. Nevertheless, not one person in attendance at the deliberation will appear to be clueless.

As a result, where conviction was lacking, an exceptional, farsighted philosophy was not held, only self-serving sophistry or a genius at arguments emerged. Consequently, the deliberations were only pretentions, became pointlessly entangled, entered into side streets for no reason, and fled into triviality. No matter how often deliberations were held, in the end, a throng never delivered one truth. Everything descended into a dead end where nothing was resolved.

"Please stop. If we question every last one of your intentions from last evening's deliberations, we will not advance one step from the roadblock of the first words from last night. Wouldn't it be better to invite Kanbei to take this seat again and bluntly ask him for his opinion? For just a moment, this is a critical matter linked to the rise and fall of our Gochaku Castle. For those uncomfortable with Kanbei, it will be a problem if you don't set aside your usual self-interest and combativeness and consult with him."

Kodera Masamoto, the lord of the castle, gave this order in a tone resembling a long sigh to the men seated in a row below him.

For the time being, the opportunistic caution, trite opinions, and fights between egos appeared to have been silenced. Then someone said, "This is no good if it's Lord Kanbei. Where is he now? We are searching for him. It's absurd for the chief retainer to sneak away from his seat during deliberations. His heart doesn't seem to have a fragment of loyalty in his humanity to lament the reversals of fortune of the clan or to worry about the lord's future. His sole job appears to be boasting."

When Sue Yoshichika, who had an important role, disparaged Kanbei, Kuramitsu Masatoshi, Murai Kawachi, and Masuda Magouemon, and other senior retainers seated in the row spoke up in agreement.

"Basically, he is glib and a samurai of slight loyalty. His rudeness should be expected."

"If that is true, it's unreasonable to ask for loyalty from Lord Kanbei. He is different from us. We are hereditary retainers. He is nothing more than a senior official connected to this clan beginning in his father's generation."

"In other words, he began life as the son of a seller of a medicinal eye lotion. Because he is the chief retainer, we are allowed to be hard on the man instead of having respect for him," said one to himself but loud enough to be heard by the lord.

These words displeased the young warriors who sat in the back seats, favored Kanbei, and supported his views. One of them could no longer bear it. A youthful voice rose from those seats.

"Please excuse me for interrupting an elder's words, but these words are also the lord's words. The lord is waiting to see Lord Kanbei and carefully question him in order to hear his opinion. I think it would be good to discuss the pros and cons and listen to his views. I may be out of line, but shouldn't we be careful about too much malicious gossip?"

While conscious of his rank, his courage was revived and he spoke his criticism. The lord of the castle Kodera Masamoto thought, It is as he says, and directed his thankless eyes toward the man in the back seats. As the lord, he did not easily overlook this man. Kodera was not a foolish ruler. He had been educated to become the lord of a powerful, provincial clan but may have lacked the ability to lead an entire clan in this generation. His keen eyes saw dismantling or rebuilding as the actions to take in these times of sweeping change. His firm belief was to act without hesitation in uncertain times. That was nothing to him.

Of course, it was unreasonable to say a farsighted viewpoint like that was desired in the lord of the castle who governed a region of no more than several districts in Harima in a remote corner of the world. The actions on that day in year 3 of the Tensho era (1575) were zealous and excessive.

CHAPTER TWO
THE MAN WHO SWIMS
WHERE THERE IS NO BEACH

1

WHAT WAS GOING to happen? How would it unfold?

Masamoto would only follow the trends. But the inescapable day finally arrived.

Of course, half of the responsibility fell on the councilors. With no solution in sight from the previous night, shades of suffering and exhaustion filled them like tainted water in an ancient pool. The extinction of the main family would also bring about their demise. They were unable to deny the obstacle that could not be left to tomorrow and clouded each man's future.

The problem was "How shall we decide the position of the Kodera clan now?"

If the problem were split in two, the debate becomes "Does the clan's future lie in staying with the Mouri clan to the end?" versus "Should the clan ally with the rising power of Oda Nobunaga?"

The time had come.

"Which action to take is not obvious. This demonstrates freedom from the usual intrigue of the

Mouri clan. If we attack Oda's power, we must be ready to respond at that moment."

The senior councilors persisted in staying with the old ways. The eyes of Masamoto inexperienced in any and all trends of the day knew the Mouri clan would certainly be disgruntled by petty machinations and makeshift plots.

From the day before yesterday, an envoy of Mouri Terumoto had been staying at a temple in the castle town to wait for the response of "I accept or I do not accept." If accepted, hostages would enter Yoshida Castle in Geishu. A rejection was fine, but the envoy would not come to Harima a second time. An unmistakable threat was also included in the spoken message. At the same time, a note from Mouri Terumoto was passed to the hands of Kodera Masamoto.

A frightened and pallid Masamoto unexpectedly gathered the clan and the key vassals as if the problem began the previous night.

He asked, "What is the best course to follow?"

The faces of everyone being consulted again burned with bewilderment, like the roof had been set on fire, as they advised him.

"If Nobunaga comes with his forces to Chugoku, first, he will demolish the frontline in this area. Moreover, he's already crushed and expelled Imagawa and Takeda and drove off the power of the Kyoto shogunate. He can never be taken lightly."

Completely disregarding these words, Masamoto said, "Well, how near is Oda's military strength? Mouri's strength begins in Aki and Suou Provinces and extends over the twelve provinces of the San'in-Sanyo region. In the strait, the naval forces of the Murakami and Kurushima clans hold back the allies and have close ties to the sect at Hongan-ji Temple in Osaka. Betrayals abound in Settsu and other places. Is the base that wielded power from the time of Mouri Motonari being shaken? Also, this castle boasts a lineage that ruled over this domain as senior government officials of the Mouri clan for ages. What is the confusion? Instead of seeking hostages or written oaths, we should seek support."

He was oblivious to the entire state of affairs. Those words were from a man dependent solely on the power of the Mouri clan.

If this crisis could be overcome in that way, of course, Masamoto would raise no objections. However, the true state of affairs was not so simple and trouble free. Some arguments displayed revulsion at the sudden rise in Nobunaga's power.

As evidence, the westward drive of Oda's forces was spoken of in terms of "temporary" or "may come." A clash between Mouri and Oda was inevitable and saturated the air closing in with tomorrow. This was not a modest affair that could be declared "a possibility."

2

During the previous month and the beginning of May in Tensho year 3, Nobunaga went to Gifu in an alliance with Tokugawa Ieyasu to crush the massive elite army of Takeda Katsuyori at Mount Kabuto and returned to Gifu in triumph.

Nobunaga's soldiers and warhorses resembled a whirlwind with no fixed direction. While opponents wondered whether he clashed yesterday with the forces of Uesugi Kenshin in Hokuetsu, he acted with lightning speed to swiftly quell an uprising in Ise then returned to slaughter Asai of Goshu, overthrow Asakura, and set fire to Eizan. He achieved far-reaching impact by driving the central cancer named Ashikaga, who held the power of the shogunate since its founding, out of Kyoto.

To think, Gifu is far away, was a huge mistake.

Nobunaga did not fight branches and leaves; he yanked out the root. This was one ploy seen in Nobunaga's battles. For several years, his mistake was not to douse the flames at the base of the fire with water. His soldiers headed only to places in the shadows of the fire. In no time, they were exhausted by constant activity. Sects rose up and tormented him in various provinces like Ise, Koshu, and Hokuriku. Resistance of remnants from the clans he destroyed, like the Imagawa, Saito, Asakura, Sasaki, Rokkaku, and Asai, and resistance in various lands controlled by the exiled shogun Ashikaga Yoshiaki shared the same motive.

Where was the source of the fire that resisted Nobunaga and had the ability to burn bright and was not the shadow of these flames? As an intelligent man, by this day, he already pinpointed its location.

Was it the Ishiyama Hongan-ji fortress in Osaka with its many believers and vast resources?

No, even Hongan-ji with only the power of a Buddhist temple was unable to confront Nobunaga for many years and disrupt his firearms business at its foundation. For the time being, the dauntless resistance of the great number of followers of the Hongan-ji Temple was recognized, but their supply lines in the background via overland or sea routes were provided by their physical and spiritual strength. In fact, they knew Nobunaga would come in time and knew in their hearts he was watching. The obvious source was the Mouri clan, the protector of the wealth and power of twelve provinces in San'in and Sanyo.

On the surface, Oda and Mouri had not yet engaged in battle, but to say they had been engaged in stealth battles for some years was no exaggeration. Through the competition to win over the powerful clans from Settsu to the San'in district, the scramble for commodities, the comings and goings of spies, and the use of travelers in a war of rumors, it was war in every way except in the spilling of blood. Of course, diplomacy ceased, and strict security was encountered at checkpoints, including sea routes.

Above all, every possible means was exhausted in the

lead-up to war with the destruction of many lords with small castles or powerful regional clans considered to be minor nations trapped between the two powers. Does a powerful clan surrounded by them rush to support the Mouri or ally with Oda? Does a small castle separated by only a river have the courage to join forces with either? For the most part, the actions were superficial, and reality was impossible to predict.

For instance, despite being a powerful clan, the Ukita clan in the province neighboring Gochaku in Harima may have appeared steadfast to the Mouri and viewed with great suspicion based on information from spies.

Therefore, the more the Kodera looked around, the unmistakable situation was the lords of the castles in this region were ultimately confused. Gochaku Castle and its lord Kodera Masamoto were not alone in their confusion.

3

"I think I shouldn't speak too soon. How about that?" The young vassal, who turned thirty this year, was Kuroda Kanbei. (His original name is used here because, at that time, he had already received the surname of his master's house and called Kodera, but that would invite confusion.) Only he exhibited extreme aloofness despite first occupying this seat the previous evening.

Even when singled out and questioned by Masamoto, "And Kanbei, what is your opinion?" he only answered, "Other than what I've said, I have no new opinions."

Kanbei grinned and listened in silence to everyone else. Then he abruptly turned his sharp eyes to stare at their faces and with spit flying said, "This is going nowhere."

Around dawn, he suggested that Lord Masamoto retire to bed, but the senior vassal Kuramitsu Masatoshi angered and took Kanbei to task.

"What do you mean by suggesting sleep before this issue is resolved? Do you think you have the standing of a councilor?"

Kanbei calmly said, "Yes," and looked down.

Then he disappeared. The others went to breakfast in shifts and returned to their seats and believed he would return. The sun rose high and noon approached, but he did not return. People suspicious of his actions came forward. Only Masamoto was a friend who had unexpectedly selected the young man to become his retainer. He never considered the possibility that suspicions might be raised in the other retainers.

"Sirs, the chief retainer has been found at last."

At that moment, the samurai squad captains Muroki Saiha and Imadzu Gendayu returned to the end plank of the back seats to cheerfully report to the men assembled. Beginning with the senior retainers, the expressions on all the faces that turned toward the voice were not mellow. The vigorous movements of the white eyebrows of several men ended in frowns.

"What? He was here. Where has he been all this time?"

They found themselves in an awkward situation. Saiha and Gendayu looked at each other and began to dither but inevitably answered frankly, "He was on top of the drum tower."

The senior retainers asked question after question.

"What is this? Who was with him in the tower?"

"He was alone."

"What was he doing there?"

"I believe he was asleep."

"I'm appalled. I will not stand for any more of this ludicrous talk. What happened to Kanbei? Did he say he won't come back?"

"No. While asleep, he was stung on the eyelid by a bee. He said he'll take his seat after he washes his face and puts on ointment."

"…"

No one was appalled or outraged any longer.

CHAPTER THREE
THE BATH

1

WATER RUSHED FROM a water pipe beside the bathroom door. Kanbei roughly scrubbed his face splattering water around like badly behaving magpies.

"Towel. Towel," he yelled back as water drops spilled from his chin and put the razor on the tray. A flustered novice, who had been standing by the corner shelf, hurried over to him to hold up a hand towel.

A little while ago, Muroki Saiha appeared at the covered footbridge there and said, "Sir, please come quickly. As always, the council is dragging on and out of control with only slander and arguments. The lord believes only you seem to be making an effort and is waiting impatiently for your return."

"I'm coming now. Right now."

Kanbei was sitting on the wood floor facing the novice who was applying ointment to the huge swelling on his left eyelid. This lump developed from the earlier sting by a bee in the tower.

"Very good. Very good," he thanked the novice, stood, and slowly passed over the bridge. He walked up and down the veranda several times and, finally, returned to the council room.

The sun was far off and the summer day was cool. Of course, the atmosphere inside was gloomy. The mood had settled into indignation over the listlessness and the stupor of last night. The discussion was exhausted. The retainers, from the senior retainers on down, who only slandered Kanbei for quite some time, were silent. They didn't move their eyes and ignored Kanbei on purpose when he took his seat.

2

Kanbei faced the lord's seat and bowed. While touching the palm of his hand to the swelling on his eyelid, he seemed overly concerned about the heat in the room.

First, the eyes of the vassal in the key retainer seat across from him then the eyes of the others stared at him. A malicious silence was often aimed at Kanbei. The unconcerned Kanbei lapsed into silence. Every last man, even Ogawa Mikawa-no-kami, a relative of Lord Kodera Masamoto, looked full of hate for him.

"Kanbei. Where were you for so long a time after leaving this crucial deliberation?"

"Oh, me?"

"No other poorly prepared samurai is in this seat."

"I went to rest but do not intend to be poorly prepared."

"Who climbs up the drum tower for a peaceful nap?"

"I knew I had to clear my tired head and take a nap. At that moment, my mind and body rested without dozing off in front of all of you. I believe it was also for the sake of the clan."

"Chief Retainer."

These sharp words came from the elder Kuramitsu Masatoshi to rescue him from the rebukes pelting him from the sides.

"Well, sir ..." said Kanbei respectfully and slightly shifted his knees toward him then said with great confidence, "Yes, what?"

The white eyebrows on Masatoshi's face turned red and instantly stood out.

"You are still young, and I've remained silent today. However, you sullied your role as a thirty-year-old retainer and, not surprisingly, are full of yourself. What you've done … Today is not just any other situation. In this seat, the rise or fall of this house will be determined by one deliberation over going to the east or to the west."

"It is as you say."

"Nevertheless, what …" said Kuramitsu Masatoshi and pointed his trembling finger at Kanbei's face and slid on his knees, "That face … what is that face?"

"My face? It's no good, is it?"

"When did you shave your beard?"

"A short time ago. In the bathroom."

"At daybreak when rest should have been ignored, tired men were told to rest by the benevolence of the lord. How can you shave and wash your face and appear as if all of this is a joke? How arrogant!"

"No, not only my face. I also rinsed out my mouth. And washed my hands and feet."

"What?!"

"Are you familiar with bathing? Am I not allowed to respectfully bathe before returning?"

"Enough of your specious excuses."

His juniors in rank Murai Kawachi, Masuda Magoemon, and Eda Zenbei were in agreement. Spit flew from them like they were about to give him a tongue-lashing.

"What do you mean bathe? Why was a bath needed? Fool!"

Kanbei took this opportunity to politely place both hands on the ground facing Lord Masamoto in apology to the row of retainers and the other warriors. One voice expressed the unanimous opinion.

"We understand the great danger of turning to a

questionable, young chief retainer for a matter as important as this. You are not bewildered but determined and, as always, will assist the Mouri clan and work for the clan's security. You will go at once as the envoy to the government office in the castle town to address this matter. All the retainers present ask this favor of you."

To the west? To the east? Masamoto's complexion reflected his ever-present confusion as he listened to the words of the group, but his will was sparked.

Kanbei exploded in a voice loud enough to bring down the ceiling, "No, I can't. I am opposed. To side with the Mouri is to invite my ruin. And it's contrary to the righteousness of a military family!"

"What?!" burst from the council seats. Forgetting they were in the presence of the lord, the council sunk into a menacing rabble. Five or six of the samurai friendly to the Mouri stood to protect some of the lord's relatives and senior vassals.

"You may be the chief retainer, but you will die."

They advanced with their swords threatening him.

3

"Please sit down," said Kanbei, who had not moved from his seat. His heavy eyebrows seemed to flush with anger. Only his words rebuked the throng ready to pounce on him.

"Stay back. Will you sit down?" shouted Kodera Masamoto.

After making sure the five or six men still in a rage and biting their lips returned to their seats in the back, Kanbei calmed himself. He recovered his usual tone of voice and said, "The truth is I will carefully convey my belief as always to the lord's heart. Therefore, even during deliberations, I will not speak to the lord again. I believe the reason for the deliberations beginning last night simply has been to seek agreement from the two factions of the clan in a ruinous division over whether to ally with the

Mouri or to join with Oda. Of those two, ..."

"Silence! That's your plot. We who fear for our clan are poisoned by your scheme and will not blindly follow your views about Oda."

"Please, tell me your thoughts," said Kanbei. This time he spoke with civility to placate the senior retainers, "I already made vows to the lord and to the gods. Your beliefs cannot defeat the dilemma faced by the Kodera clan. Please swear an oath to me."

"...?"

They looked stunned and turned their eyes to Lord Masamoto. Was he joking or serious? Masamoto did not rebuff him. Kanbei looked again with glinting eyes at Masamoto's face. His eyes seemed to be glaring back at him.

"To understand the present crisis in advance and not panic when in danger, as always, I will offer honest advice to the lord. Even if I make mistakes or am opposed, I will continue to advise without fear. I know that is the work of a retainer and, above all, the duty of the chief retainer. I'm not ashamed in any way. If a conspiracy is plotted, it will not be declared from this seat. Lord Ogawa, Lord Kuramitsu, gentlemen, I wish you would listen with quiet minds."

"Listen to what?"

"To my beliefs."

"Isn't it obvious your views fixate on Oda? We heard them last evening and again this morning. So much pestering leads me to think you may be Oda's spy."

"I don't pay the least bit of attention to slander. Even the attempt to kill me here have not altered my beliefs at all. Although I fully explained my beliefs many times last night and this morning, each time I speak, you object. Those assembled grumbled and only provoked disputes. It was fruitless. So I left before the meeting ended to take a break. I bathed before I faced this again. I knew my final words would be to change the rule of not speaking without permission. Some of you listened, but many probably fear unwanted attention. And all of you are probably exhausted. Now, I hope you will adjust your seats, fix your collars, and listen quietly."

Naturally, Kanbei sat up straight to avoid being criticized. His words seemed to resonate in Lord Kodera Masamoto's heart, and he slid off his cushion.

The family and retainers probably noticed the lord's movement but were unable to assert themselves. They hurried to align their knees and adjust their collars. In the family of the lord of a provincial castle not from a corner of Harima, only boisterous rural customs permeate deep over many years into the formal ceremonies of the Muromachi shogunate. When they straightened their postures and formed a solemn circle, they surprisingly looked like reliable samurai.

4

Kanbei stressed giving the support to Oda he had argued for over the years. The entire country was overwhelmed by the banners of Oda's forces. Despite the power of the Mouri clan or the resistance by the Miyoshi faction that held the residual power of the shogun, the repeated belief was that Oda Nobunaga was unstoppable like grass burning in a wildfire.

With this premise, Kanbei changed what he would say that day. The problem he faced was why was that necessary.

"I believe nature giving birth to Nobunaga in this tumultuous land was divine will and not from the work of humans or their minds. If this man were not here now, what single man could embody the endless struggle of his will versus the will of his countrymen in a chaotic age of vulgar crowds and unquashable mass violence? And who is the best man for this country with its Imperial Household in extreme decay and able to advance toward the current disorder with a grand scheme to bring the people to peace

17

and harmony? Is there a man to be found other than Nobunaga?"

In conclusion, he said, "The forces of Nobunaga were certain Nobunaga was their lord and never seemed to forget the position of a military retainer in the gap between the Imperial Household and the people. His thoughts are not the political tactics or pretensions from the generation of his father, the warlord Oda Nobuhide. Look at his past. He struck Imagawa Yoshimoto, dispensed with Saito Dosan of Mino, and did not make Asai Asakura his enemy. If power were quickly grabbed like it is today, ordinary people would gradually become self-important. But he always pulled back his followers when he won and entered Kyoto. After suppressing the revolt at the palace gate, he was kind to the common people, promoted memorial services in shrines and temples, oversaw the construction of roads and bridges, and resurrected various lines of the devastated Imperial Court.

"As the child who worked hard and became the center of his family, he used up his sincere feelings in serving his parents above him and comforting his lovable younger brothers and sisters below him. Doesn't his joy come from the joy of all those from all levels in society who depend on him? After tens of generations of the Ashikaga shogunate, does a survey of the daimyos of various provinces find one man like him?

"Although the Mouri is said to have a strong nation, they preserve their family's creed since the time of Mouri Motonari and do nothing more than stubbornly defend their possessions. That desire is not found among the nation's people. Lord Miyoshi cannot ignore the shogun's police and the old forces in Kii, Iga, Awa, and Sanuki, and are only people of the ancient past with old-fashioned ideas. The crime that plunged the world into disorder and tormented the people should never be taken lightly. They also abandoned gaining the confidence of the people.

"Look at it this way. It is clear that no man other than

Nobunaga should be able to gamble the fate of the clan and be entrusted with the lives of our samurai. Given our feelings and the shared feelings of the people, I am not cxaggerating when I say the entire nation recognized the appearance of Nobunaga as a new dawn. The ideals of a man with the trust of the masses because of their desires I explained must be carried out in these times. Not to mention, he is the father in times when nothing else is asked for in this world."

As expected, the listless air, the egos, and the combative spirit in the spacious room were soon swept away. Only Kanbei's voice could be heard.

CHAPTER FOUR
ON THE ROAD

1

A LITTLE PAST noon was the hottest time of that day.

In a rural castle in a corner of Harima, a young chief retainer, only thirty years old and a healthy man with dimples on his red face, walked steadily with a horse in the direction of Himeji.

He turned twice to look back at Gochaku Castle.

"The day I return here alive may never come," said Kanbei apparently embracing that sentiment.

At last, his sincerity was only missing the gesture of a bow. This conviction penetrated him. And the wish with him day and night was taking place.

The previous night's deliberation finally found agreement and relief came.

Gochaku Castle and its lord Kodera Masamoto would form an alliance with Oda. For the time being, however, this secret would be kept as much as possible from the surrounding domains.

The remaining question was who would be the envoy to Oda. Naturally, the lord and the entire clan offered this duty to Kuroda Kanbei, and he accepted.

With this consensus, he came before the lord without

20

delay to ask permission to leave. He reluctantly parted from the people assembled, quickly left his seat, and directed his horse to Himeji.

He heard Nobunaga was now at Gifu Castle. The usual route to Gifu passed through Himeji. On the road, he approached Himeji Castle, his birthplace. His mother was already dead, but he would bid farewell to his aged father Souen. And he thought he'd like to see his young wife and the face of their eight-year-old son after his long absence.

"… Well, I'll go to Akashi. If I go by boat, I can board there at the bay."

Away from the dangers of the road, he often mulled with pleasure over a variety of issues. Because no place on the overland route or the sea route was free of the military might of the Mouri clan or the spies of the Miyoshi faction, the dangers were unending. Kanbei was a sensible man but also a young man of thirty. The great hope is for the man with this mission to not reflect too much on these matters but only to bring joy to his heart.

A sudden memory of Ichian in Akashi Port came to mind because an old man he loved so much as a child lived there. His name was Akashi Masakaze, his mother's father.

Originally, his mother was the daughter of people connected to the Konoe clan. Her father, Akashi Masakaze, was that relative who went in and out of the Konoe clan and was a rival in the art of tanka poetry to the father and son of that clan. After the world fell into disorder, Ichian was connected to the coast of Akashi and used another name of Souwa or went by the name of Ingetsuou. He taught calligraphy to the fishermen's children and enjoyed the remainder of his life in solitude away from fame and fortune.

2

From childhood, Kanbei was inclined to a love of learning like his grandfather. While a youth filled with devilry, his grandfather's ideas began to mold his spirit.

He thought about first telling this grandfather about the mission but was also restless to speak with his father in Himeji Castle whose ambitions were no different than his own.

"Hey, Mankichi. Mankichi."

Who was calling him? He was being called by a name he hadn't heard since childhood. Kanbei looked up and down the sides of the road.

An elderly priest whitened by dust under the scorching sun approached on sturdy legs. Kanbei hurriedly leaped off the saddle to greet him.

"Oh, I was a student of yours. It's been a long time," he said while slapping both knees.

It was the priest of the Jodoji Temple below Himeji Castle. He was an amiable man and called Priest Peaceful by everyone in town.

Kanbei had been trained by this priest. His father Souen had not yet been granted a castle and was doing nothing after his period of poverty as a ronin who sold medicinal eye lotion. From that time, this priest was a former teacher who taught him not only reading and writing but planted the seeds of various fields in the seedbed of his youthful spirit.

While wiping sweat from his face, Priest Peaceful like a true friend asked, "Mankichi, where are you going?"

"I'm on a trip," said Kanbei and peeked around before he said, "Please be happy for me. I'm off to Gifu."

"To Gifu. Hmm … As an envoy for the lord?"

"Yes."

"Congrats. That's great. I understand."

"I can't say much but you can imagine. If I return safely, we'll have a leisurely talk."

"Be careful on your journey."

Kanbei listened to his teacher's words and looked back toward Gochaku. Kanbei's complexion showed alarm, which was unusual for him.

Priest Peaceful looked startled, too. They were staring in the same direction down the bone dry, white road and saw two warriors flying through the air toward them. Their hakama trousers were pulled up, and they were ready to fight. One clutched a short spear. The other raised his hand and shouted something to them. Kanbei never took his eyes off them.

CHAPTER FIVE
THE PATH OF BELIEF

1

THEY WERE THE young vassals Mori Tahei and
Kuriyama Zensuke.

These two were direct vassals in the Kodera clan. In
other words, they were undervassals raised from a young
age by Kanbei's father Souen who loved their genius.
Several years ago at the urging of Kodera Masamoto, he
made them senior retainers in Gochaku. He thought of
them as children but when selecting from among many
vassals he believed those two would be good to take under
any circumstances. They were particularly good men to
bring along.

Tahei and Zensuke were now approaching with
alarmed expressions. They looked like their knees were
dropping to their feet as if on the verge of tumbling over.
Kanbei wasn't easily surprised, but his voice sounding
agitated asked, "What's going on? What's happened?"

Both breathed heavily from their shoulders and took
turns recounting the following incident.

"We left right after deliberations ended. The men
who pushed hard to support the Mouri said it was
cowardly and disloyal. From machinations behind the

scenes in the castle, they used their deep influence to immediately overturn the decision you witnessed. They snatched the still small Princess Sue and handed her over to the envoy from the Mouri clan ... and like bandits, they embraced the princess like the wind and spirited her through the rear gate to beyond the castle walls in broad daylight."

"We suspect this was done with the knowledge of Lord Ogawa of the clan, and some of the wives living in the ringed enclosure were kindred spirits. Also, senior retainers like Murai, Kuramitsu, and Masuda gave their full consent, and the lord's daughter was turned over as a hostage into the hands of the Mouri clan...."

Kanbei was dumbfounded. More than anger at the complete betrayal of his trust by the entire opposition faction, he had sympathy for the stubborn old ideas and the recklessness of the senior retainers unable to support Gochaku Castle and each person's fate, but his sympathy vanished with their extreme action.

"... Oh, so that's it?" he said. In a sigh of grief resembling a groan he said, "If it's the youngest princess, that's the adorable Princess Sue who's only six. How did Lord Masamoto react when he found out? ... Did he rebuke the senior retainers? Did they respond with silence?"

"I cannot guess the lord's reaction.... Well, I didn't question the man who told me. We galloped to the temple outside the castle where the envoy from the Mouri clan had been staying."

"You're very alert. And the princess ..."

"Regrettably, she was nowhere to be found."

"Well, was there a fight?"

"If there were, he would not shamelessly hand over the princess to us even if it cost him his life. The envoy's party left the castle town early in the morning. We did not find one horse there later."

"So ... they had a secret understanding. That is

certain."

Kanbei's sharp mind instantly processed this unforeseen incident. His words ended with his usual brightness. He spun around and started to smile at Priest Peaceful who had been standing there the whole time.

"Priest. As you've heard, my trip has become more urgent. We will meet again in less hurried times. I must be off."

Kanbei brought the reins closer, gently patted the horse's neck a few times, and lightly moved onto the saddle.

2

From horseback, he looked again at the ground where the two retainers had placed their hands.

"Tahei. Zensuke."

"Yessir."

"In my absence, I have a job for you."

"Yessir."

"What is best for our residence? During my absence, you will protect the interior of the castle. Fortunately, my absence is a gift to the gang who plan to support the Mouri clan. They will probably devise every manner of scheme, flattery, and coercion. I think this group consists of about a third of those in the castle. Get close to the younger ones who agree with me and keep an eye on them. That is your charge while I'm gone."

"We understand. Until the day you return home, even if we have to cling to the castle's stone walls, Gochaku Castle will not lean toward the Mouri."

"That is my only fear.... Your words reassure me. Goodbye."

When the horse started to move, Priest Peaceful ran up to the side of the saddle.

"Mankichi. Are you all right? Is this serious?" he asked as his eyes focused on Kanbei's face.

As if comforting him, Kanbei said, "I'm fine. Don't

worry. I may be acting selfishly and with self-interest, or this may be a huge adventure. Starting with the governor-general, if everyone at Gochaku Castle leans toward the Mouri, the extreme decision would be to promptly kill my wife, child, and elderly father in Himeji.... But my mind is unbiased like this blue sky. I can't entertain the notion of personal gain and glory. I believe my actions are the sole path to saving my lord's house. This belief saves the land of Chugoku from fires ignited by war. More importantly, I pledge to god there's nothing other than this will to set the lord's mind at ease."

"I believe you, but from what you've said, does the lord's decision matter? I have my doubts."

"By nature, Lord Masamoto is a good man. I am often by his side and he permits me to speak. However, when I'm away from the castle, even for a short time, his weakness is listening to heretical opinions then getting confused about whether to join the Mouri or to trust Oda.... I believe young Princess Sue was handed over as a hostage to the Mouri clan. The lord himself may have been kept in the dark. Half of him shows agreement with that action, but his other half is waiting for good or bad news from me. For this reason, even if the senior retainers or family members of the clan concocted the scheme, the lord's position would not be obvious until I return from Gifu. First, I will fly like lightning. I believe the situation in Gochaku Castle will not change before I return."

"As you wish.... If you've put so much thought into this situation, this country priest has no need to worry. Go in health."

"Goodbye. Tahei, Zensuke. Don't forget your assignment."

They watched Kanbei move down the path between the rice fields trailed by the fog of dust kicked up by his galloping horse.

CHAPTER SIX
THE FAMILY ON THE HILL

1

HIMEJI WAS A short two and a half miles away, the distance traveled between whips on the galloping horse's legs.

This land was a strategic point near the neck of Sanyo and Kinki, but at that time, had not yet provided the imposing landscape later to be called Himeji Castle. It was no more than a branch castle for protecting the main castle in Gochaku. Its fabulous moat and enclosure were extremely simple structures. A dozen years earlier, the powerful family called Kuroda built their modest home on a hill blanketed by trees.

However, the power and popularity of that family on the hill flourished in a short time. The source was the eldest son Kanbei who surpassed his father and was not held back by him.

Some in the world badmouthed him, "He became a superior man by the power of gold. A ronin peddler of eye medicine becomes a landowner in the blink of an eye and gathers a slew of servants and horses."

Even now, malicious gossip was heard. But the superior nature of the eldest son became apparent as he

28

grew and was certainly not due to the power of money. Kanbei was only thirty years old. His small castle in Himeji was being put under pressure by neighboring domains. His eventual eclipse of his father's virtue and influence was unique.

Because the mountains and the secluded beaches of Harima were a part of the Kodera domain, the wealthy local clan lived throughout the domain and strong-armed their way to power. They mainly pursued war expenditures and manpower to subjugate insurgents and ran a chaotic government unlike any other.

Even when surveying the territories of various countries and not only within the domain of the Kodera clan, a situation like this could be said to be a typical sign of the times. In this world, a mere peddler of eye medicines owned land, raised horses, nurtured people, built stone walls on several hills in Himeji, amassed weapons and power, and grasped peace and order with the neighboring domains without going to surrounding provinces because he was able to establish a military family in this place.

Furthermore, heaven blessed the Kuroda clan with a child prodigy. The family's fate finally revealed prosperity. Kanbei was the eldest son. He had a younger brother and two younger sisters. Glimmers of Kanbei's talent first appeared around the age of fifteen or sixteen.

After his mother died, he studied literature for a time and ventured into learning how to read tanka poetry. The driving force seemed to be his maternal grandfather Akashi Masakaze. However, Priest Peaceful of Jodo-ji Temple where he served as a teacher of classic Confucian writings and Zen studies once stated his opinion, "Now, why are you reading about the beauties of nature? You differ from men like your grandfather who are at the fringe. Aren't you a young man who must stand in the fierce storm from here on? This is the time for you to ask heaven."

He abandoned tanka poetry and embraced Zen and military strategy.

When he was about twenty-two, Kanbei attacked a bandit leader named Sawakurabo from a neighboring district and put down the Mashima clan in Sayo-gun. In any case, the townspeople firmly believed that when the eldest son of Himeyama led his followers out, they always returned in victory.

The family called Kuroda on the hill strengthened each year without the power of money. In fact, local wealthy clans and thieves continued to oppose this family as the enemy.

"What kind of man is Kuroda?" asked Kodera Masamoto, the lord of Gochaku Castle, as he approached this hill during a hunt. This began their connection. Kuroda Souen later served as a high-level official in the Kodera clan. Soon the son Kanbei replaced the father in the influential post of chief retainer.

In a short time compared to the other hereditary vassals, after the Kuroda father and son became chief retainers, the rampage of insurgents in the domain of the Kodera clan ceased completely; land was recovered from the hands of enemies; and the local population submitted to the rule of Kodera Masamoto.

However, once the internal affairs were considered settled, they were soon battered by numerous pressures from beyond the province. In this small province, clarity was demanded in the positions of Kodera. Opportunistic positions were taken over the past few years, but these were stopgap measures. And now an emergency arose that forbade taking that stance one more day.

2

"Matsu, ... wait quietly. Your father will start here and pass through the capital as an envoy to the province called Gifu. All right? Do you understand?" asked Kanbei while stroking his son's head.

The child Matsuchiyo was eight years old.

This boy was born the year Kanbei married his wife and was unbearably cute.

"Yes, yes I do," said Matsuchiyo and nodded while looking at his father's face. In a child's heart, a journey to a far off land was not a simple task.

Matsuchiyo returned to his mother's side, tugged on the hand of his beautiful mother, and said, "I want to go with Father to Gifu."

Souen had been silently watching his son and his family. His expression did not reflect the slightest contentment as he accepted the harshness of ripping out a living tree in the depths of his heart.

"Kanbei, Kanbei. What is a samurai? While on a journey as an important envoy, doesn't a samurai always long for and mourn the separation from his wife and children? Ready yourself and go. If you hurry, you can board a boat at Shikama beach while there's daylight. A moment's difference may lead to a mistake that leaves behind ten years of regret."

"No. I didn't intend to stay this long, but time never stops. I will say goodbye. And Father, you be strong, too."

"Don't worry about me, not even a little. You must go quickly," said Kanbei's young wife and hugged Matsuchiyo with her knees as she twisted around to speak in a hushed tone and began sobbing.

When Kanbei was just twenty-two and she was fifteen, she married into his family. Despite being the mother of an eight-year-old child, she had not reached her twenty-third birthday.

His attractive wife was also the niece of Kodera Masamoto and had an abundant talent for poetry. She was said to be the most beautiful woman in the province.

"This parting may be for life. This is understandable but emotional."

Souen guessed her innermost feeling and was pained in his heart. However, when he considered his son's mission and the importance of the outcome, he willed himself not to look at the child or the wife from the corner of his eye.

"Wait Kanbei, wait. Are you going alone? Aren't you taking an attendant?"

"I'm selfishly going alone."

"What if something goes wrong,... Kinugasa Kyuzaemon? How about taking him?"

"No, I will not be conspicuous if I'm alone."

Kanbei was strong-willed and without a word to his wife and child, he left the room. He soon lashed his horse and galloped down Himeyama. The parting was so brief he wondered why he went.

CHAPTER SEVEN
REIJUKOU

1

SEVERAL PILLARS OF smoke rose from the salt-drying field. It was a little past noon in the harbor town of Shikama. The evening calm beginning around this time until sunset was the hottest part of the day.

The leaves and flowers of morning glories covered in white dust grew on the shadeless, sandy plain. When night fell, Kanbei could hear the thick voices of the men working on the dock or the songs being sung accompanied by shamisen from one of the houses visible on the far side. This crossing turned into a row of houses on one side of the road in front of empty lots.

Kanbei dismounted and left his horse in the grassy field. He brushed away the dust from his hakama trousers and his back.

"Oh, are you the young lord of Himeji? Kiku, Kiku! Bring the wash basin."

Yojiemon had been sitting in front of his store until he jumped up at the man's sudden appearance. He said a few words behind the shadow of the partition screen to his daughter Kiku who was diligently packing the family-made eye medicine into seashell containers. Then he hurriedly slipped on *zori* sandals and rushed to the other side of the road.

"Why has the young lord come here? Why have you suddenly appeared alone?"

Yojiemon went around to Kanbei's back to brush off the dust and removed his bamboo hat to give him a warm reception. When Yojiemon began to rise, Kanbei said, "Uncle, before tending to me, please bring my horse around back, take off the saddle, and hide him inside. That saddle stands out a little too much."

"Are you traveling incognito on an urgent mission?"

"Traveling incognito is a secret trip in fear of any public notice. This harbor town is alive with the comings and goings of people from other provinces. I'm in a hurry so I'll tell you the details later."

"Yes, yes. Hey Kiku, leave the back gate open. I'm going to pull in the horse."

Yojiemon still knew nothing but took the horse's lead to quickly pull it into the alley. While watching, Kanbei sat down in the doorframe of the store with the ease of entering his own home, removed his straw sandals, and washed his feet. The large characters on the signboard hanging from the eaves were written to advertise the eye lotion.

The Miracle of a Family Tradition
Reijukou

Kanbei gazed at the sign with nostalgia as he recalled the poverty of his father during his boyhood.

2

The eye lotion dealer Yojiemon once worked as the lone houseboy of Kanbei's father Souen Mototaka.

When the chief retainer Uragami Munenori of Akamatsu overturned his lord's house and plunged the entire country into revolt, Souen escaped the rebellion in Bizen to Harima and began his long life as a ronin. In fact, Iguchi Yojiemon passed through an age of poverty while

serving his lord well in his house from that time. Souen
soon became a high-level official in the Kodera clan and
solidified the foundation of the clan today. After Yojiemon
aged and grew infirm, his wish was to spend the remaining
years of his life in comfort in a tradesman's home. Souen
passed to Yojiemon the preparation and the sales of the
eye lotion handed down in Souen's family to save him
from a difficult life and as a reward for his service.

Given that relationship, Kanbei had known Yojiemon
since childhood and was close to him. Yojiemon helped
him blow his nose, carried him piggyback, and had a
willfulness missing between master and servant. Looking at
him now, Kanbei's words had a touch of the spoiled child
of those days.

"Uncle, Uncle, don't bother. I'm not staying long.
Night is coming and I will sleep soon. I intend to leave by
boat," said Kanbei as he sat in a north-facing room off the
courtyard and wiped sweat off his face. He sat with a
casualness that filled the room like he had no sense of
restraint or formality. He waved a folding fan in long
strokes to cool his chest.

Yojiemon did not forget the old manners and sat
respectfully in the adjoining small room separated by the
door threshold. He asked, "You said you'll be leaving
tonight by boat?"

"Yes, I cannot safely go by an overland route. Going
by boat is best.… Could you employ your genius to get a
small boat to cross over to Settsu?"

"That's easy but where are you going this time?"

"Gifu's my destination."

"Gifu."

"But it may be a gamble."

"… If you get there, will Oda Nobunaga be there?"

"First of all, my business is there …. Here in
Chugoku, eyes queerly brighten upon hearing the name
Nobunaga. If it were known that a senior retainer from
Gochaku was going there, turmoil would bubble up like a

boiling kettle. Therefore, I must go in secret. The boat captain must be absolutely reliable. Otherwise, I want you to find a fool."

"I understand. The area is identical to enemy territory until you get close to Kyoto. In that case, you'll be on your own."

"No, no matter what precautions I take, it'll be difficult to escape being killed. If my karma is inexhaustible, any difficulty I encounter will end well."

"That has been your temperament since you were a boy. Once your mind is made up, you will not bend. Well, if you think you're in danger along the way, I have an older brother in Itami in Settsu ..." said Kiku sipping tea beside him, "He's related by marriage, but my brother is a silversmith named Shinshichi and runs a small shop. You can hide there. If you give him orders, he will work his fingers to the bone to serve you in place of my father."

"So a silversmith in Itami. There may be trouble. I'll be sure to remember," said Kanbei and sipped the tea offered by Kiku, "I'd like a bowl of boiled rice before leaving for the boat."

"Kiku, prepare a bowl. In the meantime, I will go to the beach and hire a reliable man with a boat," said Yojiemon and left.

CHAPTER EIGHT
THE SAIL AT THE VANGUARD

1

TWILIGHT ENVELOPED THE town. With nightfall, the coastal breeze flowed in to chill even the back streets.

Yojiemon came back just as Kanbei finished his boiled rice. He cautioned Kanbei, "It may be a bit inconvenient, but I paid a mute but very reliable boatman to bring a boat around just below Karimatsu.... This evening more than ten seamen from the Mouri clan go ashore for drinks in the red-light district with a group of samurai from Miki Castle. Be very careful when you go out because mostly unseen samurai will be walking around town."

Kanbei bowed and said, "I had a thought while eating. I have a hunch that dressed like this may not pose any problems on the sea journey, but the walk to Gifu will not be easy. Because peddlers leave this house to sell eye medicines in different provinces, why don't you lend me the provisions for peddling? I will leave here in a little while with an altered appearance."

Yojiemon agreed with this excellent idea. He gathered slightly soiled underclothes and leggings worn by peddlers and watched Kanbei change his clothes. Yojiemon had raised Kanbei from a young age but worried deep down about Kanbei's readiness for the possible dangers and turned his face to furtively wipe away a tear.

The man himself, however, seemed to be without a care in the world and shared none of that sentiment.

Kanbei turned to show Kiku and playfully asked, "How do I look? Does it suit me?"

He added, "The baggage can't be empty. That'll be important if someone decides to inspect them. Please put in a credit notebook, the shop's emblem, and all the bits and pieces.... What? My hair? Of course, I can't wear a topknot. Kiku-san, please untie and fix my hair?"

Although in a hurry, he was meticulous.

2

Before the moon rose, Kanbei left through the back door. Though strongly encouraged not to, Yojiemon went as far as the beach. Kiku said she wanted to see Kanbei off at the boat, but he told her to come later.

He passed through the town in long strides and soon came to the shore at Karimatsu. He saw a small boat moored there. Kanbei approached the water's edge and called out twice, "Are you the boatman hired by Yojiemon? Is this boat hired to go to Settsu?"

The boatman was leaning over in the stern and stoking the fire in the hearth under some sort of stew he was cooking. He didn't turn to look.

"Aha, ha, ha, ha."

Kanbei laughed alone. He remembered the boatman was mute.

Kanbei waited alone for Yojiemon to come. For some reason, his wait was surprisingly long, but finally Yojiemon appeared.

"I'm sorry for making you wait. I followed right after you but ran into Lord Kinugasa at the crossroads of town, so ..."

Yojiemon looked back and ran away.

Kinugasa Kyuzaemon, the attendant of Kanbei's father in Himeji, had changed his appearance to become a peddler of eye medicine and, without a word, lowered his head to his knees as he held his straw hat in both hands.

"Ah, Kyuzaemon. Why have you been shadowing me?"

"By order of the lord."

"What? My father ordered this.… When we near the residence in Himeyama, I will bid you farewell, it will be brusque and I'll leave quickly. As you see me off, scold me for my reluctance to leave."

"Despite his encouragement as your father, he was probably deeply concerned about your destination this time.… After the young lord departed, he sent me in the event of an unexpected incident. The life of one child is linked to the future of the entire land of Chugoku. In words of gratitude, he told me to perform this duty I'm unworthy of. I followed to protect you so that this journey ends without incident."

"… Really?"

Kanbei looked back at the skies of Himeji. Without revealing any uncertainty, he ordered Yojiemon to hail the mute's boat to the shore.

"Yojiemon, you've been a great help. Well, I'll see you again," said Kanbei then quickly went with Kyuzaemon to the boat. The expressionless boatman had already gripped the squeaking oar and was rowing. The sea surface was calm, and a seasonal evening breeze blew. The boatman raised the sail as soon as the boat left the shore.

Below Karimatsu, the father and daughter saw them off until the white sail was out of sight.

That evening, no one knew about the goings-on in the world of Chugoku. The sail filled by the south wind stealthily moved south on the harmonious sea, and in time would drastically alter the state of affairs in Sanyo, have a lasting impact on all of Japan, and form the vanguard of a revolutionary force.

CHAPTER NINE
KAJIYA

1

THE SHORT JOURNEY from Himeji to Gifu over sea and then by land took a little over a month. Finally, near the end of July, the two eye lotion peddlers arrived. Their appearances reflected the withering hardships of a lifetime during that short time. Filth had accumulated on their collars. Their faces were burned black. Even the flesh around their eye sockets thinned. Anyone looking at them now would not see a senior retainer of the Kodera clan and his follower. They would only see two dirty men traveling by foot to sell the family heirloom Reijukou.

"Well, Kyuzaemon, this castle town is prosperous. No, it's a spirited town."

"Yes, it's a lively place. The looks in their eyes and the strides of the passersby are completely different from those in Chugoku."

"You think so? The goods gathered in a city give you a glimpse into its culture, but what's found in the city of Zhucheng or the ports in the western provinces are noticeably better."

"But passion like this is not found in Chugoku."

"Naturally, the west exhibits the conservative policies

40

of the Mouri clan and differs from the east that burns with the spirit of revolution and the casting off of the old. Isn't it obvious they're both the central forces moving this age?"

As they walked, Kanbei spoke often, sharing his observations. When someone traveling the road approached, he immediately went mum. They were adept at appearing to be master and servant to the eyes of strangers.

"However, to meet Nobunaga-sama, who is the most trusted among the elders of the Oda clan to act as the go-between to request an audience on our behalf? Do you have a plan?" Kinugasa Kyuzaemon asked his master Kanbei when they entered the land of their destination then turned his thoughts to going to Gifu Castle. They stayed at a grimy lodging house in the town of Kajiya then spent the day they arrived and the following day walking around town and selling the eye medication.

"Mmmm.... It's just as you said, Kyuzaemon. If I find relatives of my father and mother in the Oda clan and am able to make contact despite my being a stranger to them, I may meet people who would understand. But how I begin is critical. More than that, this is a serious problem. It would be best not to use a shallow man as the intermediary."

"The influential men now in the Oda clan begin with Lord Hayashi Hidesada, Lord Sakuma Nobumori, and Lord Mori Yoshinari," said Kyuzaemon.

"And Shibata Katsuie, Takigawa Ichimasu, Niwa Goroza, Ikeda Nobuteru," said Kanbei.

"And Lord Maeda, Lord Akechi, and Lord Hashiba."

Kanbei counted each one on his fingers and shook his head when Kyuzaemon mentioned Lord Hashiba.

"The heat is awful. Gifu is hot. I'm through with selling today," said Kanbei and turned at the crossroads to return to the lodging house in Kajiya.

2

In the section of back streets that was home to the many craftsmen in smithery, dyeing, and leather tanning, the red flames from bellows, the sounds of hammers, and the shouts of men working went on night and day. Even in the dead of night while the entire castle town of Gifu slept, sparks scattered in this neighborhood.

It was the summer of year 3 of Tensho, just after the Battle of Nagashino. This craftsmen's town was given to the feudal lord who had just returned in triumph after a second chance to win a decisive victory over a second-rate province and vanquish Takeda Shingen from Mount Kabuto who, for a long time, took pride in his invincible Iron Army. Naturally, the times were prosperous but not blindly competitive. Groups of half-naked sculptures with faces washed by sweat stood with menace in the workrooms in the houses and on the streets.

They would say things like, "Yeah, we won big at Anegawa and Nagashino. There's no one like our great general. Nothing scares him. He values each spear and each arrowhead forged by us. Look, everything from Echigo Uesugi, Hongan-ji Temple, and the Mouri of Chugoku, you know, was melted in the bellows in our blacksmith sheds."

These sorts of men gathered in what seemed to be a sake shop next to the cheap lodging house where the master Kanbei and his follower stayed. Kanbei thought they'd probably tire as night fell, but at that moment, their excitement seeped through the walls.

The lively voices were bearable, but the walls shook, and rat droppings fell from the ceiling beams onto his sleeping face. Kyuzaemon also seemed surprised, lifted his head from his wooden pillow, and griped, "This place is awful. No mosquito nets. That racket. We picked a fine house."

He looked over to see Kanbei whose pillow was placed on a similar straw mat awake, but he was smiling.

Kyuzaemon said, "Well, we're probably not getting any sleep tonight. We should change to another inn tomorrow. Since this is a nightly ritual, we'll never get enough sleep."

Kanbei said, "No matter where we go, it'll be the same. Heat and mosquitoes ..."

Kanbei slowly woke and sat up on the flimsy straw futon. He said, "After listening to the clear voices from next door while resting, I now understand various aspects about the prices and popular opinion in this castle town. I chose to stay here on purpose because I saw the sake shop next door. Kyuzaemon, you must put up with the lack of sleep."

CHAPTER TEN
A LATE NIGHT KNOCK
AT THE GATE

1

TOKICHIRO HIDEYOSHI WAS second-in-command in a
platoon from the Odani Castle in Kitaoumi, commanded
Konida for a short time, and arrived today in Gifu.

With a win in Nagashino, the expectation of the
dispatch of troops to Echizen coming next was the feeling
in the air in Gifu. Although the subtle plot was a secret, it
was sensed by everyone and soon had the force of the tide.
This could not be hidden from the eyes and ears of all.

At the corner of the crossroads, Tokichiro Hideyoshi
dismounted and shouted, "No, I'm not going to the inn.
I'm going straight to the castle.... Only men carrying the
packs proceed to the inn."

After the downfall of the Asai clan, he became the
lord of the castle in Odani and finally added authority to
his status and popularity, and he was only thirty-nine years
old. His build was compact, and he lacked the majesty to
make eyes light up. His face had been burned dark red by
the scorching sun. A stranger's first impression would be
an officer commanding around one hundred men.

"What? Are they going back?"

"Go back. Go back. Leave the packs."

Naturally, his officers seemed to have a prior belief that when they arrived here, they would set up an encampment, wipe off sweat, rest their bodies, and relax for a night. They reported Hideyoshi's words again and ordered an immediate return to the bend in the road. In an instant, an unbelievable traffic jam smelling of the sweat of horses and men clogged the crossroads.

The page on horseback beside Hideyoshi snapped around his spear to point down the road and screeched, "Look, someone's coming!"

A man they encountered a little earlier under the eaves of a merchant's house was galloping up to the side of Hideyoshi's mount. He held no weapons and was only burdened by a load of eye medication for sale and a bamboo hat. The other officers did not react recklessly; only their eyes turned up in unison.

"There's nothing suspicious about him. He's been waiting since this morning for your occasional passage through here as the messenger of his lord. This note from his lord is a request for you to act as an intermediary."

A letter could be seen in his hand, and a soldier on foot took it and passed it to an officer on horseback. The officer looked like he was wondering if it were some sort of trick as he turned to Hideyoshi already leaning over with his hand extended.

He read the short note in a glance. Hideyoshi's gaze shifted to Kyuzaemon wearing his straw hat and gave his response.

"Tell him to come this evening."

Kyuzaemon was ecstatic and said, "Tonight."

"You can be a little late."

"Where?"

"Ask anyone, he will tell you. The temple west of town. The one with the gate painted red."

"Yessir."

When Kyuzaemon bowed and raised his head, the dust kicked up by the horses of the officers already concealed Hideyoshi's figure. The sounds of galloping left the town at high noon headed to the front gate of Inabayama Castle.

2

Before meeting Nobunaga, Kanbei would first meet with this man, known to history as Toyotomi Hideyoshi but known then as Hashiba Tokichiro. In this case, Nobunaga would be met through that man and not through a man with hereditary wealth.

Kuroda Kanbei became aware of Hashiba of the Oda clan while back in his home country. He was obsessed with this man, and his prior expectations were bolstered by various meaningful events after coming to Gifu.

Senior hereditary vassals and high-ranking generals in the Oda clan spoke ill of him and called him a monkey. His reputation among them wasn't that he was merely not good but wholly inadequate. However, the backbone of up-and-coming officers certainly judged him to be a fair man and respected him. Most important to Kanbei, the people in the castle town trusted "that man." They had no interest in the idea of confronting Tokichiro. Everyone praised Hashiba-sama and his virtue. When speaking of Tokichiro of Odani, public opinion was unanimous.

"He is a great man."

For a time, Kanbei wondered what support Tokichiro received from the common people. Different from the support for other brave and courageous generals, Kanbei hadn't heard anyone speak of Tokichiro's bravery. Whether acting as a magistrate, building a castle, or being appointed an administrator, great successes were always found in posts filled by Tokichiro. When people who worked for him returned to town, every last one trumpeted his greatness. When sighted, even in lands ruled under occupation, everyone recognized him as the head of the clan.

Kanbei thought, He is, without a doubt, a man of merit. Even in a clan with new approaches like the Oda clan, should I risk my greatest hope by entrusting it to the sort of men who boast of being hereditary retainers? I will meet him and test his ability. If Hashiba Tokichiro is the man to ask, after I make him my puppet, I will not delay in meeting Nobunaga.

Kanbei looked from every perspective and came to this decision. A major miscalculation as he waited to meet Tokichiro (Hideyoshi) was the feeling in his heart.

"I intend to skillfully capture Hideyoshi for my great wish and to use him well."

But when he looked back to his surprise, Kanbei had not realized the tables had turned.

3

It was the middle of the night.

The master Kuroda and his follower stopped in front of the temple near the edge of the castle town.

There was a reason to say the middle of the night was good. Kanbei deliberately came late at night.

Kinugasa Kyuzaemon knocked on the small door beside the gate and said to the guard inside, "I'm sorry to keep you waiting. We're here as arranged."

The guard seemed to be unfamiliar with Hideyoshi's will and persisted in questioning Kanbei. He had good reason; Kanbei had not changed his clothes that night and remained a peddler of eye medications. Given his appearance, the guard's doubt was natural.

"Wait here," said the guard and made Kanbei stand outside the gate for a time, in fact, for about a half hour. Finally, several other retainers came and with exceptional courtesy apologized for their rudeness.

"The truth is Lord Hideyoshi has spent few nights in inns from Kitaomi to this land. He slept in camps but spent his waking hours on horseback. He has reached a state of no sleep or rest. As soon as he arrived, he came to this castle without stopping at an inn because the conversation with Lord Nobunaga will finally take place this evening when he arrives.... As soon as Lord Hideyoshi bathed, he fell asleep and began snoring loudly. That was terribly rude, but he will now meet with you. Come this way," said a retainer who held aloft a candle to guide them deep inside the temple garden.

Several men of the Hashiba clan took turns providing reasons and apologies to the guest. They were probably pages serving Hideyoshi. He believed he recognized among the young faces those who directed their spears at Kyuzaemon at noon that day. In any case, the servants appeared to endorse this elegant guest. They didn't deliberately conceal the lord's fatigue and escorted the guests to a room. The brightness conveyed by people in the house was much brighter than the lights there. One family custom of the Hashiba clan was displayed without reserve.

CHAPTER ELEVEN
THE FIRST MEETING

1

THE FOLLOWER KYUZAEMON waited in another room. Only Kanbei passed down the corridor to an inner reception room.

Three candles lit the interior measuring about twenty tatami mats enclosed by white sliding partitions. A line of pages dressed in fine clothes brushed past him with food trays as he entered. Hideyoshi appeared to have awoken and finished his meal this late at night. Kanbei guessed his days were hectic and his private life haphazard. He had to persevere without regard to time.

Hideyoshi saw the guest and said, "And this is ..." and rose from his cushion to greet him. Before Kanbei sat, Hideyoshi walked right up to him.

"Thank you for coming. I didn't expect a guest. But first ..."

Hideyoshi took his hand and greeted him like a friend of ten years. Although a proud, independent lord should have a majestic appearance, his manner showed no trace of those characteristics. More surprising, his bearing lacked dignity. Kanbei was not a big man, and Hideyoshi had a small build, too. His sole uncommon quality was his resonant, clear, booming voice. His loud voice while at odds with his body seemed to embody the nature of this man. When his guest sat, he received a simple greeting. Hideyoshi began this unexpected story.

"I've already heard many things about you. I don't consider this to be our first meeting and already think of you as an old friend. Specifically, I've accompanied Lord Nobunaga to Kyoto several times, you were often mentioned by my lord and his friend Konoe Sakihisa. Your mother's father Lord Akashi Masakaze was always respected as a teacher of tanka poetry by the previous head of the Konoe clan during his youth as well as by Lord Sakihisa."

He went on to describe everything from the recent situation in Gochaku, which was nothing more than a rural district in Chugoku, to the relationship between the Kuroda clan and the Kodera clan. The breadth and depth of his knowledge amazed Kanbei.

"Not from a few people, I've heard that the son of the eye medicine peddler in Himeji is a talented man. Not only from men in the Konoe clan but from men like Araki Murashige of Settsu, I've been told about a gifted man worthy of attention in the future. I thought if I had the opportunity I would like to meet this man one time. You can't know my joy when you intentionally came to Gifu. When I received the note from your servant today at the crossroads, I suspected a coincidence, another man with the same family name. Well, tonight is a delightful night."

His honest, cheerful figure rose above ordinary frivolous compliments or merely being sociable. He forgot the distinction between his social status and that of others or between host and guest and plainly expressed his feelings as a candid man.

2

Kanbei was a little stiff until he glimpsed this room. This could be considered normal. In the end, he was a high-

level government official who was no more than a minor
daimyo in the countryside. His companion was a man with
one castle despite serving under Oda Nobunaga. The
difference in rank was remarkable. To Kanbei, being in the
same room was an exceptional courtesy.

Kanbei never thought about the menial nature of
being said to serve under Hideyoshi. If he was the lord of a
castle, so was Kanbei who also led a military family. If he
was eminent among core military men, Kanbei also had
the self-confidence to move the state of affairs in Chugoku
to the west or to the east with one finger. He did not say it
but amply demonstrated it.

Kanbei said, "Oh, really? You know that much about
this country boy. I didn't expect that. You make me very
happy. I have no response to your words. In fact, I was
always fascinated by the name Hashiba Tokichiro while
home. Thus, every detail of the rumors from the street
entered these ears. No one in the Oda clan other than you
inhabits my mind."

Hideyoshi said, "That is mysterious. Although
unseen, there was a mutual longing. In some way, public
criticisms like those about me usually are not good rumors
but are often negative. To show such favor toward me is a
blessing."

"To be honest, before we met, I imagined a man with
a more imposing physique, but only that was a little
unexpected," said Kanbei.

"When young, I lived under trying circumstances in
the home of poor peasants. By nature, I am skinny.
However, when I glanced at you, I noticed you did not
have a powerful build. How old are you?" asked
Hideyoshi.

"Exactly thirty."

"Ah, thirty years old. I am the older brother, nine
years your senior."

To distinguish Kanbei from himself at this first
meeting, Hideyoshi used the words older brother. In his

heart, Kanbei was a little suspicious of that extraneous remark, but Hideyoshi didn't seem to think that unfair and quickly looked at the man seated beside him.

"… Well, Kanbei, there are two differences between you and I. You are the youngest, and I have the title of Chikuzen. If you think about it, at some time, I entered the class of young men. And yet, I'm unable to enter the club of young men," said Hideyoshi with a touch of self-mockery and a big laugh.

The only other person present smiled but did not say a word. His first greeting was a slight nod. Again without speaking, this warrior sat close beside Hideyoshi. His face was white and thin. His clear eyes were ready like a hawk resting his wings on a pine tree. Kanbei felt uneasy for some time and took this opportunity to ask him, "Who are you? Where is your family?"

CHAPTER TWELVE
THE HAWK

1

"OH, WHO IS he?"

Hideyoshi began to properly introduce him.

"He is Takenaka Hanbei Shigeharu. You may know of him. He's the son of the lord of the Bodaisan Castle in Iwamura in Mino Province. He is now also my teacher of military strategy, the only one in the clan. Lord Nobunaga created a special relationship for him to join the Hashiba clan. The time may come when he will be summoned to return to the lord and I will be a troubled clan member with constant panic in my heart. In other words, he is my unrivaled right-hand man. Kanbei, you two may become inseparable friends. Sworn friends would be nice."

When Hideyoshi finished, Hanbei Shigeharu quietly turned for the first time to greet Kanbei on this first meeting. In contrast to Hideyoshi, his voice was solemn like *muratake* mushrooms whispering on a snowy night. He never spoke without a reason. His bow radiated a charming intelligence and a temperament that gave one a vague desire to have a drink with him.

"Oh, you are Lord Takenaka. I am honored to meet you," said a flustered Kanbei and bowed. For some reason,

he couldn't embrace moderate self-deprecation with
Hanbei as he had when speaking with Hideyoshi. Of
course, he was the true loser by being the country samurai.
However, he realized his companion did not have the
conceit of looking down on him.

Nevertheless, he thought this sort of man would find
it impossible to be content with serving the Hashiba clan.
Takenaka Shigeharu, the son of Bodaisan Castle in Mino,
was a world-class genius whose name has been known for
a long time to all military strategists. Kanbei heard his
name often spoken since he was a boy. In a sense, Hanbei
Shigeharu's famous name may be heard more than the
name of General Hashiba Hideyoshi of the Oda clan.

Many young men were said to reside in the imperial
city of Kyoto. Most of them practiced Zen meditation at
Daitoku-ji Temple. Once word was received from their
hometowns about a battle, they mounted their horses and
whipped them to gallop to the battlefield. When the battle
ended, the figures seen on the Zen floor became the talk
of the capital.

One day on that battlefield, Hanbei Shigeharu laid
down his long sword named after Tora Gozen, the
courtesan lover of the vengeful Soga no Juro, and his
armor coarsened by a grainy varnish.

> *If this young lord is placed at the vanguard, he will*
> *play some important role in the military and*
> *strengthen the spirit throughout the entire rank and*
> *file.*

Not only did this belief about him pervade this clan,
this opinion was widely held. In that age, a man with a
profound knowledge of military science was counted as a
leader. His resolve to fight, his earnest protection, and his
generosity resembled an ocean. His divine plans of strategy
were evaluated as highly as the work of the second coming
of the Chinese military strategists Zhuge Liang and Nan.

Like Hideyoshi, he was greatly admired. Here is a

story barely known in the world. When Hideyoshi still resided in Sunomata Castle and first had possession of the fortress and a narrow territory, the young genius was quickly welcomed as an ally. Hideyoshi traveled dozens of times to urge Hanbei Shigeharu back to the active world from his seclusion in a thatched hut on Mount Kurihara.

Long ago in China, Liu Xuande, the founder of the Shu-Han dynasty, knocked on the door of the thatched hut to invite Zhuge Liang to become his military adviser. Hashiba Chikuzen's enthusiasm was drawn in by the exceptional Hanbei hidden among the masses.

At any rate, this matter did not become a problem of military affairs in this warring state. Sadly, why didn't heaven bestow strong bodies on men like Takenaka Hanbei? He had been sickly from his youth. That was lamentable. Hideyoshi always showed exceptional concern for him as if he were an exquisite fragile instrument by his side.

In the loneliness of remote parts of Chugoku, Kuroda Kanbei heard swiftly spreading rumors and forgot what he had imagined and forgotten about him. Kanbei sat up, paid solemn attention to his existence and his importance, and recalled every early opinion he heard about Takenaka Hanbei because on this night he met the man.

2

A page came to report, "The bath is ready."

Hideyoshi said, "Well, Kanbei? The page will escort you. Would you like a bath in hot water?"

Still not knowing the purpose of Kanbei's visit, Hideyoshi came to a hasty conclusion and made this offer as a reward for his guest.

Hideyoshi said, "What? Nothing is better than enjoying a bath in the summer. It's nice to wash away the sweat and put on a summer kimono.... The evening is short, but the room will be prepared and we will dine.... Did you come here after having dinner? The meals build up, but I will actually eat only half a meal. I woke from an early nap and took the opportunity to eat as I waited for your visit. I just began my meal and left half of it uneaten. First, drinks will stimulate the conversation. Be that as it may, go enjoy your bath."

As if unaware of the time growing late, Hideyoshi urged him to go and secreted himself with Hanbei in a private room. A page urged him from behind and guided him to the bathroom. With no way out, Kanbei accompanied him. He had no room in his heart to leisurely enjoy a bath. He wondered, How and when can I broach this troubling concern in my heart. While searching for the right time, he worried about missing his opportunity.

Kinugasa Kyuzaemon waited in another room and was worrying himself to death over the outcome of the conversation. As Kanbei and the page passed by his room in the long corridor, Kyuzaemon caught sight of a worried-looking Kanbei.

CHAPTER THIRTEEN
AN EVENING TALK WITH YOU

1

IN THE DEAD of night when people and their stabled horses were fast asleep, candlelight lit a room and drinks were shared.

After his bath, the guest Kanbei changed into a summer kimono that felt good on his cool skin. He freely drank more than usual and was talkative as if restored to life.

Hideyoshi loved sake and Takenaka Hanbei had a taste for it. When joined by Kanbei, the three sat in a triangle. Kanbei put up with the determined lord and his associate.

Summer nights are short. Especially when men speak frankly in a chance meeting, negotiate the ideal, squarely face reality, and talk of the joy of being born together at this time, the merriment does not fade even as the night grows late.

Kanbei asked, "I'll say it again, but what is your future grand strategy, the so-called world affairs, what is the prime target after the suppression of Chugoku? While the force of the powerful Mouri clan stubbornly guards the land and sea west of Settsu, Lord Nobunaga may raise his

banner in the land of Chugen and in Kyoto, or drive out
Shogun Ashikaga and his supporters like sweeping away
the people and the evils of the former shogunate, or one
by one conquer the powerful and minor shoguns in Kinki
who are not yielding, or attain stability in the Tokai area, or
destroy the powerful clan in the land of Kozan. In the end,
all of that cannot be said to be satisfying. These may not
be your ideal thoughts. How will the subjugation of
Chugoku end? ... The Mouri clan is linked to Ishiyama
Hongan-ji Temple. Resistance by the Hongan-ji sect is
taking various forms. If a split develops in the substance of
the sect in the northern lands of Ise in Kinki, under the
current circumstances, flames will rise and anti-Nobunaga
disturbances will erupt. So will there be more incidents?
Attacking Nagashima, attacking Hokuriku are minor
details. Why hasn't a direct attack been launched to
eradicate the Hongan-ji Temple with its puppets or the
decision made to assemble a great force to conquer
Chugoku? ... I think I'm actually the impatient one."

As the talk of the drinking conclave further livened
up, various matters were broached and veered into other
topics. The above words that burst from Kanbei's breast
were not explained in one breath. He observed his
companions' expressions, estimated suitable quantities for
their cups, and leaked out only the above essential points
many times.

Given that, his companion Hideyoshi was surely not
deaf to his problem. Hideyoshi was a better listener than
speaker. He carefully listened to a man's opinion and
displayed his enthusiasm on his face while listening.
However, his response was half-hearted compared to
Kanbei's passion.

Hideyoshi explained, "From the beginning, the
problems of Chugoku had to be neglected. For a long
time, I thought the keen insight of Lord Nobunaga should
not neglect future plans. Regrettably, the Oda clan has
been active in the surrounding provinces. The clan went to

war with Ise a few years ago, engaged in a great battle in Nagashino in May, and without a break to rest the soldiers and horses, immediately began to prepare for an expedition north to Hokuriku. Events at this pace are not caused by any weakness in our Oda clan or a collapse caused by a poor strategy. In short, like our counterparts, the work of the Oda clan still lacks experience. Think about it. The Oda clan began at the Battle of Okehazama. At that time Lord Nobunaga was a little older than twenty-five. Now he is forty-two, so that deed was a short seventeen years ago. Over those years, he advanced from the rank of a high-level official of Owari Kiyosu, swept away the long-standing vices from Kyoto, and behaved with loyalty unmatched in the world of the old Muromachi shogunate.... Gradually, no, swiftly, we retainers marveled at acts thought to be utterly impossible over the lifetime by an ordinary man being achieved in that short time. Consequently, roughness in the process was inevitable. The natural resolution remains in that rapid process. At any rate, this integrity still has not reached Chugoku. In the end, the feet go first. I think the resolution in Chugoku will be quick as it has been so far. Future rivals will be strong countries, unlike those in the past."

The intentions presented by Hideyoshi were gathered by Kanbei. But nothing more was asserted. The sake was good, and Kanbei expected his companions to be worth confiding in, but he ended up feeling dissatisfied.

2

"It'll be too late. That usual path is walked and eventually it's too late."

Kanbei's voice was tinged with excitement. The strength of the sake from the empty bottle probably encouraged him. The cup was never away from his indignant lips.

"Too late?" asked Hideyoshi.

He smiled but instantly feigned ignorance at Kanbei's

disappointment.

Kanbei asked, "Do you understand? Military preparations by the Mouri aren't finished in a day. It's longer than you imagine."

"I understand," said Hideyoshi.

"We have few allies in Settsu, Yamashiro, and Izumi but will try to take one step into Harima. Perhaps, I am a man who is mulling over whether to bow to the Oda clan or join the Mouri. First, there is the entire ruling party of the Mouri," said Kanbei.

"Hmm. Is that likely?" asked Hideyoshi.

"Even when positioned on land, which province will control the seas throughout the Settsu domain from inside the strait to the mouth of the river at Osaka? Isn't it the Mouri clan? They have several hundred regular warships and over a thousand transport ships. These ships constantly run between Naniwa and Quanzhou and maintain contact with Ishiyama Hongan-ji. No one asks the reason for one warship and a crew of seamen in the Oda clan," said Kanbei.

This time, Hideyoshi screwed up his face in disgust. Two wrinkles stood up between his eyebrows. He may have wanted to be considered the man who appears during unpleasant times.

The keenly perceptive Kanbei immediately put down his cup and was quiet. If Takenaka Hanbei beside him had not chuckled at this time, the atmosphere may have become difficult to rescue as a fissure opened between the host and his guest.

"... Kanbei," said Hideyoshi forcing a smile. Drawn in by Takenaka Hanbei, he couldn't stop himself from smiling and asked, "Would you like more sake?"

Kanbei did not answer deliberately and acted like he hadn't heard.

"No, you've had enough.... But Kanbei ..." said Hideyoshi.

"Yes," said Kanbei.

"I will speak the truth."

"What is it?"

"Of course, you are nine years my junior,"

"Are the current reasoning in the Oda clan and the power demanded in the future the power of youth and dreams?"

In an instant, Kanbei was at ease. Although young, he was the real thing. At the same time, the tone of Hideyoshi's voice was tinged with a bit of peevishness and increased slightly in volume in his attempt to reassure, "Drink, drink. I will speak on various matters in an audience with Lord Nobunaga. I am nothing more than a general who moves by the commands of Nobunaga-sama.... If permitted by the castle, even if it's tomorrow, I will accompany you to Gifu Castle for a consultation."

The ensuing conversation didn't touch on military matters or politics at all. Kanbei had enough passion and sacrifice in his heart to stake his fortune on the clan of Lord Kodera, overcome a great deal of opposition, and part with his father, wife, and child who he may never see again. Naturally, he was filled with the feeling of wanting to reveal all of this. The broad-minded Hideyoshi appeared to say the state of affairs in the Kodera clan was fine. Kanbei felt weak when forced into worry and gloom over Hideyoshi's indifference. Without saying much, he simply drank cup after cup.

Hideyoshi said, "If we're able to meet him tomorrow, you will also understand Nobunaga-sama's personality, but the lord also likes good cheer. He often offers sake and calls for a small group of pages to sing *kouta* ditties and dance. And he hums impromptu songs, too. Kanbei, do you have any talents?"

Kanbei was exasperated with Hideyoshi's digression and roared, "I also sing and dance to kouta songs and perform the *Sarumai* dance."

"You are a man of many talents. Will you dance?" asked Hideyoshi and handed Kanbei his fan.

"Here? Right now? I'm sorry ..." said Kanbei and waved his hand to decline. He went over to a sleepy-eyed page, who had retreated to a corner, in search of an inkstone case. He wrote something on the fan and returned it to Hideyoshi and said, "Lord, will you please sing?"

Hideyoshi smiled wryly at his return blow. He leaned away from his armrest to tilt the white fan toward the candle to read it.

> *We drink until late*
> *The color of sake*
> *We chat*
> *The taste of people*
> *The night grows short*
> *Who said,*
> *The wellspring never runs dry*
> *Another cup of sake*

"Hanbei, what has he written on the back?" asked Hideyoshi and nimbly passed the fan to Takenaka Hanbei who picked up a brush and on the back wrote a Chinese verse.

> *Listening to you for one evening*
> *Better than ten years of reading*

Kanbei quickly took back the fan and stared. Little by little, his drunkenness was washed away. He gently set down the white fan still wet with ink and respectfully placed both hands on the floor and to Hanbei said, "Thank you," and bowed his head.

As a smile was glimpsed moving like a ripple from the abyss in his eyes, Hanbei Shigeharu said, "I thank you," and slid both hands from his knees.

It was daybreak. The sounds of the bells for the service rang deep in the temple. Near the temple gate out front, the horses in the stable neighed.

3

The business at Gifu Castle was done. Hideyoshi had planned to immediately return to the castle in Odani but extended his stay by two days for Kanbei's sake. With the permission of Nobunaga, he accompanied Kanbei to the castle.

The audience with Nobunaga was not a formal affair. He was met with great secrecy in a small room as a secret envoy.

That year, the forty-two-year-old Nobunaga spoke with youthful vigor. He looked younger than Hideyoshi. During the hot day, only those three met in the same room for two hours.

Kanbei explained the situation. He described the urgency of the conquest of Chugoku from every perspective. He spoke with sincerity and without a bit of affectation or sophistry and did not waste one moment. His eloquence surpassed his own belief. In the end, he took no notice of his companion's status as a nobleman.

Kanbei said, "If a general is given the order to carry out the important work of subjugating Chugoku, like the Kajiwara clan of Takasago Castle and Akaishi Castle in Higashi-Harima, he will probably crouch in fear at the sight of the imposing presence of troops under the command of the Mouri. Fortunately, Kushihashi Sakyo, the lord of the castle in Shikata, is a relative of mine by marriage and can be drawn in as an ally. Bessho Nagaharu of Miki Castle was the only one to stubbornly refuse to surrender. Again in Nishi-Harima, Fukuhara of Sayo Castle and the Kozuki family of Kozuki Castle are tied to Bessho Nagaharu and are believed to have allegiance to the Mouri clan…. Of these large and small castles, Himeji Castle occupies the most strategic land and will not make an open declaration if an enemy is said to be present because I am making this pledge in your presence to be the vanguard of the allies. For that reason, Himeji Castle has been prepared from the beginning to offer help. If honored to be chosen as the base for the conquest of Chugoku, the castle will be promptly handed over."

Nobunaga was pleased with his bluntness. His scrupulous nature did not appear to harbor any suspicions about Kanbei's sincerity and passion. He said, "Because the day is near when Himeji Castle will be very useful if used with discretion, you will be in charge until that time," then he added, "That is the mark of an attendant."

Nobunaga picked up his celebrated *Heshikiri* sword beside him and handed it to Kanbei. The history of this sword according to *The Treasures and Ancient Practices of the Kuroda Clan* bore this inscription on its back:

> *This sword is the handiwork of Hasebe Kunishige. It has a length of 2-shaku, 1-sun, 4-bun. Lord Nobunaga was going to execute a man called Kannai with this sword. Kannai was terrified and tried to escape by hiding under a kitchen cupboard. The lord killed Kannai by a sword given the name The Powerful Cutter because this sword did not remember the hand that inserted it in the cupboard and provided its own force to cut.*

Nobunaga said, "For now, return to Chugoku and wait for my orders. When the time is right, the orders will come."

Kanbei carried Nobunaga's pledge and his Heshikiri sword and retreated to the castle. On that day, the castle and its town were congested with the comings and goings of several generals with their troops and horses. He wondered if prominent men such as Niwa, Takigawa, and Shibata, or Saza, Akechi, and Maeda were among them but spoke to no one other than Hideyoshi.

"I'm satisfied. You are too. First, we left the abyss and met at the edge of a storm. We encountered a genius hidden among men and finally a prudent man," said Hideyoshi, who was cheered by his happiness. On that day, Hideyoshi would return home to northern Omi. He suggested Kanbei come to Odani Castle and stay a few days.

"We'll ride together."

Hideyoshi borrowed a horse and followed behind the column of Kanbei and Kinugawa Kyuzaemon and traveled with them until Nagahama.

When they arrived in Nagahama, Hideyoshi paid a visit to Niwa Gorozaemon and borrowed two boats.

"This is better than an overland route in this heat. We should pass through the center of a lake during the night to travel to Otsu. The moon is nice, too. While enjoying the cool air, I'll see you off along the way," said Hideyoshi.

A cook and the retainer Gorozaemon boarded one boat. Kanbei and Hideyoshi boarded the other boat. Around dusk, the boats left the shore. When the moon was high in the sky, Kanbei and Hideyoshi's boat reached the center of Lake Biwa. They drank sake, praised the moon, and talked about the future. The night grew late and the boats separated. As each watched the other leave and waved farewell on the waters, they thought about what had happened, Kanbei tasted tears on his cheeks for the first time in his life. Why was he crying?

CHAPTER FOURTEEN
DEATH AS A PILLOW

1

ARAKI MURASHIGE IN Settsu held an important position. As the lord of the main Itami Castle, he was connected to Amagasaki Castle and Hanakuma Castle in Hyogo and linked together three castles, blocked travel between Chugoku and Osaka, and kept a close watch on communications between anti-Nobunaga elements and the Mouri clan. If the morning came when orders to conquer Chugoku were issued by Nobunaga, this place would become a pivotal point and the frontline base of Oda's forces.

Kanbei understood how much Nobunaga valued Murashige's bravery and depended on the honesty of that obstinate man.

"Aren't you Kanbei? Why have you come here? This is sudden," Araki Murashige asked Kanbei. He promptly granted a meeting but viewed him with suspicion.

Obviously, the place was the castle keep of Itami Castle (Murashige changed the name to Arioka Castle). For some reason, the castle was in an uproar. The generals seemed to be preparing for war. Troops were gathered at allotted locations inside the gate and trotting through various gates and down corridors.

After Kanbei finished his formal greeting, he said, "I've heard you will soon send forces to Hokuriku."

"It's as you think. Lord Nobunaga will also go. Perhaps, this time, we will not return home until the maneuvering of the ruling party managed by the Ikko Monto sect in Hokuriku and Uesugi Kenshin is annihilated," said Murashige. A beautiful maid beside him served sake, and he drank every drop. He pointed to Kanbei and said with a little sneer, "I haven't heard news of you for some time. Is your lord Kodera Masamoto as before?"

Kanbei guessed two characteristics from Murashige's appearance, like he pitied the recklessness and the incompetence of a man now praised for his influence and living in an area of Harima.

"Yes, Lord Masamoto is safe and sound."

Kanbei answered obediently as he took out a tissue tucked in his kimono sleeve to wipe the rim of his cup while respectfully turning it before Murashige. In his heart, however, he saw a small vessel of a man with a heart smaller than that cup and the misery in Murashige's demeanor.

Lord Kodera's clan had various connections to the Araki clan and a shallow old friendship. Thus, Kanbei well understood his attitude and relationship that day.

Originally, Murashige was nothing more than a subordinate of Ikeda Katsumasa of the Ikeda clan and belonged to the Miyoshi faction. When Nobunaga withdrew his forces and entered Kyoto to drive out Ashikaga Yoshiaki from the center, he had just four hundred men with him to face street fighting and gained quick support from Oda's warriors. He exhibited surprisingly bold actions in combat with the Shichijo Dojo (Kinko-ji Temple) from the Honkoku-ji Temple. That began his service to the Oda clan.

Later, when summoned to Gifu Castle, along with

several generals, he was honored with elaborate trays of food. As his usual amusement or to deliberately test the mettle of Murashige, Nobunaga pierced a bun filled with bean jam with the tip of his sword and asked, "Do they eat this in Settsu?"

As the story goes, Murashige opened his mouth wide and moved forward.

He said, "Thank you," and ate the bun off the tip of the sword. At any rate, Nobunaga observed his behavior and said, "I can use this one."

This was one reason for his promotion to a vital role.

Compared to his time as a follower in the Ikeda clan, this was an exceptional success. Before going to war even now, Murashige was an influential man with maids to his left and right waiting on the handsome young man as he listened to the military orders from a senior retainer between cups of sake and approved each decision. He asked Kanbei the reason for his visit and did not try to hold back his laughter.

Kanbei said, "You could call me a secret agent or a tactician. No, it's enjoyable work I haven't seen recently. The secret agent of that minor tactician is bestowed with the famed Heshikiri sword, the favorite blade of Nobunaga-sama. This may pique your suspicions. To reassure you, please have a look?"

Murashige said, "He gave you the Heshikiri sword.... Wh... where is it?"

"I left it next door."

"He actually presented it to you?"

"To be given his beloved sword must be for an exceptional war exploit. What should be the answer to a wish given to an undervassal in the remote countryside? I know I'm hard to forget."

"What!" said Murashige and folded his arms in a grand gesture. He correctly guessed most of Kanbei's mission. But at the same time, he could not stop thinking about Hashiba Hideyoshi, who acted as the go-between.

"Lord Kodera Masamoto and the small Gochaku Castle are probably insignificant from the perspectives of all our allies. In the past, the three bases of Itami, Amagasaki, and Hanakuma formed the front line connected to Chugoku. From today on, however, they will take the form of bases of critical points and strategies of the forces under the command of Oda deep in the enemy territory of Himeji in Harima and Gochaku. It may be an exaggeration, but this matter should play a role in creating the initial foothold that will be an important accomplishment in Chugoku. And Araki Settsu-no-kami Murashige should enjoy the implication, too.... I know this is a bit foolish, but in the future, my Kodera clan and the Araki clan must cooperate wholeheartedly as forces under the same command and with the same objective. In any case, I've had the glory of meeting you on my way home and had your ear before the described affair takes place," said Kanbei and slid from his seat and bowed.

"Forgive my intrusion at such a busy time. Thank you. Goodbye," said Kanbei, and with one hand picked up the sheath of the famous sword in the adjacent room and swiftly withdrew from Itami Castle. After that, Kanbei gave a strained smile from time to time when he recalled Murashige's face.

2

Some wished for him to somehow not return home alive, and some prayed for his safety. After he left, Gochaku Castle was shrouded by these two aspects of human nature but on the surface carelessly whiled away the summer.

The expectations of seventy percent of the people in the castle were betrayed. Kuroda Kanbei returned healthier than when he left.

"First, the negotiations at Gifu can be said to have ended with great success."

He promptly reported each detail to Lord Masamoto and presented a thorough report to the prominent elders and lower-ranking clan members.

The opposing faction of Masuda Magoemon, Murai Kawachi, and others immediately occupied those seats and, as before, roared with criticisms.

"A promise is offered only from our side. What written pledge has been carried from the Oda clan?"

"What's the point of a promise of simple words in this turbulent country?"

"Moreover, Oda's forces are not advancing into Chugoku, but assistance is being offered nervously. How will we feel in the rare event Oda is defeated in the current attack on Hokuriku?"

On that point, anxiety could be read from the coloring of Masamoto's face. However, Kanbei's conviction doubled in his heart after meeting Nobunaga and Hideyoshi, and confused minor criticisms were unable to cloud his eyes.

Kanbei said, "Please leave it to me. For this matter, if everything is entrusted to this unworthy man, before I depart, I will make a clear pledge. I firmly believe and have no doubt that with me as the envoy you saw sufficient meritorious deeds. Although uneasy about why I did not bring back a written pledge from the Oda clan, still more than us, if sincerity or action or even a sliver of loyalty is not shown to the Oda clan, Lord Oda has no reason to grant a cheapened written oath."

Kanbei sternly added to this warning, "Obviously, in the future, if this clan is outwardly the premier base under Oda's command, internal conflict between the two factions should be discreet and unseen by the Mouri. Our lord will never forget he is in the important position of waiting for the right time in Chugoku to accompany Lord Oda."

However, within several days, a dozen or so samurai serving the clan disappeared from Gochaku Castle. Even without an investigation, all of them clearly fled the castle and escaped to the domain of the Mouri clan.

Consequently, even if the secret were somehow

maintained, the situation obvious to the enemy Mouri
Terumoto would be an envoy with the mission of joining
the clan of Lord Kodera to the clan of Lord Oda. The
castles in the surrounding domains were jolted by this
shock and kept close watch on this castle.

Kanbei's life was in great danger. All those who loved
the Mouri had not fled the castle. Yet an anti-Nobunaga
faction existed among the elders in Gochaku and other
clan members. Groups friendly to the Mouri were not few.
They were vigilant in their sleep. Every night was the same
as sleeping with death as his pillow.

Then from autumn to the beginning of winter, Oda's
forces didn't seem to have the time to devote all their
power to the conquest of Hokuriku and turn back to
Chugoku. And on the Mouri side, the heresy of Gochaku
and Himeji became "a serious matter that could not be
ignored." The attack would be now while Nobunaga was
busy. A dozen warships were quickly filled to capacity with
the soldiers of Geishu Yoshida and landed on the shore
near Himeji. This landing took place one moonless night
in the spring of year 4 of Tensho more than a year ago. A
messenger on horseback alerted the castle, and a small
band of soldiers was dispatched at once from Himeji
Castle to defend. The enemy Mouri forces probably
weren't elite and beaten back in no time. By morning,
fighting intensified on one side of the town of Himeji. The
Mouri soldiers took every corner, pressed forward, and
eventually were seen everywhere. An air of crisis
enveloped the entire castle town.

CHAPTER FIFTEEN
THE IRON WALL

1

AS SOON AS he woke that morning, Kanbei at Gochaku Castle already knew a strange event had taken place at Himeji.

The night lookout in the tower hurried down to report, "Heavy clouds of smoke are hovering over Himeji."

His alert preceded the knock at the castle gate by the messenger on horseback sent from there.

"Good. Forget about the watch. If you see anything unusual, tell me immediately."

First, he opened the armor chest and put on his armor with the heirloom navy leather straps. He arrived as the trusted associates who were summoned entered the samurai room.

"Is Mori Tahei here? Kuriyama Zensuke, Inoue Kuro, and Goto Emon are coming. If Miyata, Nagata, Mihara, and Kitamura are not here, summon them right now. Everyone, go out to the big veranda."

One by one, they answered, stood, and rushed out. In a short time, thirteen or fourteen strong men trained by Kanbei were gathered on the veranda.

"At last, everyone's here."

The faces Kanbei saw every morning appeared before him smiling. As he tied the straps of his armor, he said, "An urgent message from my father Souen now in Himeji states Mouri's forces number two to three thousand. He wrote that after a cunning landing from the sea before daybreak, the enemy carried out a sneak attack. The enemy set the town on fire, but he said not to worry because the enclosure on Himeyama though small was determined. I tended to think of him as an ordinary old man, but, surprisingly, this time, he is more daring than I."

After a brief chuckle and quickly issuing explicit orders to each vassal, Kanbei turned around and ran to the living parlor of Lord Kodera Masamoto.

2

Not only had the lord of Ogawa Mikawa, the elder Kuramitsu Masatoshi, Masada Magoemon, and others who usually formed the faction opposing Kanbei already assembled around Masamoto, each one, including Masamoto, was dressed for battle. Kanbei looked at them with surprise and wondered about their quick transformation and how they found out before him.

His suspicions were natural, but he saw the obvious distress and his own qualms that could be called his answer in Masamoto's eyes looking into his eyes suggested something Kanbei could not overlook.

"I will not abandon my intuition," thought Kanbei who believed in his own will. He gave orders on the spot.

"Masuda Magoemon, Murai Kawachi, Eda Zenbei. Take your troops as fast as possible to provide relief to Himeji. If the old man is there, Kuramitsu Masatoshi will protect the inner enclosure. Lord Sueyoshichika will go and take positions outside the castle and communicate at the entrance to Himeji. I have ordered my men to do everything else, and they've already given orders to their respective squads. There's no time to waste. Go quickly."

The enraged Sueyoshichika refused his orders.

"What do you say, Elders? We are seasoned fighters. Should we leave the lord's side and scatter? We will steadfastly protect the castle gate and our lord. Others should provide rapid support to Himeji."

"There's no one," said Kanbei.

"What?"

"I cannot leave the lord's side for even a moment. The number of soldiers in all of Gochaku Castle does not reach one thousand. Except for the men under my command, you are the generals, and the commanders are second in command. Other than the troops being dispatched, where should the troops be in the castle?"

Ogawa Mikawa-no-kami of the clan felt compelled to speak.

"Why have you taken command? Himeji is protected by your father Souen, the chamberlain. Even in this castle, your father and you have the support of many followers."

However, with a look that said he was not intimidated, Kanbei said, "This is an emergency. My men are already positioned to defend the castle gates. The castle keep is my responsibility and a key position. My orders are the lord's orders. The lord's orders are the same as military orders of Lord Oda. Until this war ends, men in opposition will be jailed. In today's battle, what man will disrupt military discipline? Show yourself. The decision has been made."

Everyone was silent.

However, greater than the fierce fighting outside the castle, Kanbei was engulfed in a great battle inside.

What were the feelings of the men around him who seemed to be thinking, If he gives us the chance, … When Kanbei issued the strict order, he moved forward to stand before Masamoto.

"Folding benches have been set up in the large garden under the tower. And the *jinmaku* curtains have been erected. The vassals have completed all the fortifications.

74

Shall we go and sit on the campstools?" suggested Kanbei. He took Masamoto's hand and together they passed through the sharp eyes on both sides to the garden.

3

Shouts came continuously from the tower to give moment-by-moment updates on the situation in Himeji.

Around this time, the sun finally broke through the morning clouds and faintly dyed the field of vision.

In the field of campstools in the garden, the samurai squad captain Muroki Hassai and the commander Imadzu Gendayu arrived with fifty castle soldiers to fortify the area. Men suspected of secretly supporting the Mouri were kept from approaching this position.

Under Kanbei's command, the generals Kuramitsu Masatoshi, Masuda Magoemon, and Murai Kawachi had no choice but to leave the castle. Earlier, Kanbei assigned a company to Mori Tahei, his trusted associate, and fearless men like Kuriyama Zensuke and ordered the commanding officers to immediately engage in sword fights and kill dangerous allies conspiring with the Mouri on the off chance they behaved suspiciously.

"First, the allies are prepared."

While standing outside the military curtains around the field of campstools, Kanbei munched on a rice ball of brown rice from his provisions. He thought about the true danger at the border at that moment on that morning and sighed in relief.

"No, it's too soon to be relieved. The battle starts now," he admonished himself. He picked grains of boiled rice off his fingers with his lips and finished eating.

His confidant Goto Emon received a very early order from Kanbei this morning to scout the mountains. He returned with his sweaty hand gripping a riding crop to give his report.

"The situation was not what you hoped. Soldiers definitely under the command of Nagaharu Bessho from

Miki Castle numbered around three hundred. I infiltrated nearly five miles north to the edge outside the territory, passed through the surrounding forests and mountains, and watched for signs of betrayal inside of Gochaku Castle. There was nothing unusual in the area of the boundary with Ukita Castle to the west. But if I see a change like smoke rising from this castle, I won't be able to make sense of the movements."

"How will you handle this?" asked Kanbei.

"I will follow orders. Kitamura Hassai will lead one hundred fifty soldiers and move with Miki's forces. Nagata Sansuke and his seventy men will keep a close eye on the other border. Mihara Hayato will position the foot soldiers for communications along the way."

"Very good. You stand here and protect this stool."

Kanbei turned and went up the tower. On this morning, even if he had more than one body, they would be inadequate. If he stood there and looked toward Himeji, black smoke swelled to darken the morning sun.

The skies above the northern mountains were bright and untroubled. The longer he looked it became clear to him that the enemy that should be feared lurked in the wrinkles of the mountains and the shadows of the mountain streams under those clouds.

The clan of Bessho Nagaharu who provided the swords of Miki Castle in Kita Harima in the backcountry was professed to be the most powerful accomplice of the Mouri in Harima. During the previous night, the Mouri navy and the mountain soldiers of Miki Castle approached Himeji by sea and land. Needless to say, they emerged with a strategy of cooperation on land and sea founded on intricate plans.

The enemy believed skirmishes would break out and surely thought half a day was wasted in the occupied area of Gochaku Castle.

Why? This castle alone has troop strength and strategic importance, as well as, powerful accomplices of the Mouri inside. Thus, attacks will not come from the outside.

He could not help thinking about the situation of his elderly father, wife, and son, How is my father in Himeyama? Matsuchiyo is still young. He looked at the sky filled with the black smoke from war fires. His heart was with the vassals engaged in desperate battles there.

Again at the foot of the tower, Kanbei ran into Kinugasa Kyuzaemon. Of course, Kyuzaemon raced by horse from Himeji. A surprised Kanbei asked with a slight reprimand, "Why have you abandoned Himeji? They're probably in the midst of savage fights. If defenses are breached there, we will also be in crisis. This is not the place where they should die."

"No, Souen-sama raged that Himeji is not important and was worried about Gochaku. He ordered me to investigate. So I took my whip and came to report on the battle and inquire about the situation here," said Kyuzaemon.

"Tell my father we are not worried here, and I am the son of Souen," said Kanbei.

"Yessir."

"You've seen this place. It's an iron wall. Now go!"

"Yessir! Goodbye."

He started to leave but Kanbei called to stop him and asked, "Are all the tradesmen at work? Is Iguchi Yojiemon, the Reijukou peddler, safe?"

"The entire force is fighting hard," said Kyuzaemon.

"I see. Give them my best," said Kanbei.

Kinugasa Kyuzaemon saw him nod and left for Himeji.

4

The assault on Himeji was a decisive act carried out by the naval general Urahyobu Jo of the Mouri clan. The landing was a success, but they suffered a crushing defeat in battle.

The street skirmishes carried on into the night. They

were stopped in one section of town and their advance halted.

Kuroda Souen of Himeyama gathered his old bones to not only command forces engaged in battle but to strengthen and train his subordinates. To repay his unfailing kindness, they fought the enemy with no concern for their own lives.

At first, the intensity of their hostility confounded the Mouri forces. More than that, their defeat in the desperate fighting was rooted in their ignorance of the distinct nature of the castle town of Himeji compared to the castle towns in other provinces.

There, invasion by enemy soldiers was considered odious. Every last citizen of the castle town transformed into a soldier. They doused fires, sheltered the old and the young, clutched his own specialized weapon, and clashed with unforeseen fighting power brought by the Mouri forces. At first, the enemy Urahyobu Jo was bewildered and wondered what was going on.

Like Iguchi Yojiemon, who hung up a signboard for an eye medication called Reijukou in town, the figure of an ordinary shop owner instantly changed into the old general of a squad, the so-called Tradesmen's Division, and displayed the bearing of a warrior remembering days of old.

Other men like him, several dozen of them, lived in this town. Not only tradesmen, but soldiers also lived in this fishing village.

There had never been an organization that could be called a naval force of seafarers. But when night came, the Beach Gang launched an unknown number of fishing boats. These boats closed in on the Mouri vessels tied to mooring lines on the beach to attack and set them on fire.

No real sailors or provisioned soldiers rode on the boats from shore. On this battlefield, Kuroda's Beach Gang was crushed. Several boats burned up and sank. The remaining boats fled in confusion far from the coast.

Of course, the fires on the sea led to extreme despair in the fighting spirit of Urahyobu Jo on land. The rout began at that moment. Urahyobu's forces were ripped apart and reluctantly fled down the main road to Miki Castle. At that time, Kuroda Kanbei and selected elite soldiers left Gochaku Castle and lay in ambush everywhere. In the roads, the fields, or the forests, everywhere the defeated enemy was captured and nearly exterminated.

"… They were wiped out," said the father Souen and his son Kanbei while drawing deep breaths. While lost in their many thoughts as they scanned each other's unharmed faces, the night ended and morning came.

"First, a fleeting danger was avoided.… But the enemy will come again with more determination. With your permission, I will leave now," said Kanbei in celebration with his father and returned immediately to Gochaku. He returned without seeing Matsuchiyo's face or to the safety of his wife.

Although Gochaku Castle and his home in Himeji were separated by just short of two and a half miles, would one day over a period of six months come for this family when the wife would see her husband and the child be near his father again?

CHAPTER SIXTEEN
TWO PLANS

1

AT THE START of the new year, Nobunaga began the construction of Azuchi Castle.

His engineering works mimicked his wars. They were huge in scale, daring in design, and designed by him and not another. He gathered the wisdom of many and surpassed it. His large, impressive works destroyed the conventions of the Higashiyama style and grabbed the attention of the world. In addition, the construction was pushed to a rapid pace both day and night. In less than a year, most of the frame was completed on the hill on the lakeside. The expanse of mulberry plantations and crop fields became the new castle town.

Niwa Nagahide, Akechi Mitsuhide, and others took charge as the building magistrates. Today, Nobunaga climbed up from Sojitsu Temple at the foot of the mountain.

"Is my home ready? Even if it's just the seven stories of the keep, work together and finish soon."

He looked around impatiently, urged them on, and surveyed the site like a battlefield.

Niwa Gorozaemon Nagahide who guided him was

always overcome with worry. He only said, "As you see, we are working together both day and night with deliberate speed."

Particularly in the seven-story tower of the keep in the center of the structure, the construction work demanded great care. Nobunaga's orders were intricate.

The underground level was a storeroom. The second floor had a total of 280 pillars, a width of 20 *ken*, a depth of 17 ken, and divided into many rooms including a 12-tatami-mat drawing room, next to a 4-tatami room, a 32-tatami room on the north side, a 32-tatami room on the south side, next to an 8-tatami room, a 20-tatami room on the east side, next to an 8-tatami room, and a 3-tatami waiting room. All the openwork screens and barriers were lacquered. The papered sliding *fusuma* partitions were decorated with the ink brush drawings of Kano Eitoku and other masters of the time. The paintbrush enlivened the rooms that were appropriately called the Geese Room, the Hibiscus Room, the Plum Room, and the Bell Vesper Room.

The higher up the tower, the fewer the number of rooms. The craftwork structure was precise and enhanced its elegance.

"Gorozaemon. On New Year's, we'll drink spiced sake here."

"Campstools were placed in the corridor on the third story still missing the sliding partitions. While indulging in the view of Seta, Hira, and the lake's waters, again Nobunaga hinted about having Nagahide make a pledge concerning the deadline.

Nagahide had been silent but said, "By the new year …" then continued, "The new spring is coming earlier in this fifth year of Tensho. We will sit side by side on new mats smelling of trees and be served congratulatory drinks to enjoy."

Nagahide unknowingly made the promise to meet that deadline.

Nobunaga had a reason to be in a hurry. He handed over Gifu Castle to his son Nobutada at the beginning of November. He took his personal belongings and his tea utensils and moved into Sojitsu Temple at Azuchi. In other words, his miserable dwelling was a rented room in a temple. He did not want to spend New Year's in that temple and, in fact, would not.

Because of this prodding by burning one's bridges, each of the many times Nobunaga came to look around was time wasted and a nuisance to the magistrate Nagahide who was needed to look after and escort him. Today, however, was his lucky day.

"Lord Hashiba of Nagahama has come," said an intermediary who appeared before Lord Nobunaga. This provided Nagahide a good opportunity to withdraw. After greeting Hashiba Hideyoshi with his eyes, Nagahide disappeared.

2

After the end of the conquest of Hokuriku last year, Hideyoshi moved from Odani Castle to Nagahama Castle.

Azuchi and Nagahama hugged Lake Biwa. The lord, Nobunaga, and his retainer, Hideyoshi, would live on the edge of the same body of water.

"Hideyoshi? When did you see it?" asked Nobunaga.

"I just arrived. The construction is quite far along," said Hideyoshi.

"How is Nagahama? Can you live there?"

"I am unworthy."

"It appears you have sent for your mother. You are a truly dutiful son."

"Because she is a woman of the countryside, after moving to Nagahama, she is simply confounded. She was sure it would be enjoyable but it hasn't been, so she lives with a slightly aggravated look. I brought a bit of the harvest from the fields grown by my elderly mother as a small gift for you."

KURODA JOSUI

"Harvest from the fields?"

"Yes. When my farmer mother neglects her farm, she says she feels unwell. After moving to Nagahama, she cultivated a field inside the castle grounds and grows a variety of vegetables."

"That is commendable. Thank you. Well, let me see them."

"Oh no, we will pass through the construction site. I left them in the kitchen of the Sojitsu Temple.... Incidentally," said Hideyoshi looking up at Nobunaga's face, "There's something I'd like to discuss...."

"Is that so?" said Nobunaga and anticipating his companion's thoughts immediately ordered the pages beside him to leave, "Go downstairs."

"Chikuzen, what is it?" asked Nobunaga.

"It's about Kuroda Kansei of Chugoku," said Hideyoshi.

"Hmm. Him?"

"He's in a difficult situation."

"In what way?"

"Because of the pressure from the Mouri clan and the machinations of surrounding clans, he is alone and without support."

"He was probably prepared for that from the beginning."

"Of course, but the plan was to decide the outcome once and for all by Oda's forces going west. However, the Mouri clan anticipated their move and, instead, defended Harima and were given time to defend against the enemy. It's regrettable. This was told again and again through letters."

"Has he made an urgent demand for military forces?"

"His perseverance under these circumstances is admirable. Once this February and again at the end of May, the navy of the Mouri clan attacked Himeji in an attempt to excise the internal heresy in one stroke. Both times, fortunately, the brave fighting by the Kuroda father and son beat back the enemy. This was previously reported to you. My lord awarded a scroll of appreciation."

"Can't he hold out any longer?" asked Nobunaga.

"I would not say that because he's a man unwilling to admit defeat. But if forces are not dispatched soon to Chugoku, under pressure from and through strategies devised by Mouri, all of Harima will eventually fall...."

Nobunaga laughed, "Ha, ha, ha,..." and said, "And eventually he'll give up in despair."

"No, he is pragmatic," said Hideyoshi speaking up until the end on the side of the father and son.

"From the perspective of this clan, he may be our sole ally among rivals in all of Chugoku and must not die."

"However, my substantial forces cannot be sent out to save Kanbei and his father. Chugoku is the reason for building Azuchi."

"I understand your thoughts. Therefore, my formal reply will be in writing. Given the situation in Kinki, it is still not the time, but the time will come soon. With patience and waiting a little longer, I will work to appease. If you wish, with a word from My Lord, the father and son's loyalty will be further invigorated. I know they will wait for the day you go west."

"I have to believe that. The Kuroda father and son are retainers of Kodera Masamoto. If he is not listened to inside the Kodera clan, that will secretly reach the ears of those favoring the Mouri clan. At the same time, the heart does not forgive. Before my written oath, shouldn't a hostage be sent from the Kodera clan to this house?"

"Yes. That is absolutely in the imperial message. If a letter demanding a hostage is sent immediately, they will surely send one."

"Come to the temple. The vegetables cultivated by your mother will be steamed. While having a drink, we will carefully consider the situation," said Nobunaga and left his campstool and led the way down the stairs that smelled of lacquer.

CHAPTER SEVENTEEN
THE HOSTAGE

1

THE FIFTH YEAR of Tensho passed. The red seal of Nobunaga was sent to the Kodera clan to formally request a hostage. Hideyoshi communicated the purpose beforehand in a private message to Kanbei. That was expected. The clan head Kodera Masamoto asked, "What should be done?"

For a problem like this, his upset appeared on his face, and he asked a large number of people for counsel.

Of course, among the family and the retainers, an unpleasant atmosphere hung over this contract with the Oda clan. Another reason was the pain of parental love for Ujimoto, the heir of the Kodera clan who was a son unworthy of his father. He had a weak constitution and could not be sent out to the world.

"Don't worry," said Kanbei, who had a seat in the deliberation and declared in his usual tone, "Lord Hashiba heard about Ujimoto-sama's frailty. Surely, Nobunaga is not saying to hand over a sickly child. In place of the heir, my son Matsuchiyo is just ten years old and will be sent as the hostage. If Matsuchiyo is the substitute, this affair will not bring anguish."

As always, his statement was not a lie. Substituting his child for the child of the main family impressed many of those present. Even the elders usually in opposition agreed and said, "We understand your feelings Kanbei, and accept."

This day was the first time Kanbei saw the council deliberate and come to a quick decision in Gochaku Castle. He recalled forcing a smile.

However, Kanbei was a shrewd man. The hostage was not sent without delay. Kanbei exchanged letters with Hideyoshi several times. Naturally, they concerned the pledge to go west. The letters from Hideyoshi were always written with the sincerity of a friend.

> *I too wish a prompt conclusion. As always, I am striving to advise you. Therefore, I assume the hostage will finally be sent in accordance with Nobunaga's wish. Sending a hostage will prove fruitful. My simple advice is to distance yourself from the wild rumors of the enemy. I am relying on you with all my heart like a rock at my feet.*

In one letter, Hideyoshi went as far as to write:

> *You are doing fine at this time, like my younger brother Koichiro (Hashiba Hidenaga). Everyone is asking what will I do, I should come to a decision through direct negotiation with you.*

Kanbei mulled over Hideyoshi thinking of him as his younger brother Koichiro. When did Hideyoshi come to regard him so?

Kanbei was in a predicament and felt only that Hideyoshi had not turned away from him.

2

"I will see the capital. I will see Azuchi," said the ten-year-old Matsuchiyo and jumped around while watching the preparations for his journey. His young mother and his grandfather Souen were unable to suppress their tears.

His young eyes gleamed with the joy of a trip. In fact, he was gleeful. He put on straw sandals, wore a sword, and held a bamboo hat. His traveling clothes also gallantly drove his youthful dreams. He raced forward taking no notice of his nursemaid since infancy and the retainers who were seeing him off behind tears and ignored his mother.

The party rode on horses from the castle gate. Tears of separation were wrung out at the sight of his small figure. How many sent far away as hostages have returned home safely?

No more than four or five vassals accompanied him to Azuchi. They feared the enemy would seize him along the way. Every front was strengthened while they waited for the boat to be prepared on the Shikama coast. If they made it to the shore in Hyogo, his father Kanbei would be waiting.

Kanbei racked his brains more over inviting tens of thousands of Oda's forces and one general into Harima than sending off his only son. He believed the day he would see that reality was not now.

A lone rider hurried along an overland route to meet Araki Murashige to inquire about the situation in Kinki and confer about possible preparations for the invasion of Chugoku. He hid in a fishing village on the Hyogo shore and waited for his son to arrive.

CHAPTER EIGHTEEN
THE LONG-AWAITED DAY

1

THE AUTUMN SCENE at Azuchi was a notable change from the autumn scene a year ago. The castle keep was finished. The castle town surrounding the eight towers and ten gates nearly had the look of a new cultural capital.

Matsuchiyo's eyes opened wide when he arrived with his father. Compared to the small castle in Himeji, even his young eyes drank in the splendor and magnificence of the very different Azuchi Castle.

This boy would later become known as Kuroda Nagamasa. Whether he appeared with his father Kanbei before a crowd of Azuchi vassals or in an audience with Nobunaga, Matsuchiyo was always shy, but his timid figure answered any question in a clear voice.

"He is better looking than his father Kanbei. I think he favors his mother. His disposition is pleasant. He's a good boy. A very good boy," Nobunaga declared.

Kanbei's absence of treachery was reconfirmed when he promptly brought the unsuspecting hostage. Kanbei probably garnered great praise for his action.

Of course, Hideyoshi was present on that day. After the formal meeting for transferring the hostage ended, a banquet was held in the 42-tatami-mat Plum Room. To the child hostage and the parent who would return home without his son, this banquet signified a meal of separation until the unknown day they would meet again. The blood father and son's emotions were immense.

Thus, few underlings were seated with Nobunaga. From his seat, Nobunaga said, "The situation in Chugoku in the west will definitely soon come to a head. At that time, Chikuzen will command. Chikuzen and you will cooperate on all matters."

Hearing this, Kanbei felt leaving his only child was not a problem. His long-standing ambition had been achieved, and he received a pledge directly from Nobunaga. He could not suppress the heat in his eyelids like he saw the truth. Furthermore, Nobunaga said with sympathy, "You and Chikuzen are compatible. You've had this rapport from the beginning and are sworn friends. The hostage Matsuchiyo will be kept close to Chikuzen. If he is raised by the hand of Chikuzen, you will not worry."

"Thank you."

Kanbei only knew those words and felt more respect each time he met Nobunaga. His friendship with and respect for Hideyoshi permeated to his marrow with the samurai spirit of "I will die for a man who knows himself."

And to Nobunaga, he said, "Naturally, my foresight did not extend that far. The expectations told to me are not betrayed," and felt he climbed a mountain, did not lose hope on the mountain, and finally, knew the beauty and height of the mountain.

Of course, the mountain is the sword, but there is also a valley. Kanbei acknowledged Nobunaga's hard-to-please disposition, his mysterious temperamental nature, his short temper, his selfishness, and many other human flaws. In those matters, Hideyoshi always stood in the middle to placate both of them. He would say "That's his nature" to put Kanbei at ease. He could not see the few shortcomings among Nobunaga's flaws.

2

Kanbei stayed at Azuchi Castle for two days. On the third morning, Kanbei spoke his parting words to Nobunaga. Hideyoshi took his hostage son back to Nagahama.

Takenaka Hanbei, who came with Hideyoshi, had taken charge of Matsuchiyo the previous day. When Hanbei departed, he said, "As Hideyoshi-sama said, your son will be taken care of at Bodaisan Castle in my hometown of Mino. It is a remote but safe place. There's no need for you to be the least bit concerned about that place."

Kanbei thanked him from his heart and spoke with resolve, "No, I apologize for this unexpected burden on you. If he receives his education in the hometown of the Takenaka clan, his training will be better. However, this worldly experience will not protect Matsuchiyo's life even a little, only the lord's intentions will. In any case, whatever the outcome, this father's heart will not resent you."

Kanbei vowed the day they would meet again in Chugoku would be soon then he departed.

Hideyoshi and his servants returned by boat to Nagahama. His houseboat was the only one floating on the lake from the sluice gate at the shore.

At exactly that time, Kanbei also left the town of Azuchi and walked west toward a row of pine trees on the shore. An attendant samurai said, "The Lord Chikuzen is waving his fan. Kanbei stopped his horse to look. The rising sun on the fan was moving. He spotted Matsuchiyo by Hideyoshi's side. He could also see Takenaka Hanbei.

Kanbei waved back. When he looked back, the lofty gold and blue colors of the castle top of Azuchi were the spectacular sights of unifying the nation by force. The deep interior of Kanbei's heart was not equal to the rising sun fan being waved in the distance that somehow was accompanied by Hideyoshi's usual humanity. Could he make a man with authority submit? Is this linked to his kind heart? Kanbei privately imagined Hideyoshi had both.

On the way home, Kanbei abandoned his attendant and his horse and took a detour from Tamba to San'in. The reason for this action was to carry out the secret plan devised with Hideyoshi over the two days in Azuchi.

A faction of the Amago clan was hiding in various locations in San'in and waiting for the right time to come. Their strength was said to be small, but the conflict between the Amago family and the Mouri clan actually originated during the Daiei era (1521 - 1528), ever since Mouri Motonari seized Amago Tsunehisa's territory. Over the long fifty years since then, from the children to the grandchildren, the Amago family never stopped their fight to overthrow the Mouri.

Without a domain and without a castle or even strong men or military force, through sneak attacks, a spirit pierced the Amago ronin who anticipated their revenge and to this day worried the Mouri clan. The man who protected Amago Katsuhisa, the youngest son of Masahisa, and often called The Windy Day in San'in was Yamanaka Shikanosuke Yukimori, the right-hand man of Masahisa.

Shikanosuke Yukimori and Azuchi were already connected. This connection was not direct but through Akechi Mitsuhide and Hosokawa Fujitaka, who were active throughout Tamba and had signed a private agreement on another day. Hideyoshi recognized the importance of this power. He surmised he would meet Kanbei in Azuchi next and, for the most part, Nobunaga's intentions had been set. He suggested to Kanbei, "Shouldn't you meet Yamanaka Shikanosuke Yukimori one time to familiarize yourself with his wishes?"

Of course, Kanbei was familiar with the situation from all perspectives. Hideyoshi's words convinced him the day to go to war in Chugoku was approaching so he promptly changed his plan to return to Himeji and went to San'in on foot and alone.

He embraced several other schemes. Despite having

the men to carry them out, he lacked the spirit. He wandered for about one month resembling a ronin.

He also met Amago Katsuhisa and held private consultations with Shikanosuke Yukimori. He visited the illegitimate family lines of the former Akamatsu clan scattered over Tajima, Hoki, and Harima. He explained his belief that the world must move. This must be the future of the world. He boldly went to meet Bessho Nagaharu at Miki Castle with this belief.

From the beginning, Miki Castle could be called the leader in support of the Mouri and planted the obvious anti-Nobunaga banner, but the passionate belief and sincere eloquence of Kuroda Kanbei chafed Nagaharu, the lord of the castle.

"If the ambition of the Oda clan is sincere, as you say, when Hideyoshi goes west, working to become a part of the Oda may be the right move."

After Kanbei obtained this promise, he returned home.

The Bessho clan was also an illegitimate line of the Akamatsu family. The Kodera clan descended from the Akamatsu and had close blood ties. In other words, the lineage of the Akamatsu clan reached as many as thirty-six clans in Chugoku alone. He had never said so until today, but on that important day, even if half of the thirty-six families were persuaded to join as allies, a new force would be awakened. This was one scheme he adopted long ago.

3

On the one hand, Hideyoshi came into contact with the life of Nobunaga in the middle of October and, as quick as lightning, gathered his force in Azuchi and entered Harima in the capacity as the overall commander of the Chugoku battle camp.

This shocked the enemy Mouri clan and struck the hearts of the experienced generals of Azuchi like a huge wave.

The dissatisfaction of many, including the senior retainers, was seen in the sole criticism of "An inexperienced general like Chikuzen was sent as the commander on the important mission of conquering Chugoku. Wasn't that slightly drastic assignment unprecedented?"

In other words, they felt Hideyoshi was very much junior to the likes of Shibata Katsuie or Niwa Nagahide. Why?

Akechi Mitsuhide seemed surprisingly alone. His expectation when leaving for Chugoku or for himself seemed to be an unspoken conceit. For the plan for the San'in region, in particular, his offering of opinions and mediation with the Amago clan were surely the results of his conceit.

However, the man more hopeless and annoyed than anyone may have been Araki Settsu Murashige who was stationed for a long time in Itami Castle on the critical border between Chugoku and the Kyoto region. He had always been filled with pride. He was unable to fight and suppress the alarm that gripped him upon seeing the huge force commanded by Hideyoshi pass through Settsu.

4

It cannot be said for the Kodera clan but for Kuroda Kanbei, Hideyoshi's forces were precisely these long-awaited warriors.

As promised to Nobunaga, all of Himeji Castle where his family lived was offered as the "headquarters for Oda's forces." Hideyoshi and his forces were invited in. The families moved to an enclosure in a corner of the grounds.

Hideyoshi entered Himeji Castle, assessed the overall situation from local observations, and promptly wrote the following in a report to Nobunaga.

> *The subjugation of all of Harima will begin in the middle of next month and be resolved.*

When the banner of the Oda clan was raised here, the preliminary work of Kanbei was answered by an important fact. Sincerity was shown in sending the hostage.

Hideyoshi was in Himeji and saw a dozen or so hostages. However, they were nothing more than the children of weak but wealthy local clans. Men with true power do not easily surrender. In the future, who will be the true power? With the speed of a strong gale, his soldiers entered Tajima, Yamaguchi, and Iwabuchi, and Takeda Castle fell.

Acting in concert, the forces of Ippyo that started from the San'in region were the soldiers of Amago faction. Yamanaka Shikanosuke Yukimori and Kuroda Kanbei gripped each other's hands at the encampment at Kumami River.

"The day I've been waiting for has finally come."

"Yes, it has. The dawn of Chugoku …"

As the two men talked, news came that a large number of soldiers under the command of Ukita Izumi-no-kami with the support of the Mouri clan were behind Kozuki, a castle of the enemy.

"With the addition of Ukita's forces, what kind of fight will ensue?"

Yukimori wished for an advance guard.

Of course, he was allowed one. Kanbei consulted with Takenaka Hanbei Shigeharu, who was always in the camp, because he strongly believed Hanbei had far greater knowledge of battlefields than he.

Kozuki Castle fell within ten days. The lord of the castle was sent to Azuchi from Himeji. Hideyoshi had an audience with the lord and the retainers of Amago.

"I understand the long years of hardship. But you will be rewarded for that hardship. Today cannot be said to be the day of the fruition of our long-cherished plan but only a link," said Hideyoshi with sympathy and appreciation of his pain. That evening, they drank sake together. Later, Amago Katsuhisa and Yamanaka Shikanosuke entered Kozuki Castle that had been attacked by the enemy to guard the border abutting the enemy. Lord Katsuhisa was still a young twenty-six-year-old. The chivalrous Shikanosuke Yukimori, with a lifetime as his solitary loyal retainer, possessed the rugged physique of a thirty-nine-year-old.

CHAPTER NINETEEN
THE FINE HORSE SHOSHAZAN

1

HIDEYOSHI RETURNED IN triumph to Azuchi. With news of victory, he personally requested orders from Nobunaga for the next stage in the war strategy.

"Meritorious deeds at the beginning of the war are satisfactory. It's a great burden. Spend a leisurely New Year's in Azuchi," said Nobunaga because the year was coming to an end. Then Nobunaga gave Hideyoshi his treasured ceramic cup.

At that time, the gift of a tea container, a teacup, or a tea kettle was the same as being awarded the highest medal. This honor not only had useful value, Nobunaga gave the gift with the claim of "With this sort of object in your possession, during a lull in busy times, you can restore your spirit." Tea was very popular, but there were few examples of receiving this sort of official recognition from one's lord.

February began in the new year of Tensho year 6. Hideyoshi went to Harima again. He created more impressive and stronger preparatory battle formations.

The local ruling party and a group of Oda's men left to meet in Kakogawa. Originally, this event was the clever work of Kuroda Kanbei and was nothing more than his faithfulness to illuminate the entry of Hideyoshi into Chugoku.

Above all, among the attendees, Bessho Yoshisuke, the uncle of Bessho Nagaharu, the lord of Miki Castle, entered the clan with Miyake Harutada.

The Bessho clan governed 430 thousand koku of land in eastern Harima and had the largest force. Having been friendly to the Mouri clan at one time, Kanbei had difficulty persuading them despite his eloquence. Finally, without the use of a single soldier, they were drawn into Oda's camp. To what extent were the advantages this brings to the state of affairs and the brilliance of Hideyoshi's forces understood in Harima?

"Now, now, it'll all be fine ..."

At first, Hideyoshi was like this with anyone. He had no particular doubts about the family members of the powerful clans or the retainers of the small castles.

However, when he went out on the first campaign, he arrived at his post through remarkable brilliance. Joy plainly flowed from his face.

That evening in the Kakogawa encampment, a huge banquet was held for the Harima allies. When the banquet ended, seats were rearranged to transition to a war council. If only the foundation of the default policy and the attitude of undefeated victory in the Oda clan were declared, tonight would be a success. This was the first vague thought of Hideyoshi who also occupied a council seat after the banquet.

However, there were men who spoke eloquently in the council. They were Yoshisuke, the uncle of Bessho Nagaharu, and Miyake Harutada.

From time to time, Hideyoshi threw sharp glances at them. And, surprisingly, he fretted at times.

2

"Now, Lord Hashiba instructed or explained the ambitions, but lords, what do you think? You often say the center, the center, but if spoken from the Mouri crowd, Chugoku cannot be said to be the center. The eyes of the Oda crowd conform a little too much to our own. Does the Mouri's power seem slight? … I'm rather worried," said Bessho Yoshisuke.

Although drunk, while licking their lips, not only the men to the left and right of his seat, the men across from him constantly called to him.

"The wealth and the armaments of the Mouri clan are not mere fancy. The navy, in particular, is overwhelming. They've been assembled since the days of Mouri Motonari. Apart from the current lord Terumoto, Kikkawa Motoharu and Kobayakawa Takakage do not look particularly skilled but each one has superior talents."

"Wait. Wait a moment. Nagaharu's uncle …"

Unable to endure it, Hideyoshi called to him from the head seat like he was about to yank his ear, "Why are you grumbling? What is the point of what you're trying to say? What does it mean?"

"Well, have you heard something?" asked the uncle, Bessho Yoshisuke, who had his brazen moments.

He was a veteran around the same age as Hideyoshi's father and did not flinch.

"In fact, I have. I will say it for your sake. My concern is a rash incursion into Chugoku will lead to a grave situation. After we harden our armaments in good time and attack and defeat the small castles and branch castles of the Mouri, I think it would be better to judge between fact and fiction and move a great force."

"I am not saying that is not needed," said an angry Hideyoshi.

He looked straight into the faces of Bessho Yoshisuke and Miyake Harutada and spoke these heroic words.

"My work is to take the initiative and yours is to follow my orders and fight hard. The fundamental plan and strategy are to receive orders from Nobunaga and to take them to heart. I will not permit your meddling."

"Ah, that is so," said the calm Yoshisuke then to Harutada beside him said, "... That's so. Is there any reason for us to be here? Shall we go?"

They both nodded and left together.

When he left Kakogawa, from his horse, Yoshisuke turned to Miyake Harutada and said, "Tonight's trick was a bit of gambling your neck. But first, the reason for moving the lord was achieved.... A shift in Hashiba's view or the Bessho clan instead of foot soldiers being driven at the beck and call of Kuroda cannot be tolerated. Ultimately, our reputation will not be tainted in the eyes of the Mouri."

He was Mouri's man from his guts. Kanbei explained the situation to Nagaharu, the lord of the castle who promised to accompany him to Oda. However, these words were ample proof of the presence of many strong anti-Nobunaga partisans in the castle.

3

Bessho Nagaharu, the lord of Miki Castle, was young, twenty-five years old. He watched the glory of the rising Oda forces and remembered being dissatisfied with the Mouri of Chugoku. Last year, he encountered the persuasion of Kuroda Kanbei and clearly communicated benevolence toward Oda.

His Uncle Yoshisuke denounced Kanbei directly to him, "It's deception. All of it."

"I met with Hideyoshi in Kakogawa and trembled when confronted with his arrogance and rudeness," he said with exaggeration, "Bessho Nagaharu and his followers all said they will not permit meddling with matters at the field headquarters or with the war strategy and think of it as nothing more than Chikuzen's first trick. Their views are public knowledge. He seems to think little of every last person in Harima."

After Nagaharu's expression changed sufficiently, Yoshisuke attacked the point he was most cautious about.

"In the end, Nobunaga's true intention is to use the power of our family. The day of the subjugation of Chugoku will bring on the self-destruction of each one. Is his real intention to present Miki Castle as a prize for Hideyoshi? Crafty heroes throughout the ages have employed the same plan," explained the uncle.

Nagaharu was unable to believe his uncle's theory. In an instant, Miki Castle betrayed Kanbei. The estrangement from Oda was referred to as "a breaking off of negotiations," the banner of revolt was raised. These actions relied on the rapid emergence of power supported by the Mouri. Again their cooperation was conveyed to Mouri Terumoto of Geishu Yoshida.

When news of the reversal at Miki Castle spread, several powerful clans based in small castles like Kanki, Kajiwara, Ougo, Kinugasa, and Nagai followed and responded with a banner with the declaration: "Wipe out Hashiba's forces in Chugoku."

In one morning, the bloodless strategy at the tip of Kanbei's tongue and his hard foundational work went up in smoke.

Kanbei was close to tears. He grabbed Hideyoshi and spilled out his heart. Kanbei said, "I thought of you as an expert who obliged men not only in strategy but in diplomacy, but you angered Bessho Yoshisuke and he returned home. That was an unimaginable failure. Miki Castle has many brave warriors and is impregnable. This situation will take a long time to resolve."

Hideyoshi asked, "Was there a choice?"

He recognized the regret in his own emotions but did not express dismay at this result. Hideyoshi added, "On the other hand, I can say it was a good outcome. Miki

Castle is already filled with the dangers of several fires of defection. I don't think your service in gaining submission through clever words was careless. However, the great work of administering Chugoku will not be a house built on sand. Therefore, wasn't this, in the end, a good thing?"

He was not willing to admit defeat. Perhaps his ideas could be said to reflect a determined mind. Kanbei seemed unable to be moved by him a second time. As he gradually came to see the strengths of Hideyoshi, he was handed a piece of paper on which Hideyoshi had written:

You are like my younger brother Koichiro.

The truth in those words penetrated his body.

4

Despite an unwillingness to admit defeat in words, Hideyoshi was unable to gloss over the sudden change in the established strategy of the forces caused by the breakaway of Miki Castle.

The second campaign was planned for Bizen as the objective from the beginning. At the time, the Ukita Naoie clan in Bizen was the largest fortress and becoming the vanguard of the Mouri.

Now, however, the sudden change in events might plunge them into peril if the heresy close at hand was not defeated. Following Kanbei's recommendation, Hideyoshi rushed to move his headquarters to Mount Shosha and commanded from the temple there.

The enemy swiftly learned this information.

The naval forces of the Mouri saw their chance in the area of Kii and Awaji and had several thousand soldiers board over one hundred ships and attacked the coasts.

"Accept the challenge. Lord, please attack the enemy head-on."

Kanbei took four to five hundred soldiers to his trusted associates like Mori Tahei, Takenomori Shinjiro, and Kuriyama Zensuke in order to confront the Mouri forces coming ashore. They struck a severe blow and defeated the enemy generals Kajiwara Kagetoki and Akashi Motokazu then returned.

At that time, Hideyoshi said, "Patience Kanbei. Patience."

When Kanbei doubtfully asked, "Why?" Hideyoshi in his customary frankness said, "When I praise you as I usually do by saying you are a man with a silver tongue or a strategist carrying the sword of eloquence, I was being flippant. Lately, however, with the attack on Kozuki Castle and your valor at that time, I understand you are more than a tactician or strategist. Therefore, I apologize. Forgive me."

Hideyoshi slipped on his zori sandals and abruptly went out to the garden. He seemed to be wondering what to do and approached a black colt tied to a huge chokeberry tree in the temple garden. He grabbed the muzzle and pulled the horse to the front of the hall.

"This is a fine horse, Kanbei."

Kanbei went out to the veranda, lowered his head, and placed both hands on the ground in respect. He said, "He is a chestnut horse. His hair is glossy. His legs, buttocks, and shoulders are symmetric, and his hooves are sharp. Best of all, his eyes are quiet. He's a fine horse not seen these days. What is he, close to ten years old?"

"No, he's a young horse. A seven-year-old. He will be ridden for many years. I think all will go well if he's ridden onto the battlefield. Well, would you like him?" asked Hideyoshi.

"Yes, I would," said Kanbei.

"Then I will give him to you …. In fact, he was a gift from Lord Nobunaga to go west this time. I rode him and tied him up at the camp for the first time. I named him Shoshazan and adore him. However, I can say that my distinguished service was mostly your work. Kanbei, come down and take hold of the reins. This horse has a beautiful gait," said Hideyoshi.

"Thank you," said Kanbei.

Kanbei stepped down into the garden and dropped his knees to the ground to receive the reins. He did not mount the horse but pulled him to make one round and watched him. With deep admiration and joy from his heart, he said, "He surpasses the matchless Red Hare loved by the warlord Lu Bu of the Han of long ago. The name Shoshazan is fitting. If he came from a stable in Azuchi, the omen for this mount is most auspicious. We will surely advance in the world."

Seeing this, Hideyoshi returned to the veranda and his seat. They looked at each other. Hideyoshi encouraged Kanbei with "The work begins now."

Kanbei bowed again then called over the garden fence to his retainer Mori Tahei. When he came running from somewhere, Kanbei hurriedly said, "Your recent actions at Kozuki Castle and in the pursuit of the naval forces of the Mouri were spectacular acts of your loyal service. This fine horse I received from Chikuzen-sama has experience on the battlefield, and I am giving him to you. Please thank Chikuzen-sama."

Mori Tahei was more than overjoyed and speechless. When the reins were pushed toward him, tears poured from his eyes.

Hideyoshi evaluated Kanbei's actions again and again in his heart.

"This man also knows how to treat a retainer. For that reason alone, it will be a bit difficult to use him."

CHAPTER TWENTY
A FRIEND'S KINDNESS

1

THE SWORDS AND the power of resistance at Miki Castle resembled cavities with strong roots in the gums.

Moreover, to leave behind that hardship, if the small, satellite castles of Shikata, Kanki, Takasago, Noguchi, Ougo, and Hataya were not captured first, the root of the tooth forming the base of the enemy would never be shaken.

In the strategy of Hideyoshi, who made Mount Shosha his headquarters, the outlying enemies were attacked castle by castle in a so-called established tactic. Noguchi Castle fell and Hashitani Castle was taken. In turn, whatever base of Kanki Naganori in Kanki or clan of Kushihashi Osamu in Shikata was attacked to strengthen the hand for arson, clearing away the enemy, and mortar attacks over the vast territory of the Bessho clan.

Both the strategist Takenaka Hanbei and the wise Kuroda Kanbei helped by the influence of Hideyoshi. But with a small force of fewer than ten thousand, a quick success was doubtful in contrast to his geographical advantages.

Situation dire. Send auxiliary force west without delay.

This was the urgent message sent by Hideyoshi to Nobunaga in Azuchi. In order to not weaken fighting morale, the warhorses must rest and the exhausted spirits fed from time to time. He expected a long war.

There were opportunities for days of a cease-fire. Hanbei came to Kuroda Kanbei's encampment. He looked elegant carrying a bamboo cane and dressed in his battle surcoat.

"Is he here?" Hanbei asked and looked inside the camp.

Many living quarters for monks were located on Mount Shosha. Kanbei's camp was in the temple. Occasionally, while bearing arms, he read the *Analects of Confucius*. He cheerfully welcomed an unexpected visit from a friend. Right after greetings were exchanged, Kanbei inquired about his friend's health.

"How are you? Camp life is harsh. Food is hard to come by. Doesn't that promote sickness? I'm always advising Chikuzen-sama about this, but …"

Kanbei always greeted Takenaka Hanbei with that question. Hanbei had not been well since he came to the battlefield. In the presence of the heavily bearded men with skin burned like steel by the sun, only his white face stood out. At the time of the war council, he was taciturn and always beside Hideyoshi like a single white camellia flower blooming in a thicket.

However, if Hanbei's words were heard, those listening were always delighted. He was obviously ill, but he never communicated his pain or melancholy to others. Today too, he quietly displayed his never-changing smile.

"Oh, thank you. This illness is not so painful that you would guess it is chronic. It's become normal."

"Now, should the reinforcements in Azuchi move quickly?"

"I wrote a letter describing the situation to the lord. Based on that, the forces of Araki Murashige will join and are already headed here. The oldest son Nobutada-sama of Lord Nobunaga has also joined."

"Well, that provides a bit of relief. The deliberations in Azuchi were concerned about what may happen."

"No, there is no relief. I believe the difficulties begin now."

"So you're saying …?"

"Lord Niwa and generals Akechi, Takikawa, and Sakuma all have the strong conceit of generals. Are they willing deep down to receive our general's commands and act under his direction? I think they will present problems in leadership."

It was April. Spring came late to the mountains, and the bush warblers were in mating season.

2

In the heart-to-heart exchange, even in the absence of sake in a jug, the talk did not become tiresome. While watching the petals of wild cherry trees dance, the pair's entire conversation was restricted to military matters. Finally, Hanbei Shigeharu said, "Recently, because of your many war exploits, Chikuzen-sama gifted you with the fine horse Shoshazan."

"That reward was excessive. Moreover, my service relied entirely on the actions of my men. I gave the horse to Mori Tahei, a retainer of the clan. It was the lord's wish, but, in truth, I was put to shame," said Kanbei.

"Oh, no, no. I have no opinion on that matter. However, I am worried about a letter expressing true feelings, like between two brothers, that Chikuzen-sama sent to you."

"Oh yes. Those immaterial opinions were in the letter. Why does that trouble you?"

"Do you have that letter now?"

"It is a family treasure. I always carry it."

"If you have it on hand, will you let me see it?" asked Shigeharu.

"That's simple enough," said Kanbei; he took the letter from the armor box to show him.

Hanbei Shigeharu carefully read the letter in silence. When he finished, he said nothing as he put the letter in the hearth fire.

"... Ah?" slipped out of the shocked Kanbei as the letter turned into a sliver of white ash. His slight upset changed to reproach.

"To me, that letter expressed the favor of my lord and was a unique family treasure. Why did you throw it in the fire? Such insolence is not like you. Is there some hidden agenda?"

Hanbei Shigeharu withdrew slightly on his knees and, in an apologetic posture, quietly offered this admonition.

"One as wise as you will immediately understand my rashness. You could say this is a friend's kindness."

"In what way is this a friend's kindness?"

"Importance is given to this sort of written oath. Compared to its possible usefulness in the future, it's filled with deficiencies and becomes worthless. The result is unsatisfactory and inadequate. Am I saying this will be the source of your destruction? I think for the sake of both the lord and your family, the letter was unimportant and I burned it".

"Oh, yes ... of course."

Kanbei slapped his knees and was moved to tears by his friend's words. He felt the retainer had never offered instruction as severe as this.

Shigeharu searched the sleeve of his armor and pulled out a particular piece of paper. He passed it to the hand of Kanbei who was frozen with contrition.

"You lost an important item and are probably crestfallen. I believe this too is an exceptional letter. Read it later at your leisure," said Shigeharu.

Hanbei Shigeharu looked at the twilight sky and left. He could be summed up as a man who comes quietly and leaves quietly. Kanbei saw him off at the camp gate. When he returned, he remembered the letter in his hand.

He wondered, Who wrote this? Then he sat down and broke the seal.

The letter was from his son Matsuchiyo.

Since he took his son to Azuchi to be a hostage, he expected to forget them every day and night, but these were the childish characters written by the eleven-year-old he saw in his dreams on the battlefield.

The awkward characters of the letter included an innocent farewell poem and described his current situation. He wrote:

> *The castle on Mount Bodai in Mino of Takenaka Hanbei-sama is on a taller mountain than the castle in Himeji. Snow is deep in the winter, and spring comes late. I was lonely at first, but everybody in the castle takes good care of me. Many children in the castle gather every day to study with me, and now I'm not lonely anymore.*

He ended with, "I want to go soon with you Father to the battlefield."

CHAPTER TWENTY-ONE
A GENERAL'S HARDSHIP

1

THE CONQUEST OF the stronghold Miki Castle remained incomplete. At that time, an urgent report arrived at Mount Shosha.

Large Mouri force has taken Kozuki Castle.

Kozuki Castle was a pivotal ally and closest to enemy territory. After it was occupied, strategic positions were protected by the so-called Amago clan of Amago Katsuhisa and Yamanaka Shikanosuke. Naturally, they could not be abandoned.

The support force from Azuchi arrived, and Hideyoshi swiftly gathered the forces of Araki Murashige and commanded a total of twenty thousand men. To provide rapid assistance, they marched straight to the enemy and camped on Mount Takakura to the east of Kozuki Castle.

"Hideyoshi will form the rear guard here. We will brave it until word comes from the castle."

Hideyoshi sent out spies to infiltrate the enemy and urge on the Amago clan in the castle. However, in the valleys between Mount Takakura and Kozuki Castle, stockades had been erected, abatis obstacles laid out, and trenches and ditches dug to build the line of defense. They were constructed until there was no way to take one step forward and possess the summit.

Furthermore, the enemy was more than double the size of Hideyoshi's forces. A count of only the leaders in the large force like this with the might of Mouri's province would number about twenty thousand in the forces of Kobayakawa Takakage, fifteen thousand in the forces of Kikkawa Motoharu, and fourteen or fifteen thousand in the corps of Ukita Naoie. Hideyoshi had a bird's eye view of them and knew he could not start an utterly reckless war.

Reluctantly, every night, huge bonfires were built to do nothing more than build the fighting spirit far away at the isolated outposts of their allies.

In contrast, Mouri's troops also displayed their grand forces on the seas. Every last one of the more than seven hundred warships with fluttering banners cruising off the entirety of the shores of Settsu and Harima was a naval ship of the Mouri clan.

2

Warned about the emergency, Nobunaga in Azuchi sent his son Nobutada and several other generals, but the second front of the Mouri clan surrounded Kozuki Castle and split the allies in two. Nobunaga decided to go himself. However, a few days of rainstorms in Kamigata flooded the rivers, and reports arrived of dangers along the way. They lost sight of how many days passed.

> *The current situation is inescapable. The best strategy is to abandon Kozuki Castle, pull back Hideyoshi's forces and combine them with the military might of Nobutada-sama to confront a powerful enemy and launch a full-scale attack on Bessho Nagaharu at Miki Castle.*

Takigawa Kazumasu and Sakuma Nobumori offered
their opinions from the front line to Nobunaga in Azuchi.
As friends of the hereditary retainer Oda, their envy over
Hideyoshi's exploits was already brewing since the war
began in Chugoku. Secret feelings of hoping for one crisis
to frustrate Hideyoshi were harbored by more than a few
generals.

Nobunaga's order was rushed by messenger from
Azuchi to Hideyoshi's forces on Mount Takakura. It said,

*Attack the rear guard of Kozuki Castle to create a
second front for the enemy. Pull back immediately
and unite with the military forces of Nobutada-sama
to attack Miki Castle.*

When Hideyoshi received the order, he was
discouraged for a time.

He wondered whether by abandoning Kozuki Castle,
did Nobunaga intend to leave Amago Katsuhisa and
Yamanaka Shikanosuke, who were in the castle, to their
fates? How could he say that? That would be unacceptable.

Kanbei was not in this battle formation. He had
secret orders and infiltrated Okayama in Bizen. He invited
the strategist Takenaka Hanbei Shigeharu. However,
various orders flowed from Azuchi, so what was his
counsel?

Hanbei's words flowed like water.

He said, "You should retreat. Don't turn away from
Azuchi's orders."

"Why is that all there is?" asked Kanbei.

"The only time to withdraw is over one night. During
that time, a messenger will sneak into the castle. Make a
death-defying escape from the castle and meet up with our
allies. There is no other plan than the final communication.
I am well aware of the difficulties."

"I'll assign Kamei Shigenori."

He waited all night to escape the castle but failed. He
was unable to penetrate the deep encirclement by the

Mouri.

Finally, until the army evacuated in retreat, Hideyoshi stared at the ally of the isolated castle and lamented over and over.

He said, "Fighting with our sworn enemy the Mouri has gone on for the long period of fifty-seven years, since year 4 of Taiei. Beginning with the father and the son, the second and third generations, the revival of the Amago has been the long-cherished wish. With the chance for Oda's forces to move west, they clung to Lord Nobunaga and became allies who served with distinction. Now, he was going to abandon them. Amago Katsuhisa and Yamanake Shikanosuke were both left to die. From the position of a general like me, the name of Lord Nobunaga will be dishonored until the outcome in Tsukushi in Chugoku and until the distant future when the siege is achieved, and become the seed of slander in the world.... This is truly regrettable."

Araki Murashige in the allied forces already left for Mount Shosha without hesitation. Hideyoshi left the rear guard and gradually began to retreat. His feelings conflicted with his spirit on this battlefield. No experience is more bitter in war than a retreat out of futility. War strategy was always easily disrupted. However, the general of a great army was not as embittered and greatly frustrated as much as when the disruption came from an ally.

CHAPTER TWENTY-TWO
THE CASTLE
OF THE ABANDONED CHILD

1

NEITHER LIFE NOR war progresses smoothly. Adversity is always present. No, it is better to say adversity is always found within steady progress. Hideyoshi's adversity began here. Looking back, until now everything had gone well for him. Serving as the commissioner of Chugoku, he could employ his wits as he liked as the supreme commander.

However, Oda Nobutada went west aided by his generals Niwa, Akechi, Sakuma, and Takigawa. The fundamental strategy changed completely by direct orders from Azuchi. His orders and intentions were no longer what they had been. But first, Nobutada had to be obeyed. All the generals at Nobutada's field headquarters were senior to him and continued to regard Hideyoshi as an upstart. They also took to calling him That Monkey.

Unlike his father, Nobutada did not respect him. Before anyone noticed, the headquarters of the army besieging Miki Castle was not at Hideyoshi's camp but had been moved to Nobutada's location. When he abandoned the futile rear guard at Kozuki Castle and withdrew,

Nobutada immediately gave him the order "The soldiers under your command will enter Tajima and sweep away the ruling party of the Bessho scattered throughout Tajima."

Nobutada was a young general at twenty years old. This sort of simple strategy was reasonable, and Hideyoshi obeyed his orders with a smile.

He said, "Yessir. I understand," and set out that day for Tajima. A clear intent of Nobutada's orders was to give control of some of the troops to the experienced generals of Sakuma, Niwa, and Takigawa at his field headquarters.

"This is Lord Nobutada's order, but why is this unexpected news readily accepted?" asked Hideyoshi, showing obvious concern when he spoke to his commanders. Takenaka Hanbei's military command was unyielding. He warned, "You cannot refuse. First of all, a worthless man debates in the military."

In the end, the generals directed their dissatisfaction in another direction and began the sweep.

The sweep of the minor enemies scattered throughout Tajima lasted about one month. By then, it was already July. During a short forty days of hard fighting in the remote regions between the mountains, the faces from Hideyoshi and his commanding officers were burned black by the sun. Only the face of Takenaka Hanbei stayed white like a morning glory even after laying down in several mountains and fields and being scorched while riding on a cart in the intense heat. Hanbei's illness suddenly took a turn for the worse. According to his subordinates, "He coughed frequently during the nights the field troops lay on the grass. Between battles, he was seen frequently spitting up saliva like blood into tissue paper."

The samurai side of Hideyoshi didn't show one instance of a pained brow. For example, he laughed as he said in his usual quiet voice, "Battlefields are enjoyable. I can't remember anything when off to war. If you think about the lives of several thousand warriors hanging on one command from the field headquarters, like Hanbei's illness, there's not a spare moment to remember even if one tries."

2

During this period, Kozuki Castle, the base of the Amago clan and the abandoned child at the border between Harima and Bizen, was left to its inevitable fate and fell.

Amago Katsuhisa committed seppuku and pleaded to spare the lives of the castle soldiers. Yamanaka Shikanosuke Yukimori surrendered and kneeled at the camp gate of the Mouri.

"I will give you an estate worth 5,000 koku in Suou province. Can you forget the old grudges and have the heart to serve the Mouri clan for many years?"

Kikkawa Motoharu and Kobayakawa Takakage gave instructions to treat him favorably. Shikanosuke said, "I have no hope," and accepted the favor. He was escorted with around thirty people including his wives, children, and vassals to Geishu.

Because of their tenacity and hope of reviving the main family, he confronted the powerful Mouri as the enemy, surmounted all obstacles over dozens of years, and was undaunted by any trial. With this complete reversal, his demeanor should have been wretched and miserable.

But until his last moment came, hidden in Shikanosuke's heart was the idea that death will not come easy. After being pulled into enemy territory, he would stab to kill and be killed by Kikkawa Motoharu or, if given the chance, Mouri Terumoto.

From the beginning, however, the Mouri were skeptical of his surrender.

They wondered what kind of man he was?

His lord Katsuhisa was already dead by seppuku. The blood ties to the main branch of the Amago clan were severed. Shikanosuke Yukimori probably would not unashamedly take a handsome stipend and steal half a lifetime living in luxury. The followers of the Kikkawa clan already sensed that. As their convoy was about to cross Kawabe River at the foot of the mountain Bitchu Matsuyama, at the instant Shikanosuke wiped sweat from his face while waiting for the ferry, a long sword descended on him from behind.

Shikanosuke dove into the river as he had planned. Spears flew down from the shore and the boat. One man after another jumped into the river to grapple with him and eventually took his head.

For a time, Shikanosuke's blood stained Kawabe River red.

He was thirty-nine years old.

When Hideyoshi heard this news, he said, "Poor man …" He looked back at Kanbei and Hanbei and clicked his tongue like he was pained.

Kuroda Kanbei quickly answered to soothe his despair.

"Kozuki Castle was finally given to the enemy. Soon they will try to take ten more. This situation will never defeat our allies."

"…Hmm, is that so?"

Hideyoshi held those feelings. They were the attitude of Ukita Naoie of Bizen who was passed a secret message by Kanbei after he slipped out of camp.

CHAPTER TWENTY-THREE
AUTUMN ON MOUNT HIRAI

1

WHEN HIDEYOSHI RETURNED to camp from Tajima,
Nobunaga's main force added a wing and set up a full-scale
siege of Miki Castle.

Kanki Castle and Shikata Castle, the satellite
fortresses of Miki Castle, fell in no time.

However, the base of Miki Castle where the Bessho
clan protected over seven thousand people was
impregnable. Strong warriors were linked by blood to the
clan and its vassals. Furthermore, the latest, most powerful
weapons and provisions were brought in by the Mouri
over sea routes. In the short term, there was no prospect
of attacking to defeat them.

The Azuchi plan prepared for the long term and only
attacked their stamina and their provisions. When August
began, Nobutada temporarily withdrew to Azuchi,
accompanied by almost all of the generals and their
military units.

"This will be a long siege. I will leave it to you," he
said to Hideyoshi upon his return.

Hideyoshi readily answered, "Don't worry."

A military force much smaller than before was

stationed at the headquarters in preparation for the long siege on Mount Hirai in front of Miki Castle.

There was another reason for Nobutada's withdrawal. The huge forces of the Kikkawa and the Kobayakawa attacked and defeated Kozuki Castle in a short time. They understood the enduring nature of the war. Kikkawa Motoharu went back to Izumo. Kobayakawa Takakage returned to Aki.

The war situation appeared to have unexpectedly become complicated.

The public sentiment amid the chaos of war still had no regrets about their unwavering dedication. However, their uncertainty was exposed in their concerns over whether the advantage lay in depending on the Mouri or whether victory belonged to Oda. Engaging in the morning and retreating in the evening was difficult to predict.

Mouri forces appeared to withdraw from the border between Bizen and Harima, but that was the treachery of the Ukita clan.

He seemed to be offering the entire province of Bizen for the Mouri forces to withdraw and engage with the Oda clan. This altered the grave state of the war and was an unprecedented, favorable turn of events for the Oda clan. Nobutada and his generals presented this gift of a new advantage and returned in triumph for now. But the legs and tongue of Kuroda Kanbei understood this exceptional gift.

Naturally, Lord Hideyoshi's consent and the considerable workings of Takenaka Hanbei's brain created a unified force of lord and vassal. However, that power was moved to act after many visits by a man carried by his legs and using his tongue. This man who exposed his life to the dangers of enemy territory that lurked in his many secret missions was Kanbei.

He maintained an excellent contact inside the Ukita clan. This man's name was Hanabusa Sukebei, a vassal of

Naoie. He was called "The Sensible Man" and often enlightened Kanbei and was enlightened by Kanbei. He pushed aside the confusing, different opinions in the clan and made Lord Naoie a follower of Oda.

2

The large military units of the allies left, and the forces of Hashiba Chikuzen-no-kami were determined to carry out an extended siege at the impregnable Miki Castle. Early autumn had arrived in the camp at Mount Hirai.

The Chinese bellflowers bloomed on the mountain, and eulalia grasses budded their ears.

Hideyoshi said, "Today is the one hundredth day since Yamanaka Shikanosuke Yukimori's death. When he died crossing Kawabe River, they say a Taikai tea container hung on his chest. Even his majestic bones showed an aspect of his simple elegance. This evening, I plan to offer a cup as comfort to his courageous and loyal soul burdened by many grudges. You are welcome to join me."

The white moon shone through the pent roof of the camp headquarters. Hideyoshi often humbled himself before the boiling kettle. There were often tea gatherings in the camp, but Hideyoshi was not seen submissive and silent.

Only two men came. Of course, they were Hanbei and Kanbei. The two were grateful that Hideyoshi had not forgotten the anniversary of Shikanosuke's death. They deeply felt his death was not regrettable to this man.

The night passed.

Takenaka Hanbei leaned into the white path of the moon on the return to his camp and sat down to rest for brief periods.

"How have you been?" asked Kanbei.

His fellow retainer peeked at his face whitened by the moon and knitted his brow. Still walking, Hanbei said, "I'm fine."

However, he threw away tissue paper stained with

119

blood. He was coughing up blood. After that night, he came down with a fever and was confined to bed in the camp for more than ten days.

At his bedside, the visitor Hideyoshi said, "Your stubbornness frustrates me. I'm asking you to take care of yourself. The battlefield is no place to recuperate. Go to Kyoto and get treated by a good physician. Go see Manase Dousan. He is a noted doctor these days.... My path would darken if you died. You must go to Kyoto for six months or a year to restore your health."

He encouraged using what resembled scolding, egging on, and begging.

"You're wasting your words," said Hanbei wiping away tears. Kanbei understood his feelings and hung his head.

The autumn day was filled with the cries of shrikes. The sickly military specialist Takenaka Hanbei said he could not leave the camp in Mount Hirai even if he died, but he eventually returned to Kyoto. Hideyoshi and Kanbei saw him off.

A new mountain palanquin was built for him. This was a product of Hideyoshi's compassion. He left the gate and went down the mountain road. His shadow was seen off by Hideyoshi's and Kanbei's eyes burning with tears.

"Kanbei, he's a young man but a great talent and erudite. If heaven sent a man like him to this world, why did he carry that illness when born. I can't bear thinking about the feelings in the heart of Hanbei as he leaves this place ..." said Hideyoshi and strode back to the camp headquarters. When he felt spasms on his face like he was about to cry, he hid away like a child.

The autumn of insects deepened. Beside Hideyoshi's seat was sadness like pulling a tooth. As much as possible, Kanbei did not gossip about Hanbei.

As expected, this loneliness was broken. He was put under pressure by the addition of greater isolation when General Araki Murashige in the army withdrew earlier

along with Nobutada and commanded the strategic
position of Settsu where he was stationed. Suddenly, an
express dispatch by horse messenger reported the flying of
banners of revolt against the Oda clan.

"Murashige?"

"Lord Araki?"

In an age when the human heart was difficult to
gauge, the shaken lord and retainer looked at each other.
Before ten days passed, another urgent message was
delivered to the surprise of Hideyoshi and Kanbei. The
message from a spy stated:

> *Kodera Masamoto in Gochaku was invited to switch
> sides by Araki Murashige in Settsu. Evidence of
> reinforcements requested from the Mouri. About eight
> to nine tenths of this matter are certain.*

On that day, a similar urgent message also came from
Kuroda Souen in Himeji. They had no doubt what was
unfolding.

CHAPTER TWENTY-FOUR
THE STRAIGHT ROAD

1

"**SIR, I HAVE** an earnest request for several days off to rest," said Kanbei and placed both hands on the ground before Hideyoshi. The result was a night of worry. His eyebrows swelled with serious determination from self-reproach.

"Where are you going?" asked Hideyoshi who wondered how he should handle this crisis. Hideyoshi seemed to still be deliberating. Obviously, he would not say things were fine.

Since yesterday, a pensive look rarely seen on Hideyoshi's face reflected his predicament. Pained by having to ask him in this state, Kanbei frowned and said, "I'll whip my horse and rush to Gochaku. After I assess the situation, I will handle the outsiders in the clan once and for all, express my opinions to Lord Masamoto, and put an end to mindless defections."

"Now what should I do? Even if you go, now is ..." said Hideyoshi.

"No, if you send me, I will risk my life," said Kanbei.

These were not mere words. Kanbei thought hard about the risk to his life and stared at Hideyoshi's lips.

Gochaku Castle had to stand firm in Harima, but Kodera Masamoto's conviction easily crumbled. Coupled with the treason of Araki Murashige, without warning he called for succession and, through the Mouri clan, deceived the world and switched sides. Kuroda Kanbei could not stop crying. If you saw his eyes reddened the previous night by this immensely regrettable, stupid, and unprincipled act, you would understand his extraordinary indignation.

After pondering the circumstances from the beginning, his position was shaken at its foundation. How could he face Nobunaga in Azuchi, Hideyoshi, and the people of Harima he convinced to join Oda? He had the faith of a military family. He had a living moral duty. If he were a meek man, the only path would be to slash open his stomach to demonstrate his integrity.

"Please, give me these few days. I will quickly go and return," repeated a sincere Kanbei. Hideyoshi's eyes jumped and studied his face. Kanbei's reflection resembled mourning.

Hideyoshi's answer did not come easily. He did not say yes or no or forbade him from going. Did he silently fear deep in his heart that Kanbei would never return to camp from Gochaku?

From Hideyoshi's perspective, he had some trepidation. It's times like these; it's the mind of the general public. The current outlook for Oda was definitely poor.

He said too much. Kanbei was well aware that Hideyoshi's concern centered on his quick return. When he raised his head to bolster his sincerity, "Go," said Hideyoshi and suddenly slid off his cushion.

Kanbei placed both hands on the ground and focused his strength.

"It may be hard, but go. No matter what, Kodera Masamoto is your master and no better friend to me," said Hideyoshi.

"Do I have your permission?" asked Kanbei.

"I will allow you. Who can assume your responsibilities? My only concern is for your life. Danger is everywhere."

"I will prepare in advance."

"That's impossible."

Hideyoshi took away his sweaty hand and moved forward on his knees. He said, "In addition to substantial fear of harming the Kodera clan internally, I am also gripped by the fear that you will choose death. A man who once spoke of breaking away is not easily forgotten no matter what the explanation is because of fear of the consequences. For instance, despite your sincerity, as a man of Gochaku Castle, you may not hold fast ... Kanbei, what do you plan to do?"

" ... "

"You will die. At that time, cut open your stomach and do not apologize to Lord Nobunaga or to me. If you don't have narrow-minded thoughts, then go. Achieve great deeds then return," said Hideyoshi,

"I will not die," said Kanbei again but sounded on the verge of tears.

As the tears and the muscles fought on Kanbei's face, he found his resolve.

"Goodbye for now," said Kanbei.

"All right," said Hideyoshi in a full tone and gave a large nod. Kanbei promptly left.

"I will come again another time."

2

When he returned to camp headquarters, Kanbei called out, "Tahei, lend me your horse. Shoshazan over there."

"Take him. Where are you going?" asked Tahei.

"To survey some of our allies' camps."

"Then we'll go together."

Mori Tahei walked behind his lord's horse.

Kanbei left the headquarters on Mount Hirai and observed the enemy stronghold, the front line of the allies confronting Miki Castle. He made one observation pass and returned.

A burgeoning fighting spirit was felt with no center in the castle of the enemy hardened with more than seven thousand elite troops. The unexpected betrayal of Azuchi by Araki Murashige was clearly reflected in the fighting spirit. The joy of the songs of triumph was seen in the enemy.

One after another in Murashige's plan, Takayama Ukon of Takatsuki in the Settsu region and Nakagawa Kiyohide of Ibaraki raised the banner of rebellion. Even in Chugoku, the Kodera clan in Gochaku acted in concert with them. A celebration in the associated camps of this series of schemes was reasonable as an uncommon diplomatic success of the Mouri.

"I think this place is in crisis. Mount Hirai is the divide that determines whether Oda or Mouri wins."

Kanbei's heart was muddled, but he also felt his responsibility.

He turned his horse and went to speak with Hideyoshi again. He proposed a serious plan to deploy troops he noticed during his patrol of the camps to the front line.

"Starting with the east and west roads passing through Miki Castle, recent allies are blockading the roads entering Miki from the shore of Harimanada to cut off the enemy's supply lines. Today, I observed the enemy's fighting spirit, and the geography worries me. This plan does not address, even a little, the enemy's fighting spirit and must be rethought," said Kanbei.

Because this was the enduring long-term strategy in Hideyoshi's eyes, he was astonished to hear Kanbei's words. He stared and impatiently asked, "Why is cutting off the supply lines pointless?"

"In the following months, more than two hundred supply ships of the Mouri clan will approach the shores of Uozumi. Any attempt to go to Miki will be driven back.

Smuggled rice provisions are seized continuously. In truth, the blockade is so complete water cannot leak through. It's a serious matter that this has not delivered a heavy blow to the enemy soldiers."

Kanbei's words were filled with dissatisfaction, but he emphasized their thoroughness.

He said, "No, that was fine until yesterday, but today all of Settsu has joined with the Mouri, and a huge fissure is developing."

"What? ... Is that so?" asked Hideyoshi.

"It is reasonable not to notice. I was born in Harima and first noticed the secret road. That place is Sessho in Nibuyama visible about two and a half miles south of Ougo. It is the border of the two provinces of Harima and Settsu. There are no roads that look like roads. If passed through there, the transport of the goods of Settsu to Miki and the passage of soldiers from Miki Castle to Settsu would face no obstacles," said Kanbei.

"Today, the day Araki of Settsu changed sides, a new base is already being constructed there. The soldiers of either Miki or Settsu will surely be stationed at this base. Also, transport routes are being cleared. Even our allies are not considering measures to address that. Even if the three roads to Miki are blocked, the provision ships of the Mouri will supply provisions from the area of Hanakuma in Settsu, cross over Niwa, and pass through Awagawa. Goods can probably be sent with ease to the castle from that direction."

Hideyoshi's opinion was spoken with gratitude from his heart. Kanbei was distressed by the predicament and on the verge of going to a more painful place than death. His strong emotions overflowed with a passion that offered ample heart in these last moments.

"You've taught me so much. Thank you. Thank you. It somehow seems so," said Hideyoshi.

"Well, I will be going soon," said Kanbei.

"You're going already?"

"I believe a little sooner is better."

"Be careful of mistakes and be vigilant. Again, take care of yourself."

"You too, even in camp."

"Don't worry. I'll be fine."

"The enemy shut up in the impregnable castle and the allies in the exposed camps seemed to have the same number of warriors. In addition, the allied warriors were hidden and given an advantage by the lay of the land. The enemy soldiers are provincial samurai who aren't confused by the roads in this area even on moonless nights. Their fighting spirit may swell, so try to estimate the danger of them hurtling out of the castle in a sneak attack. Especially during long encampments, the enemy bores easily, and carelessness becomes a possibility."

Kanbei turned on the saddle of the fine horse Shoshazan and watched the sun set in the west behind the Chugoku mountain range and, filled with emotion, slowly descended from the headquarters on Mount Hirai.

3

When he reached the foot of the mountain, Kanbei looked back and said, "Tahei. You can see me off here. Go back now."

For half the day, Mori Tahei followed Kanbei's horse on foot. He vaguely sensed the extraordinary nature of his master's destination and his feelings.

"No, I will make the entire journey with you. To Himeji or to Gochaku," said Tahei.

"This is far enough!" snapped a scowling Kanbei,

"Each soldier here is crucial. The camp on Mount Hirai cannot be defeated even once or the entire core of the Oda may rupture. Compared to the castle, the camp is undermanned. One hundred men can fight during my absence. Now go."

"Yessir."

"Go back."

"Yessir …"

The despondent follower who cared for his master returned to the mountain camp.

Kanbei watched Tahei return and looked up at Hideyoshi's camp. The hardened heart of a warrior like Kanbei felt sharp pangs. And the follower who was scolded and driven away was pained by thoughts of Hideyoshi's loneliness.

Kanbei thought, Not even a dozen days had passed since the sickly military strategist Takenaka Hanbei, Hideyoshi's reliable right-hand man, descended the mountain to recuperate in Kyoto. And now, I'm leaving the mountain. Not to elevate myself, but in times of leisure, the lord Hideyoshi often said he thought of Hanbei as his right hand and me as his left hand. And frost may come early with snow this autumn on Mount Hirai where a hard fight will be faced. He stopped his horse for a few moments then resumed his journey.

"I will not die."

He took a moment to make this pledge. However, if he imagined the situation at his destination and the difficulty of his objective, he did not wish for the good luck of living to return home. He could say one in a hundred is impossible. With that firm belief, he unknowingly and unwittingly glanced back at the figure of his beloved follower like this separation was for a lifetime. He paid respect to Hideyoshi and stared at the darkening mountainscape of Mount Hirai.

"I'm complaining but I must not delude myself. Hojo Tokimune once said, 'There is no looking back in a military family. The road is straight.'"

He cracked the whip. For the whole night, the horse galloped until it panted for breath.

CHAPTER TWENTY-FIVE
THE PAPER BALL

1

INTELLIGENCE FROM THE lookouts with eyes open in
all directions came swiftly.

Voices without sound passed like the wind from
station to station along strips of roads.

"Kuroda Kanbei left Mount Hirai."

"Kanbei is rushing west."

"Kanbei is returning to Himeji."

From the day this was heard in Gochaku Castle,
Kodera Masamoto and his followers acted with the
urgency demanded by a crisis.

"Why is there panic? If focused on preparations for
war on Himeji, there would be no uproar. A crisis at any
time will draw in the huge forces of the Mouri clan as the
rear guard."

Ogawa Mikawa-no-kami of the clan, the senior
retainer Masuda Magoemon, and Kuramitsu Masatoshi
encouraged the clan. Although the only name heard was
Kanbei, Lord Masamoto was shaken and lost all color.
That name rebuked and restrained him.

Out of necessity, Masamoto and the senior retainers
deduced the reasons for his behavior. They concluded,

"After Kanbei returned home and made Himeji Castle his
base, he would rally the military power of his father Souen
and nearby allies. Then he would seek the support of the
Ukita clan and probably attack us here in Gochaku."

That morning, however, a scout entered the castle
gate nearly flying in on a fast horse encouraged by the lash.
His words upset their speculations.

"Kanbei arrived at Himeji last night. Why didn't he
enter the castle on Himeyama? He stayed at the home of
Yojiemon, an eye medicine dealer in the village. This
morning, he seemed to be headed here to Gochaku."

Although adequate preparations were made for battle,
all the senior vassals reddened and asked questions one
after another.

"What? He's coming directly here? How many men
are with him?"

The scout answered, "He's alone. There's just one
horse."

"What? Kanbei's alone?"

"If that's so, he's not with an attendant."

"That's odd."

They looked like they had been tricked although one
burden had been thrown off. As their doubts turned to
fear, everyone's eyes were blinking when Murai Kawachi-
no-kami in his intimidating voice warned, "Do not let your
guard down. That man may be harboring some ingenious
scheme. I say to each one of you, be vigilant."

2

Kanbei rushed to Himeji the previous evening but was
relaxed this morning. He swayed from side to side as his
fine horse Shoshazan carried him more than two miles to
Gochaku. He gazed occasionally at the mountains and
valleys of late autumn.

"The ripening fields are a blessing. This year looks
good. This is the best time for viewing the autumn leaves.
The farmers look happy, too," nearly shouted Kanbei's

traveling companion.

His companion was on a Buddhist pilgrimage to a destination beyond Himeji. In other words, he was a man from the roadside teahouse but was turned into a conversation partner by Kanbei in a lively, aimless conversation during the tedium of the journey.

"Forgive me. I'm on a pilgrimage to Sekison-sama in that mountain, so now ..." said the pilgrim just as Gochaku Castle came into view. He gave an unexpected farewell and left down a side road.

Kanbei forced a smile and said goodbye. He was certain the man was a spy from Gochaku. Kanbei had no idea how this man appeared like an autumn fly along his route.

Finally, he tied up his horse at the castle gate.

Kanbei identified himself to the samurai out front. He greeted everyone with a hello and returned bows with his usual animation and immediately passed to the parlor in the castle keep occupied by Masamoto. A samurai rushed to block his way. He said, "Please wait a little while. The lord was not feeling well earlier and shut himself away."

To push back, Kanbei said, "No, if he is ill, I'd like to see him at once."

"That is impossible. Please wait a little longer," said the samurai and offered a cushion and brought out tea and pastry. By the lord's orders, he had no choice but to wait.

Meanwhile, in Masamoto's parlor, he was conferring with his family and senior retainers in confidence.

"It is best to kill him. This time, he came here to kill. He is who he is and certainly planned with Hideyoshi to come here harboring some elaborate plan. He also came with no companions and returned alone. This is truly a perfect opportunity. If the man who is the root of the calamity befalling this clan is not stabbed to death, the regret will last one hundred years," said Ogawa Mikawa-no-kami of the clan and was backed by Masuda

Magoemon and Kuramitsu Masatoshi. On the other hand, one or two retainers of Kodera Masamoto said, "If the source of his breath is stopped here, a huge obstacle will be removed. And for the Mouri clan, this would be very useful in stating our attitude.... If it becomes known that he was stabbed to death in Gochaku Castle ... Souen in Himeji and the Kuroda faction in the neighboring villages would immediately attack us here. Naturally, we would have the support of the Mouri clan and could wait for aid from Bessho Nagaharu at Miki Castle. Without support for this castle, it will be very difficult .... Kanbei's visit was too soon. Who can we contact because the signal won't arrive in time?"

This other opinion adopted the principle of being overly cautious. This consultation would not easily come to an agreement.

"Well, what should we do?"

"Even if you ask what to do ... isn't this sudden?"

Without a plan and without an escort, Kanbei quietly entered a place where he could leisurely compare the pensive faces. Did he believe he had waited long enough or did he intend to surprise them? From behind everyone, he loudly said, "Well."

More than the senior retainers and the family, more than anyone else, Kodera Masamoto was rattled. His face laid bare his panic. His cheeks looked like they were dyed red.

As a senior retainer, Kanbei had not changed at all from the days he worked in this castle.

"It's good to be back. The lord is in good health as always. In my absence, the rest of you have been loyal in many ways. I thank you all.... Ah, it's been so many years, ten or so years, we have not seen each other."

He was nonchalant, like he was comforting them in their distress, and worked hard to recall earlier friendships.

3

On that day, Kanbei negotiated directly with Lord Masamoto and discussed the situation face-to-face with the clan and the retainers. In his heart, Kanbei thought, Now the temptations of Araki and Mouri are being pulled apart. It was a good idea to return. He felt some relief when he returned to his residence outside the castle that night.

He returned home with his principle of unwavering candidness. He did not come with a plan. He showed no anger. As for the main Kodera clan, its beliefs as a military family were constant. Through sincerity, he would persuade the lord, the clan, and the retainers. He clashed with the feelings of humility of whatever will happen, will happen.

Through that sincerity, the next morning, Eda Zenbei and Murai Kawachi-no-kami came, spoke frankly, and returned home. However, close to noon, Masuda Magoemon came to greet him as Masamoto's envoy.

"From your words yesterday, the lord is deeply ashamed given your unceasing loyalty. Breaking away this time is not a crime of the lord alone. The beliefs of our comrades were weakened by your absence.… In any case, the lord is eager to speak with you. Will you come with me?"

Kanbei said, "I will go. You may have noticed, but I am not very happy."

Kanbei immediately prepared and left for the castle. He met only with Lord Masamoto who confessed, "As you know, Araki Murashige of Settsu and my clan have been connected by ideology and beliefs since my father's generation. In my generation, the bond is still unbreakable. Without knowing details about the situation, Murashige broke from Nobunaga and rose in rebellion. The Bessho family in Miki Castle secretly contacted Gochaku through the Mouri clan. The situation was explained in detail to

Hideyoshi in Chugoku, and a proposal came. I heard his ardent admonition yesterday, and my response was guarded. In fact, I feel ashamed. I feel quite ashamed. For that, I apologize to you."

"No, that's ridiculous. There is no need for you to confess to a vassal like me. If you open your eyes to that, I will die here without malice," said Kanbei.

"I'd like to place a great hardship on you. Will you do it?" asked Masamoto.

"What is it?"

"I'd like you to meet with Araki Murashige. Meet with him one time to explain my mental anguish. As you believed, the revolt against Lord Nobunaga was nothing more than rash behavior or only seeing the powerful figure of the Mouri clan. Based on that, I wish you to speak convincingly to persuade them of an unreliable state of affairs."

These words of his lord roused Kanbei's passion and belief.

His first thought was "This was a noteworthy mission. If explained to Araki Murashige and he abandons his recklessness, it will be a major contribution to the whole affair of the conquest of Chugoku."

Without hesitation, Kanbei said, "I would be happy to take on this mission. When Lord Murashige abandons rebellion …"

"Of course, I will absolutely not break from the Oda clan," said Masamoto.

"In the rare event, I'm inept and am unable to convince Lord Murashige to reconsider, what will you do?" asked Kanbei.

"Although the connections with Araki Murashige are old and deep, my ties of friendship have been exhausted. It's better for the agreement sent earlier to become wastepaper."

"I am honored. After hearing your words, I feel strong as if backed by one million warriors. Well, if I hear the situation in Settsu takes a dangerous turn, I will leave today," said Kanbei.

"I wrote all of my feelings in this letter. When you meet Murashige, please hand it directly to him," said Masamoto and gave him the letter.

4

As the autumn colors of the mountains and fields faded to black, Kuroda Kanbei raced down the roads outside of Himeji.

Whether coming or going, he passed Himeji but did not approach the castle on Himeyama where his father and wife lived.

His wife was informed the previous day by Yojiemon from the castle town about her husband's actions and objectives. Today, she heard from a messenger that her husband would rest his horse for a short time at Yojiemon's store then start off again to Settsu. At least, she was able to linger in the shadows of a row of trees by the roadside teahouse and wait for her husband to pass.

Yojiemon knew where she was and held his horse to deliberately delay Kanbei until they reached the edge of town.

"Go home already, old man. I expect the envoy this time to have a harder time and will face difficulties escaping danger to return home alive. But if I return alive, I will go home to Himeyama at some point. When you say goodbye and leave, please tell my father, too.… That's it, we will part here, so go home now," said Kanbei when he stopped his horse to send Yojiemon away. He left the horse's side but did not leave and frequently wiped away tears. Kanbei took note.

In the shadows of the row of trees in the twilight, he could see the white face of his wife covered by a straw hat.

He looked in her direction and scolded her from his mount.

"A woman has many duties in the home. Even when

she has free time, shouldn't she keep busy even if it's beside my father? Your husband is a man on the battlefield. When will I take off my armor and return home in triumph? Silly!"

While scolding her, he searched for and took out something beneath his surcoat covering his armor. He flung the object crumpled in his hand like a paper ball at his wife.

It was the letter from their son Matsuchiyo passed to him from Takenaka Hanbei at the headquarters on Mount Shosha.

The paper ball did not reach her. The crying young wife chased after and picked up the paper being rolled around and nearly carried away by the evening breeze. The swift departure was left to the fine horse Shoshazan ridden by Kanbei. When his wife looked down the road again, his shadow was obscured by the mist of the autumn evening.

CHAPTER TWENTY-SIX
DARKNESS

1

ALONG THE WAY, Kanbei stayed overnight in Kakogawa where he struck the lamplight in an inn, wrote a letter, and put it in his sleeve.

The next morning, he went to the gate on the street and met the forces of Hashiba protecting the important roads. Kanbei took out and handed over the letter.

"Please give this to Chikuzen-sama," he said and hurried on his way.

Needless to say, the letter probably described in detail the latest news and urgent reports from Itami Castle of Araki Murashige.

"I want to see your eyes and face ..." he turned back to look at Mount Hirai. But two or three days were not insignificant, the situation in Settsu would not wait even half a day and will be everchanging after Gochaku. No one knew how it would change, thought Kanbei and believed it best to hurry and not even stop for a cup of hot water at a teashop along the way.

"I better be quick."

As expected, passersby on the street felt the severity of the current state of affairs when they took one step to enter Settsu. The soldiers at Hanakuma Castle from the Hyogo region commanded the streets, built fences everywhere, and connected checkpoints.

"Where are you going? What is your business there?"

The questioning on the roads was unsparing.

"I am a vassal from Gochaku, Kuroda Kanbei. By order of my lord, I am going to Itami Castle."

He did not speak a word about being an attendant of Hideyoshi. However, there was not a man who did not recognize the name Kuroda Kanbei. Although he was not stopped, he passed through sharp looks. His horse brushed passed and galloped to the destination.

Itami was getting closer. Kanbei gently prodded his horse until he reached the row of pine trees near Itami. Someone from a roadside teahouse yelled, "Master, it's been a long time."

Kanbei turned to see a man walk up to his saddle in a humble posture to greet him.

2

"My goodness, aren't you Shinshichi?" asked Kanbei and dismounted. While wiping his sweaty face, he rested on a tree stump at the teahouse and asked, "How did you know I was coming?"

The silversmith Shinshichi lived in the castle town of Itami and was a relative of Yojiemon, the eye medicine peddler in Himeji. When Kanbei displayed ambition and left his home country, on his first visit to see Nobunaga in Gifu, at Yojiemon's recommendation, he stopped at the silversmith's home along the way. There, he changed his clothes to travel incognito from Kyoto to Gifu.

"This morning, everyone in Itami is gossiping about your arrival. I also heard from someone inside the household of Araki-sama," said Shinshichi.

"You've got sharp ears.... All right. Early notices came one after another by express horse," said Kanbei.

"At any rate, the roads are a challenge. We live in this

castle town and can't venture one step outside the domain."

"That's it. The situation in the domain leaked to the Oda clan, and it is bad."

"Will the battle with Oda finally begin?"

"Murashige is focused.... Naturally, he's probably prepared for a fight because the flag of rebellion against Nobunaga is flying."

"The men of Miki Castle and the envoy of the Mouri clan will enter the gate of Nobetsu Castle."

"The men of Miki Castle will cross the mountain to enter, but from where will the Mouri men come from?"

"They will come up from the sea. A large number will be from Hongan-ji Temple."

"They're very active. Lord Murashige is probably an imperious man.... Shinshichi, you've lived in Itami for a long time and worked in the castle. You may have heard rumors. Why did a man like Araki Murashige rise in revolt out of the blue against Nobunaga through the benevolence of the Mouri clan? ... Have you heard anything?"

"No, assorted rumors about that were advanced in the world."

"What, for example?"

"Was jealousy of the war exploits and successes of Murashige-sama connected to Akechi Mitsuhide-sama's secret slander directed at Nobunaga? No, it was the influence of the Mouri clan, and the temptation of a promised extraordinary reward."

"Did the public believe this was necessary? Is that the truth?"

"No, the truth seems to be very different. From what I've heard, the cause was two or three senior retainers at Itami Castle conspired to avoid scrutiny by the Oda clan and sell a lot of rice provisions and grains on the black market, but Azuchi was alerted."

"It seems so. Osaka Honga-ji Temple cut off roads in Kinki on the Oda side, and food provisions dwindled rapidly. That is an essential point of Oda's strategy. They probably wanted it regardless of price. If sold to him, I believe a huge profit would be gained."

"Murashige-sama may or may not return from Chugoku with Lord Nobutada. He was summoned to Azuchi for a stern rebuke by Nobunaga and reprimanded to his face. Then he was informed of your wish for him to hand over the criminal, but Murashige-sama stubbornly refused. That criminal will somehow strike at your fine father or a relative you love."

"Hongan-ji Temple or the Mouri clan saw an opening that led to that advantage. Have they easily gained profits?" asked Kanbei.

"I don't think so," said Shinshichi.

"I understand the gist. However, envoys from Azuchi are often seen at Itami Castle."

"Over the past few days, when the rebellion became widely known, envoys with warnings came one after another. Matsui Yukan-sama, Akechi Mitsuhide-sama, and Manmi Sencho-sama received orders from Azuchi. They came in vain many times to explain and persuade them to return home."

"You've told me a lot. It's good we met before I entered the castle. That information fits well with my preparations. Shinshichi, thank you."

"In any case, my home is squalid. Please rest here for a short time while I go and tidy up."

"The visit to Itami this time is different from my previous one. It's not a stopover during a journey. I must go to the castle right now. If the affair ends as I hope, I will be sure to stop by on my way home.... I want a decision today. Goodbye, Shinshichi," said Kanbei who stood, untied his horse, and mounted the saddle, leaving behind Shinshichi who had taken great pains to meet him. Kanbei entered the town of Itami and headed for the castle gate.

CHAPTER TWENTY-SEVEN
BEHIND THE SEAL

1

"DID YOU SEE it, Kanbei?" asked Araki Murashige revealing his grave mood. Rather, his mood was close to flamboyance. He sat like a warlord with his knees spread wide and leaned forward slightly to place his long bent arm on an armrest. In contrast to the fierce bulges of his muscles and the traces of his blue beard, the woman by his side fanning him was delicate and elegant.

"You haven't changed at all. No, you look healthier,"

"What are you saying, Kanbei? Was the change too fast? Some time ago, I met you at the Chugoku camp."

"Yes, when I was leaving Kozuki Castle, we met for a short time in front of Lord Nobutada's camp."

"You're right. I'd say we haven't met in several years."

"Why does that concern you? Perhaps, mistaken identity."

"Why do you say that?"

"Even if a man is no different than another man, and not much time has passed, a man's heart will change. That's my belief."

"..."

Murashige made a sour face. A young girl had packed

tobacco imported from the south into a ceramic pipe and been timidly holding out the pipe for a while. He looked at her but did not take it.

After he switched the armrest on his left to his right side and reversed his pose, Murashige started laughing and immediately changed the topic. He asked, "Is Chikuzen an able man?"

Kanbei avoided giving an answer and ignored the earlier topic, but said, "Lord Kodera Masamoto earnestly sends his greetings."

Murashige blinked his lightly pockmarked eyelids and asked, "Are you at Gochaku or Mount Hirai?"

"I returned to Gochaku."

"Is that so? When?"

"Recently," said Kanbei.

"In that case, today you came as an envoy for Lord Kodera and not Chikuzen."

"Yes, that is my failing. Please read this letter from Lord Masamoto."

"Where …"

He turned to a maid and signaled with his chin for her to bring the pipe from the hand of the young girl and drew in a long drag.

He immediately broke the seal of the letter as Kanbei watched. Araki Murashige's face expressed complicated emotions as he read. He was essentially a man of integrity. He was incapable of concealing his feelings while reading.

Kanbei watched. Of course, he could not read the letter, but he had no difficulty reading Murashige's expressions.

Rather than being a wise man, he was a man addicted to wisdom. In retrospect, the blunder of Kanbei's life was his misreading at this time.

2

If Kanbei thought Kodera Masamoto advised Murashige to submit to Nobunaga in that letter, the changes in

Murashige's expression were reasonable. Instead, he alone nodded like he understood what was emphasized in Lord Kodera Masamoto's letter.

But what was the plan? The content of Masamoto's letter was unimaginable.

In other words, Masamoto imagined the horror of stabbing Kanbei to death with his own hand and uprisings all around. He wrote:

> *The chief retainer Kanbei of this clan was sent to you as my envoy. However, from the beginning, he has been a strong, loyal follower of Oda and would find it difficult to carry out an honorable covenant with the Mouri clan. Please take this opportunity to deal the decisive blow. I would prefer no plan for him to return to Chugoku a second time.*

Because the man was in front of him, the honest Murashige looked nervous. He was agitated. However, Kanbei allowed for resourcefulness in himself and in others; nonetheless, he misread Murashige.

Later, when faced with this danger, he lamented not confirming the intent of the letter along the way. He was a retainer carrying the lord's letter. Even if he knew the letter was sealed with the witchcraft symbol of death, the son of a military family was forbidden to break the seal to peek. The shame would crush him.

In any case, Kanbei was now in Itami Castle that flew the banner of revolt and saw the world through crazed eyes. A battle was another place filled with the menace that tomorrow may be the end. Already, Kanbei's life was no longer his. His life and Masamoto's letter were in Araki Murashige's hands.

"Uh, what does Lord Kodera think of us? I am honored, but the Lord of Settsu includes details in this initiative that cannot be spoken…. Kanbei, relax and we will talk at leisure. Well, can you move over there?" muttered Murashige and ordered food and drinks to be prepared for the vassal. He abruptly stood and spoke again hidden in the room across from Kanbei, "We'll have a serious talk later. I have plans, too. For now, wait in there for an escort."

A petty samurai came and offered a bath. Kanbei declined but asked for hot water.

The hot water was brought by the tea master who performs the tea ceremony. Kanbei politely sipped the tea.

"Preparations have been made in another room. It's cooler there. Would you please move there?"

"Are you my escort?"

Kanbei followed him. Despite being the end of autumn, the lingering heat of summer on that day was nearly unbearable. It reminded Kanbei of a chilly autumn in the camp on Mount Hirai. Hideyoshi's figure floated to his mind.

"This way please."

As he wondered where he was, the tea master again urged him to enter an adjoining room. The room had many walls and nearly twenty tatami mats and no obvious personal effects. As soon as he sat on a cushion, the agitated tea master immediately rose and said, "The lord will come soon," then exited as if fleeing.

3

From the arrangement of the room and the behavior of the tea master, Kanbei's intuition was overwhelmed with suspicion.

"Wait. Wait, master," Kanbei called to stop him.

Despite being called from behind, the master disappeared like he was tumbling away. Kanbei was determined not to go out to the hallway. Araki Murashige's retainers came and lined up their unsheathed spears.

They flew into the other room like hawks. One crouched down and on the alert quickly then leaped up to violently grapple with Kanbei.

Kanbei frantically freed himself. The house rattled

like the ceiling beams were shaking. Kanbei threw him but toppled over with him. In an instant, four or five samurai charged in. Kanbei's two legs kicked at his enemies at least four or five times but soon recognized the futility. He could no longer see the walls and sliding doors of the room because they were buried behind the samurai and swords of the Araki clan.

What should I do? thought Kanbei and sat straight up. Of course, both of his arms were already bound behind his back with straw rope. Blood dribbled from the scrapes on his cheek after being dragged over the tatami.

"Get up. We know nothing, but by order of our lord, you are to come with us," said a samurai.

Kanbei only asked, "Oh, by order of Settsu-no-kami?"

He said no more and allowed himself to be hauled off.

His destination was not in the castle tower, he was led down two flights of a dark staircase. Kanbei had a hunch like he smelled his own blood but could do nothing about the chill at the roots of his disheveled hair. Step by step, he descended the stairs as he mocked himself. Although a man should always be prepared for death, a peek at that place filled him with visceral terror, and he realized he would not win.

"Hey, who's that? Get a light and go ahead."

The samurai huddled together and stayed for a time.

The darkness and cold felt like he had dropped to the bottom of a marsh. Kanbei looked around an underground room where only thick pillars could be seen and said, "So this is where I'm going to die."

He noticed his spirit was finally at peace.

CHAPTER TWENTY-EIGHT
SUSPICION

1

NOBUNAGA WAS STRENGTHENED by adversity. Each time, adversity became the first step. Next, his destiny swept away people's surprise and he persisted in moving forward. He confronted a grave situation for several tens of days during this crisis.

Needless to say, Araki Murashige's rebellion was thrust before the lord like a bitter cup. He was enveloped by rage to the bottom of his heart. To crush the rebellion, he suppressed his own personality of patience and strategy despite a firm belief in patience and strategy as well as the possibility of patience with military tactics.

How many times had he sent an envoy to Itami to appease and placate Murashige? First, he wanted to limit this situation to an internal matter. He struggled to see beyond these two months. He was weighed down by the serious blow of Itami's breaking away and its consequences.

In the end, his attempts to appease and his conciliatory measures had no effect.

Nobunaga had to endure sending out three envoys to politely warn and to prod Murashige's wisdom. They were

Kunaikyou Hounin, a close associate of Murashige; Akechi Hyuga-no-kami; and Manmi Senchiyo. Murashige must have been aware that he had placed Nobunaga in a serious predicament.

The work at Chugoku had just begun. A favorable change in outlook saw an unexpected failure. Finally, the power of Hongan-ji Temple in Osaka prevailed. He planned to take the offense if the time arrived. When he looked back and gazed at the eastern country, is there an opportunity to form a marriage with Takeda Katsuyori, who is tied to Hojo Ujimasa, and form a new alliance between the two countries of Kai and Sagami? To the Oda clan, a dark north wind came with another concern.

"… I've blundered," Nobunaga realized.

"While the sun moves and conciliatory measures are taken, inevitably, the worst catastrophe may occur when every measure has no effect. In that case, it's best to trust my innate ability," said Nobunaga and abandoned his lenient handling.

He left Azuchi and readied a large force at the Nijo annex and deployed troops throughout Settsu.

2

This was the moment.

Nobunaga took this stance when told the news about Kuroda Kanbei.

"What? Kanbei has been taken prisoner at Itami Castle? …"

Nobunaga also heard the circumstances, but his suspicions were aroused the moment he was told.

As usual for a man with keen intuition, sometimes he strayed and his suspicions multiplied. Nobunaga did not hear the truth but only the superficial reasons and the root cause.

"Who ordered Kanbei to advise Araki Murashige? I did not give Hideyoshi permission. How can I understand his carrying the letter from Kodera Masamoto? Because

Kodera in Gochaku again acted in concert with Murashige and exposed his treachery, why was Kanbei ordered this time to present his views to Murashige?"

His suppressed rage burst from this small crater onto the generals on his left and right.

"Ah, he definitely deceived Chikuzen and entered the castle in Itami. He entered Murashige's field headquarters, and with his ingenuity, it seems he successfully gained entry through Kodera's words and Murashige's invitation. Anyway, Murashige will simply be active inside the castle. Murashige will value Kanbei's knowledge of the details about Hideyoshi's military situation where he is headed and the internal circumstances of our Oda clan. Being a schemer, that may be the case...."

Nobunaga mumbled to ridicule himself. But when he opened his lips he was biting shut, he coldly gave this cruel order to Sakuma Uemon beside him.

"Take this letter to Chikuzen immediately. Behead the hostage Matsuchiyo, Kanbei's son in Chikuzen's custody."

"Yessir."

Sakuma Nobumori slowly lowered his head upon hearing the lord's order.

As expected, this order was entrusted to Nobumori, but Nobunaga dictated a series of other military orders for Hideyoshi in Chugoku to a secretary. The order was:

> *Attack Kodera in Gochaku. And crush Kuroda*
> *Souen in Himeji Castle.*

3

Takayama Ukon at Takatsuki Castle and the chamberlain Nakagawa Kiyohide at Ibaraki Castle were the two wings of Araki Murashige with Itami set at the center.

After a huge force was deployed and headquarters moved from Yamazaki to Mount Tennou, Nobunaga was successful in luring in both of them.

Because Takayama Ukon was an ardent follower of

Jesus, Nobunaga adeptly used his spiritual father Organtino to convince him to surrender Takatsuki Castle. Originally, Takayama Ukon disagreed fundamentally with Murashige's plan; therefore, he immediately came to Nobunaga's camp gate and apologized for his crimes.

"I fully understand. A warrior realizes his error and corrects himself. I hold no grudge," said Nobunaga.

For his own joy and to reassure them, Nobunaga rewarded the two defeated generals immense quantities of silver and gold and other bounty.

For some reason, this incident plagued Nobunaga. If the problem were solved, he would be overjoyed, and these rewards revealed his deepest feelings.

Finally, the all-out attack on Itami Castle began. It was already December. But the castle did not fall. As expected, that was only the power of Araki with his stubborn conceit. During that impossible-to-win battle, his foe General Manmi Sencho died. Despite numerous ferocious attacks on the castle walls, Itami Castle was impregnable.

"Going any faster is foolish. The defeated are abandoned …"

Nobunaga erected auxiliary castles for launching attacks on important roads. In other words, he carried out a plan for a prolonged siege and returned to Azuchi at the end of the year. Half of the military force was divided into auxiliary troops in Harima and rapidly descended to sever communications with the power of Hongan-ji Temple. This provided the chance to reorganize the entire battle formation based on the expectation that the huge Mouri force would head east from the coast.

In short, Murashige's show of strength seen by Nobunaga was not Murashige's strength but the great naval force of Mouri Terumoto coming to land on the shore of Settsu. This action was surely promised before the rebellion because Nobunaga quickly saw through these inner workings and grasped the entire situation.

CHAPTER TWENTY-NINE
LICE AND WISTERIA FLOWERS

1

MEDITATE ... MEDITATE. I will stare at this wall and meditate again today. Will the sun come out if I stare at this darkness for several days? thought Kanbei in his isolation.

"When did morning come today?"

Year 6 of Tensho has already passed. He believed it must be year 7 of Tensho, but he doubted spring had come.

"A man who does not see the light of day is a weak man. A bath of sunlight is unthinkable.... Let me see, through Zen and preparation of the mind, I will see the sun. That's it."

His smile was sour.

Counting on his fingers, he has spent six months since October of last year like a corpse living in the same darkness as his solitary thoughts. How many days have passed in that time?

At first, his body was strong and robust, but he had lost confidence in his health. He had not taken one bath or washed with a wet cloth. His dirty skin began to resemble a pine cone in the winter cold. When he thought he was feeling warmth, mysterious swellings erupted all over his body. Lumps also emerged at the roots of the hairs on his head.

Twice a day, once in the morning and once in the evening, a guard slid what passed for food for the prisoner through a sturdy, coarse, lattice window. By chewing brown rice and vegetables stuck fast to the inside of his mouth ten times longer than usual before swallowing, he was able to extract most of the nutrition. However, the problem was he could not exercise. Sometimes he walked slowly like a tiger in a cage. Recent weakness left him exhausted. His food rations were scant. He was pained by the rage in his stomach empty from near starvation.

"I will endure."

He sat in Zen meditation. His practice of Zen began in his youth and enabled him to sink deep into his mind, but he appeared to only be pretending. It was easier for his psyche to stir up fantasies rather than consciousness. Eventually, his existence became slow and simple. He slept if he slept lightly. If his eyes were tired, he opened them. If his eyes were half open, they stayed half open.

"Life is precious."

His tenacity was laudable. While alone, he wondered why he was alive and decided death may be best, but of course, he didn't want to die.

However, this regret did not become shame as he assessed his life. Even when he looked up at the sun, he was unwilling to idle away his life.

"I have too much to do."

That belief was unshakable in him.

My life burns for worldly work because my conceit says who would do this work but me.

"Sadly, I will die in this place," he said.

"I can't help thinking … don't squirm or grind your teeth."

Rather he reconciled himself to his life. On days he was illuminated by faint beams of outside light from a high window, he watched the lice walking on his knees and feet and lived with no interests. The wind was his only friend offering comfort to him.

2

"... Ah! A wisteria vine is entangled up there."

One day, Kanbei opened his eyes in wonder. He found the tip of a vine with young leaves of beautiful wisteria on a bar made from a thick zelkova tree in the high window cut out on the east side.

"Aha, there may be a wisteria trellis outside."

He realized this for the first time.

"... All right, now I understand. A cascade of wisteria grows on the trellis near the lake. Every night and sometimes during the day, I thought I heard strange sounds from outside. I thought they were the sounds of the fish in a lake hitting the water and jumping. All this humidity makes sense now ..."

This day was enjoyable. He was comforted by the young vine and their tenuous connection. The moment he woke early the next morning, he immediately looked up there. Although it was one in the morning, finally, the faint sunlight shone beautifully. The vine grew three to six inches without fail.

"But even looking at that, spring has passed and summer is near. From here on, I will only hear the sounds of the leaping fish in this castle. But how will events unfold in the world?"

He remembered a tinge of mental anguish. No, he lacked spirit for anything other than lamenting.

More than thoughts of his child or wife, his tears did not stop when he thought of the world. He thought about the future of Hideyoshi in the camp on Mount Hirai, his imagination had no limits. He thought about the position of Nobunaga, the movements in Kinki, the situation in the west country, and the state of affairs in the east country.

For several days from the beginning of December of

last year, he heard alarming sounds centered on this castle.

At that time, his heart leaped with the thought, This is the battle. The forces of Lord Oda are approaching. At the same time, he prepared his mind, but instead of the arrival of the day of his certain death, he no longer heard the thrilling battle cries of an attacking force.

Kanbei was tormented by the thought, The situation is bad for Oda. In the rare chance, Mouri's naval forces are lined up from stem to stern and land on the shore near Settsu, they can't be stopped alone by Araki or Takayama or Nakagawa Kiyohide. One after another, men holding aloft banners of rebellion will come from everywhere. Azuchi seems to lay a close siege on the interior.... No, no, the worst may be over.

With each passing day, his will to live eroded. No matter where he searched in his soul, he had difficulty finding anything other than loss.

One day, the thought, I prefer death! popped into his head. He did not have an arrow or a shield nor did he want to die.

The bones and the flesh of the skin supporting his life struggled with daily pain. When he knew his mental strength had run out like the burned out wick in a light dish, his body would fall over with a thud like a rotted tree, even without applying a blade or other force.

"Wait," he said to himself.

An urgency like dripping cold sweat called to his flesh.

"I will die one day. I will wait a little longer.... Oh, that wisteria vine on the high window has thickened. And the short tufts of flowers on it are blooming.... Of course, I will see those flowers bloom into white wisteria or violet flowers."

It may have been a bad spot for sun or the tuft was drooping, but the flowers bloomed late.

"Ah, they bloomed this morning.... Are they violet?"

On a sunny morning several days later, he saw vibrant

153

wisteria flowers. He crawled until he was under the window and reached out but could not reach the flowers.

In the faint morning sunlight, Kanbei drunk from the scent spilling from the tuft of violet flowers and blanketing his face. Pointing his face upward, he opened his mouth like an idiot in ecstasy.

"... It's a sign of good luck," he cried out. He lacked the strength to jump up, but his entire body remembered an impulse greater than leaping up. A rare blush shined on his forehead.

"The blooming of wisteria flowers in jail is impossible. I've never heard an example of this in the stories of China or Japan.... I will not die. This is a revelation from heaven. It's saying if I wait, I will bloom. Yes, it's a revelation from heaven."

He placed his palms together to worship the wisteria flowers. Lice crawled out from under the shackles on his wrists to play around in the shadows of the faint morning sun and the scent of the wisteria.

CHAPTER THIRTY
UP IN YEARS AND RETIRED

1

KANBEI'S UNFORESEEN MISFORTUNE created a huge ripple in the world for many reasons. He was a leading player who leaped onto the world stage. The world's suspicions were plausible given his sudden disappearance.

In the end, however, the people most dismayed were the people in Kanbei's hometown and his birthplace Himeji Castle. Foremost were Kanbei's elderly father Souen and young wife.

"Was it a premonition or the scolding he gave me on the day he departed about my usual etiquette before I was mentally prepared to say goodbye, I went out to the line of trees just beyond the castle town but … thinking now about his complexion and … his appearance at that time, he looked different," his wife repeatedly lamented. She hugged Matsuchiyo's letter tossed to her by her husband. Everyday she lay crying on her sickbed unable to get up.

"Why all this crying? You are the wife of a samurai …"

She was scolded with no trace of kindness by her father-in-law Souen. On the other hand, more sympathy may have left her woman's heart forever distressed. For the past ten days, this man, who had been kind to his daughter-in-law, only scolded her like a demon.

No, it was not only his daughter-in-law. He was already advanced in years and retired from active life, but once his son was imprisoned in Itami, his later life and death became hazy. The old gray-haired crane said, "Challenges to the fortunes of the clan are imminent. They may say I'm old, but am I weak and should sit by and watch the downfall of this clan?"

He recalled his youthful spirit of twenty years ago. Like a craggy rock, he glared at the members of the family depressed by the sad news. He urged them on day and night with "Don't get upset! Don't panic! Don't give up! I am here at Himeji."

In any case, once the bad news spread, all comings and goings of people from the towns centered on Himeyama were conspicuous. If everyone's eyes were bloodshot and they entered the gate, they felt like boiling cauldrons. The loyal vassals of the clan, who pledged to die here, came running on each other's heels to assemble.

These men made a blood pledge to defy death and rescue Kanbei.

The major and minor deities of Heaven and Earth in Japan stipulated the punishment to be suffered when Hachiman Daibosatsu, Atagoyama Gongen, and the guardian gods are disobeyed in the written oath of Kumano Goou. The signatures signed in blood below the oath are all loyal retainers.

Mori Yosobei, Kitamura Rokubei Katsuyoshi, Kinugasa Kyuzaemon, Nagata Sansuke, Fujita Jinbei, Mihara Usuke, Mihara Hayato, Kitamura Jinzaemon Katsuyoshi, Ogawa Yosoemon, Kuriyama Zensuke, Goto Emon, Miyata Jihei, Mori Tahei

The oath was addressed to the keeper of the castle, Souen, and dated November 5 of Tensho Year 6.

2

In no time, a secret covenant with the alliance of the death-defying squad to rescue the lord came to be. However, until the course of action was agreed on, the clan was steeped in anguish and confusion, and any discussion was chaotic. Extreme measures emerged and were seriously considered in actions demanding honorable death.

"Is there some way to put pressure on Murashige to save Kanbei-sama? In that case, we must be prepared to recognize that the life of the hostage Matsuchiyo-sama handed over to Nobunaga is inessential. Because of the difficulty in protecting Matsuchiyo-sama's life, in the end, if the faction shows no treachery toward Oda, Kanbei-sama suffered from Murashige's trick, and saving his life in jail will be thorny."

Earlier, this agony preceded the decision of the path taken by the faction in the clan and was the turning point in the discussion.

In reality, problems lay ahead. Can the lord be saved? Can the young lord be saved without leaving Kanbei's hostage son to his fate, or will the life of the imprisoned lord end? ... What will break this quandary? The bitter tears being shed and the cutting indignation gave birth to a viable plan to safely bring back both of them.

Over several days, a concern rose in the secret discussions among the clan's vassals.

"Who is going to visit the retired Souen-sama and Kanbei's wife in her sickbed to ask the heartrending question of which one should it be ...?"

At last, the group gathered one night to ask Souen, who appeared before them. He was relaxed and had come to a decision.

He serenely asked, "Are you confused? I already know in my heart."

"Kanbei will be abandoned. You ask, Why? Kanbei was charged with the lord's orders and traveled to Itami

Castle. He was trapped by a dirty scheme concocted by Murashige and imprisoned. Good and bad dignitaries, the eyes of the public, or anyone probably would not hate him as the wronged party. If my son Kanbei is killed in jail, his duty as a samurai is to sacrifice himself for the sake of his lord's orders. I will mourn him.... That creates indecision with inklings of longing. If our faction in Himeji now breaks the pledge to Nobunaga, would that be honorable abandonment in the face of betrayal? For example, if Kanbei returns alive, our name as a military family would no longer be a source of pride. A warrior burdened by shame lives only by taking a salary. When standing in the path of a born samurai, any life would be horrible.... I am not confused. Kanbei will be left to his fate. The obvious plan is to forsake him."

When he finished, Souen immediately went back inside. He seemed oblivious to the sounds of the solemn, sobbing crowd.

The written pledge with a temple seal listing thirteen names signed in blood was promptly held out.

"Souen-sama, your prepared mind gives you the strength of one hundred men. You hold no duplicity toward Oda. In time, we will strike at the injustice of Araki Murashige. However, as vassals, it is out of the question to abandon the imprisoned lord and allow him to die in a jail cell. We, the thirteen signees, will change our appearances and conceal ourselves in Itami Castle in enemy territory. We will persist against every hardship. The great gods of war and the gods of our birthplaces are also witnesses. Even in exchange for our lives, we will rescue Kanbei-sama."

They swore to Heaven and Earth with one mind.

Thus, the decision was for only these thirteen to leave Himeji and infiltrate Itami. Before departing, the defense of Himeji Castle was necessarily tightened.

The guards of the castle keep, centered on the retired Souen, consisted of men left behind selected only by the men in the death-defying rescue squad. The reason was past relationships had brought in many vassals with outside affiliations who came as attendants from the Kodera clan in Gochaku to Himeji.

Souen declared, "This is not what I originally sought, but both the Kodera and Kuroda clans ended up in this feud. Today is the day for the confrontation of opposing forces. Thus, the many vassals and attendants who came to this clan from the Kodera clan have no need for restraint. Preparations have been made for them to return to their previous lord. They've served here for a long time, and today's separation was not their true intent. However, the world today is only inevitable disorder. The task today is to overcome distressing obstacles together and to meet the turbulence ahead to peace…. We will have a drink on our parting, and tomorrow, meet with exuberance on the battlefield."

A festive party ensued, and cups were passed out to those present.

Even after the farewell banquet ended, nobody prepared to leave and declared he was returning to Kodera. The following morning, almost all of the former attendants of the Kodera clan carrying bundled oaths appeared before Souen and asked to be detained by the Kuroda clan.

Souen was the first in the clan to be delighted and accepted their requests. From that day on, he added them as pure vassals of the clan.

"I'm counting on you."

The death-defying squad of thirteen carefully checked the hardened iron wall before leaving. From the end of the year to the spring, each one left on his own for the enemy territory of Itami.

CHAPTER THIRTY-ONE
RIDING A HEARTLESS DONKEY

1

"**IT'S NOT LIKE** Kanbei to err like that ..." lamented Hideyoshi to himself after hearing the news.

"It's not like a wise man to be tricked by Murashige's odd ingenuity," he mumbled.

He meditated in his worry but thought it might not be so bad. Most men called sages or schemers in the world are frivolous and smart. Kanbei is not like that. That is the evil of favoritism. He is honest. Even his face could be described as stupidly honest.

"As a warrior, this failure is definitely not his shame. He understood that Araki Murashige did not kill him probably due to a lingering attachment to him and a plan to make him a tool as an ally. Heaven will grant him life."

Before the camp on Mount Hirai and before Miki Castle, which takes pride in being impregnable, and engulfed by a gloomy worry, Hideyoshi prayed every day from afar over Kanbei's fate. He waited many years for Lord Nobunaga's forces to sweep down and attack the treacherous vassals of Itami.

An unexpected order arrived from Nobunaga.

Kanbei is suspected of treachery. Divide the soldiers and immediately attack Himeji. And arrest his father Souen and his family.

Hideyoshi's lonely thoughts roused a smile that didn't appear on his face. From the beginning, he already understood Nobunaga's suspicion.

Hideyoshi only wondered, Does that man understand?

When he considered the current predicament at Azuchi, what does Nobunaga feel? But instead, he deduced the sorrow in the heart of his distant lord.

"It's best to wait for daylight. The crime of not promptly carrying out the order is my carelessness. If I ready myself for a reprimand in the future ..."

He concealed that matter in his heart. But another problem arose that could not be hidden.

The problem was what to do about the hostage Matsuchiyo.

As Nobunaga's envoy, Sakuma Nobumori visited Takenaka Hanbei who was living a solitary life inside the compound of Nanzen-ji Temple in the capital intent on recuperating from his illness. He returned with a detailed report from Hanbei. The gist was:

As Lord Nobumori said, "Lord Nobunaga became enraged at my behavior concerning Lord Kuroda." The reason for the merciless order of immediate beheading of the child may be that the young Kuroda hostage is now close to Chikuzen. If Lord Sakuma and even I were told to participate in that punishment, because we had essentially no reason to decline, we responded respectfully with the reasons for our agreement. Around the time this letter reaches you, a similar order will probably be passed to you from Lord Sakuma, but do not delay in reading the rest of the report.

This bewildered Hideyoshi. Out of nowhere, his tears overflowed with rage over the intense chilling of his love for Nobunaga. Even without going that far, Nobunaga must hate Kanbei. However, Hideyoshi's feelings reversed instantly, and his heart lightened.

"Nobunaga's personality is like fire. He is usually genial, but flames flare up and burn people and burn us.... When he burns, he listens to no one."

Hideyoshi calmed himself and in his reply to Takenaka Hanbei wrote the following:

> *Ignore the order from Azuchi. I have a few ideas. I will strive to engage all my wits.*

2

In the cold, snow was still visible on the tops of the plum trees. Spring came during the early part of February. A group arrived from Nanzen-ji Temple in Keage valley gripped by penetrating cold. These men appeared to be young, private citizens and rode their horses out the main gate of the temple.

Since autumn of the previous year, the sickly Hanbei Shigeharu was shut up in a monk's living quarters and worked with the aid of medicines to rest.

Only one soldier came with him as his attendant. The soldier carried a bundle on his back that contained his master's medicines.

The soldier asked, "Are you getting colder? You're coughing a lot."

"Naturally, it's cold outside. I'm getting used to this cold spring wind. My coughs are stopping now. And the sun will warm everything."

"Will you wear your hood?"

"No, people's eyes are sharp. They may whisper what trick is Hanbei Shigeharu up to, walking around in broad daylight with his face covered."

Perhaps, he was also troubled by this incident with Kuroda Kanbei. At the same time, he keenly felt a cold breath like the easterly winds of February affect his view of life.

The young man had been convinced by Hideyoshi to seclude himself in the mountains, but he eventually left the mountains. For over ten years, he had walked all the roads, the streets of blood, and the dangerous roads of the world, still in his heart, he was not a man of the mountain country.

His only wish was for the day to come soon when Chikuzen-no-kami-sama would somehow achieve the position he's destined to attain and share his understanding of the joy of peace and harmony to the many clans.

Hanbei prayed only for that result and took on the responsibility of providing assistance, but the progression of his illness each year was not good.

Recently, he resigned himself to the view that his health made living an ordeal.

Consequently, he thought his hope will be satisfied by first seeing a pause in the battles of the Chugoku forces. Without informing his friends or Hideyoshi, he placed a monk's robe and rosary beads among the objects always at his bedside. If that day came, he would ask Hideyoshi for time off. His cherished wish was to climb to a high plain and hear the voice of the mountain bush warbler.

"Whether I'm able or unable to achieve this, I enjoy embracing the wish … although it may never happen. The conquest of Chugoku will not be settled in that short a time. If so, I'm a man who wants to die on the battlefield like a warrior."

The sickly horse lodged for two nights then followed Mino Road. It moved forward on slow legs like a donkey into the western mountains.

He arrived at the castle on Mount Bodaisan in Iwamura in Mino Province.

The castle was nothing more than a small castle in the mountain forest. However, the lord returning after a long absence was heartily welcomed home. The entire clan stood at the castle gate to receive him. Hanbei entered the castle and immediately visited the senior vassal.

"Has there been any change in the hostage Lord Kuroda? Did he make it through winter without catching a cold?"

The senior vassal looked around the flat garden of the castle from the edge of the veranda and pointed out the area that looked yellow of the grasses deep in the mountain.

"Look there. Today, the children in the clan have gathered over there to play."

"Well, well …"

Hanbei got up from his cushion and went out to the area. In his heart, he was waiting for orders from Azuchi. His deeply wounded spirit that could not be hidden forever was concealed in his eyes.

CHAPTER THIRTY-TWO
THE CHILD ON MOUNT BODAISAN

1

ROUGHHOUSING WAS RAMPANT inside the residence. Although the children had parents, they were hostages from other provinces and far from their parents' homes. One of them was Matsuchiyo.

"… Aah! Uncle."

Matsuchiyo had been absorbed in playing with a group of children until he caught sight of the figure of Hanbei Shigeharu standing at the edge of the castle keep. He cast off his friends without a glance and ran toward him.

"Uncle. Welcome home?"

"Yes, Matsu. You look healthy."

"I haven't seen you for so long, Uncle. I'm a little lonely. Uncle. When did you get back?"

"A little while ago."

"Just now? Oh, I didn't know."

Matsuchiyo in the garden stood on tiptoe and clung to the hem of the hakama trousers of a man on the edge of the veranda. He played by wrapping his face in the hem.

He's a friendly little fellow. Isn't that natural given he's separated from his parents and being raised by

165

strangers? thought Hanbei overwhelmed with sympathy for him.

"Well, here. A gift from the capital," said Hanbei and gave him candy from Nanzen-ji Temple and played with the child for a short time.

Already two years had passed since Matsuchiyo came from Nagahama to be raised in the mountain castle. He was already twelve. Iguchi Heisuke and Ono Kurouzaemon were sent with him as tutors from the Kuroda family but he was treated, for the most part, in the same way as the heirs of Lord Hanbei in the Takenaka clan. Teachers in the interpretation of texts, archery, and horsemanship were also brought along to protect and cultivate him like a pearl.

Hanbei returned home the next day. He walked alone to the foot of Mount Bodaisan to visit the graves of his ancestors.

Waiting for him on his way back were two samurai bowing on the side of the road. They were Matsuchiyo's tutors Iguchi Heisuke and Ono Kurouzaemon from the Kuroda clan.

"It is quite rude of us to be at this roadside."

"But Sir, we have an earnest request."

The pair buried their faces in the withered grasses. Before saying what they came to say, Hanbei sensed the feelings of the one already welling up with tears.

2

A shrike let out a shrill cry. Spring in the mountain forest was new.

Hanbei walked with the pair to a sunny area in the shade of the sparse woods. He sat on the warm, withered grasses. The two crying soldiers prostrated themselves before him.

"… You don't have to say much. I understand your feelings."

Hanbei listened to the gist of their heartfelt request

and consoled them. As he guessed, these men already heard the fast-moving rumors about Kanbei's misfortune in Itami Castle and Nobunaga's bitter order to dispose of Matsuchiyo.

The men had been waiting beside the road for Hanbei, the lord who braved illness to return. Hanbei sensed their shock about the order from Azuchi that would be hard to disobey. They pleaded for him to take both their lives in exchange for the lord's son they were educating and nurturing. The order became known in the clan and, naturally, a debate arose, including the belief that the order should be ignored. Thus, they decided to make a direct appeal.

"I formed a deep connection with your lord on our first meeting. In light of the order from Azuchi, the head of the important heir to Kanbei must hastily be presented.... Don't worry. Please leave this to me."

His comforting words were gracious and the two vassals shed copious tears for his compassion. Hanbei could not bear the sight of them.

He thought misery was the fortune of a hostage in this world, but the hostage did not yet know about the world and was innocent. Although they were outsiders who bent their knees to another to protect an innocent boy being raised in another clan, the way of master and servants was not violated. As Hanbei sympathized with the pain and difficulty of the tutors willing to sacrifice their lives, he found them more pitiful than the hostage.

3

Hanbei often walked to the castle town. The castle was a small castle, and the town was a mountain village. If the lord is recognized, the people in the roadside teahouses and the figures in the fields hurried to prostrate themselves on the ground. However, Hanbei's excursions were better described without exaggeration as traveling incognito. Hanbei hated ostentatious men who walked around like the lord of a castle.

When he went out in those days, he had a goal in his heart. As long as that remained unsolved, every day he felt a worsening of his illness.

"... Another man's child will not be killed. If the child of a poor native, the compassion will increase and he will not be killed. If seen as the beloved child of a tradesman, only his parents and his innocence are seen. My thoughts even frighten me."

On the day, he wore coarsely lacquered armor and laid down the long war sword named Tora Gozen as the strategist of a great army and one thousand soldiers would be captured in one plan, one hundred in another, and be annihilated. Hanbei Shigeharu's eyebrows did not move as he sought the head of a child. Despite seeing a child well suited to this purpose, he could not bring himself to kill him and return home.

In spite of himself, he was shocked when he found a child resembling Matsuchiyo on the road. He saw the child around the same age in the fields but thought about the people in a nearby thatched-roof hut and lost his determination to kill.

"Well, this plan is worse than a dreadful plan. Is there some other idea?"

He mulled over this for several nights, but, in the end, Nobunaga's impatience said to kill him. Sadly, the only substitute for a child's head is another child's head.

He believed the only ray of hope was to ostensibly comply with the order from Azuchi by presenting the head of a boy who was not Matsuchiyo. Nobunaga saw Matsuchiyo two years ago. And almost none of the vassals at Azuchi knew what he looked like.

He was reminded of his duty to Sakuma Nobumori but he was not being closely watched. Furthermore, beginning with Nobunaga, the leaders of the Azuchi people were kept busy by their military duties and the battlefield.

"If he is placated even for an hour, all will be resolved in time. My present restraint is good, but ..."

This was Hanbei's firm belief. Nevertheless, he needed the head of a child to give to Nobunaga. The head of a child. He unexpectedly sighed.

"I have an idea."

One evening, without waiting to be announced, the two tutors Ono and Iguchi hurried to the edge of the veranda of Hanbei's sitting room. This behavior should be inexcusable, but Hanbei soon noticed something tucked in Ono Kurozaemon's sleeve and invited them in.

"Enter ... and close the door."

He looked pitiful when he asked, "Is that a head?"

"Yes...." they said and presented it to him. They wiped the sweat off their foreheads. With it covering Kurozaemon's knees, he said, "The truth is a child drowned and was fished out of the river rapids. We came across the parents hugging and crying. We immediately visited the head priest of Bodaiji Temple and revealed our true intent and appealed to them as they cried.... Our hands did not kill him."

Iguchi Heisuke's face showed strain.

"We respectfully watched unseen from a distance, it was as you can imagine. However, from the kind heart of mercy, we embarked on a difficult pursuit and a true hardship. Our ordinary minds understood and devised a plan. Through this action, Matsuchiyo-sama's life will be saved.... Both of our names are those of vassals in the Kuroda clan, but for the rest of our lives, we will never forget this favor inscribed with courage. In lives like ours, at any time we can be of service, we will be there. If you please, ..."

A page brought over a candle.

Hanbei stood up with a start and said, "Will you two join me in the garden?"

It was already late spring. Every evening, the new moon rose over wild cherry blossoms in the garden.

That evening, a small plain-wood box wrapped in white cloth and Hanbei's letter were delivered by a vassal of the Takenaka clan by post horse to Sakuma Nobumori in Azuchi.

A few days later, the vassal returned with Nobumori's acceptance. The vassal reported tension concerning another matter hanging over Azuchi. The small box was passed to the castle from Nobumori's hand. In the end, Nobunaga barely gave it a second glance.

CHAPTER THIRTY-THREE
THE HIDEOUT

1

SIGNS OF FRESH greenery were visible. The summer sun was appearing, and people were starting to dress for the summer. For some reason, the town of Itami was missing an air of freshness and newness. It was stagnant and anxious.

The nerves of Araki Murashige, the lord of the castle, and the others confined in the castle were reflected in the townspeople.

"When will there be battles in the street?" asked tense voices. The anxiety within the Araki domain was rooted in the complete blocking of the borders and the intense suffering of those bogged down.

Actually, it was more than that. Everyone in Itami did not necessarily support the rebellion of the lord. That may have been the source of this town's stagnation.

However, in this town, the ones who looked prosperous and seemed to be enjoying the times were the merchants awarded the contracts for war munitions, like the armorers, dyers, painters, metalsmiths, and harness makers.

The silversmith Shinshichi could be counted among

them. He owned a small mansion and had a workshop located right inside the earthen wall. The small braces for armor, decorations attached to swords, small metal fittings for horse harnesses, and various silver and gold works were crafted there by the hands of craftsmen of ornamental gold. Amid the sounds from small bellows, fine chisel hammers, and files, sixteen or seventeen men were hunched over in the workshop hard at work.

Once in a while, Shinshichi came out to the workshop but usually stayed in the main building. He often invited friends to play a game of Go or to have a drink of sake. The interior of the building and the workshop were separated by garden trees to inconvenience falling rain.

"Kiku. We seem to have a guest. At the back gate."

He leaned into a private conversation he was engaged in with his two guests. These two travelers were friends on their way home yesterday from the Arima Hot Springs and had spent the night.

"… A guest?"

The travelers heard the back gate's noisemakers and turned to look. The guests hesitated before the new arrival. His eyes were a little too grim.

"No, a reckless man should not come from the back gate.… Please go and see," said Shinshichi quietly.

While stretching his body a little, he spied the back view of his sister-in-law wearing sandals leaving through the kitchen door.

2

From this spring, Shinshichi's life in the main building changed entirely. The usual people living there were ordinary.

His wife and many children had been swiftly sent to his home in the country. On the surface, the reason was uncertainty about when the war would start.

In her place, his pretty sister-in-law Kikujo, who was around twenty years old, came to help with the household duties. People who bought the famous eye medicine Reijukou at the main house in Shikama, Harima would recognize the young woman. However, Kikujo rarely went out to the streets. She was the daughter of Yojiemon of Shikama and concealed her identity to come here.

When old Yojiemon found out the retainers favored since the previous generation made a pledge to join together to defy death and rescue Kanbei following the calamity faced by the lord of Himeji, he joined their alliance of thirteen men. The old man paid no mind to his comrades' opinions that he may be a hindrance. He made a relative's silversmith shop in Itami a hideout for his comrades.

Everyone thought about Kiku-san's participation. Using a woman would be a great advantage in any secret plan.

After that meeting, the entire death-defying rescue squad traveled incognito to this region, while Kiku came on her own.

In time, Shinshichi believed she was the right person to bring to his home because she's a relative and an attractive woman rarely seen in Itami, many of the people in the workshop and eventually the next-door neighbors spoke groundless rumors like, "No way she's his young sister-in-law!"

Shinshichi became aware of this and secretly rejoiced.

The reason was it disguised the hideout.

"Oh … Welcome."

Kiku opened the door of the back gate from the inside and discovered a traveling monk standing there. She mumbled something then silently showed him in and gently closed the door behind him. She announced, "Kinugasa Kyuzaemon-sama has arrived."

The two guests were townsmen, who happened to be there, looked at each other with a yearning and said, "What? Kinugasa-san …?"

One man was Mori Tahei, and the other, Kuriyama

Zensuke. To successfully rescue the lord imprisoned in Itami Castle, these men took great pains to transform into horse drivers, peddlers, and street performers, and even altered their appearances.

"Oh, Zensuke-sama. Is Tahei-sama here, too?"

The monk Kinugasa Kyuzaemon followed Kiku in but first left his dirty bundle and bamboo hat at the edge of the veranda. He weakly sat between his friends.

"It's been a while since we've seen you. From what far off place, have you come? We've heard news today, too," said Mori Tahei when he peeked in and saw his face. Finally, Kyuzaemon listlessly turned and answered, "What is going on in Azuchi? This small castle already provoked a large army and began explorations to launch a general assault.... I've only heard sad stories on this trip."

"What do you mean by sad stories?" asked Tahei.

Kyuzaemon said, "It's about Matsuchiyo-sama. You probably know already. The human heart is hard to trust … but is reliable. Hanbei Shigeharu of Mount Bodai seems to have carried out the order from Azuchi and cut off Matsuchiyo-sama's head.... I was disgusted with that scrawny priest. He is a false gentleman. A damn tactician does not understand a warrior's sentiment.... It's a shame, a pity. There are no words."

His curse began like fire but ended like he was choking on water. He wiped the cuff of his borrowed sacred robe over his tearstained face.

CHAPTER THIRTY-FOUR
THE NIGHT TALE TOLD
AT KOYADERA TEMPLE

1

MATSUCHIYO'S EXECUTION WAS widely believed. They worried day and night about the lord and his son rather than themselves and had no time to reflect. Therefore, it was reasonable for them to be easily convinced.

"This grudge will be satisfied. Until Kanbei-sama is saved, we have a duty, but the time will surely come for Hanbei Shigeharu to learn about great sorrow."

Joining Kinugasa Kyuzaemon in making this oath were Mori Tahei and Kuriyama Zensuke while shedding tears of mourning.

Kyuzaemon in priestly attire borrowed the room holding the home's Buddhist altar.

"We will now hold a memorial service," he said and wrote the worldly name Matsuchiyo on a mortuary tablet. Tahei and Zensuke worshipped in silence and respectfully offered incense and flowers.

Before long, twilight came. The evening cicadas' songs were loud.

"Kiku-san, show in the Koyadera Temple monk.

Bring him through here," yelled a craftsman in the shop over the moonflower hedge toward the main building.

Shinshichi saw Kiku and frantically waved his hand.

He signaled with his eyes that it was not a good time and not to bring him yet.

She said, "Yes, I'm going now. Please wait a moment."

Kiku's expression showed she understood her brother's feelings. After some time passed, she returned with a letter.

Shinshichi looked at it then passed it to the others in turn. The letter was from the priest from Koyadera Temple. It appeared to be a simple invitation to a tea ceremony but was charged with another meaning.

"Perfect. We will show up separately."

As promised, the three eventually went home through the back gate. By this time, evening had settled over the town.

After Shinshichi made an appearance at the workshop, he took a bath then went out for a walk to nowhere in particular. He walked over ten blocks west from the edge of town and ended up at the ancient Koyadera Temple in the Koya district in a copse of trees. The priest of Shingon Temple and he had been friends for years, but the priest did not appear, an acolyte came out to escort him.

"Everyone's in there," he said and pointed to a section of the priest's living quarters. Around one dim candle sat the righteous gentlemen worrying about their lord. The gathering included the more than ten men who left Himeji and infiltrated enemy territory. Mori Tahei, Kuriyama Zensuke, and Kinugasa Kyuzaemon came here a step ahead of them.

2

The fourteen comrades gathered here needed to maintain an air of coincidentally meeting and parting. But that was beyond their control because this castle town was in enemy territory. The priest of Koyadera Temple always offered this location and its facilities to these men.

"I overheard a fellow stable worker in the Araki clan say that Lord Kanbei-sama is being held in the northern corner of the castle grounds in the armory near the wisteria trellis near what is called Lake Tenjin. Regrettably, there's no way to obtain a drawing," said the comrade Kitamura Rokubei.

Fujita Jinbei added, "I've heard that rumor, too. Tenmangu Shrine, which was enshrined long ago, is located in the northern corner of Itami Castle. His jail cell may be in that area."

"In that case, the only certainty seems to be the lord's life is secure ... but this is no time for congratulations," said a discouraged Goto Emon. Soon after, from the mouth of Kinugasa Kyuzaemon came the fact that the lord's son raised as a hostage in Bodaisan Castle was executed and passed to Azuchi from the hands of Takenaka Hanbei. The entire group remarked on the cruelty and drew their lips into hard lines. They drank tears of resentment. For a short time, feelings of indescribable despair filled the air.

"It was inevitable," said Mori Yosobei, an elder in this party, and said in a changed tone to encourage the others, "That is a problem for later. Although concerned about the dismay of the keeper of the castle [meaning Kanbei's father Souen] who, from the beginning, wanted the safety of Matsuchiyo-sama even if Kanbei-sama died ... This is not the time to grieve. This regret should become heaven's whip. Even if fastened to a rock, we will save our lord from the jail cell in Itami Castle. Our mission is urgent. We cannot turn away."

"Yes, this only stirs our determination," said Mihara Usuke.

That said, what was the plan? Regrettably, they had been there for over half a year, but absolutely no method or clue had been found to sneak into Itami Castle and get close to the imprisoned lord.

They made one request of the silversmith Shinshichi who ran errands as the armorer that took him inside the castle. When would he have a chance to go into the castle? At that time, he secretly waited to become an apprentice or a craftsman and enter the castle in that role, but that opportunity didn't easily come.

That night, the squad separated in vain. They parted to find each and every possible method and clue for the day they would meet again. When Shinshichi hurried home alone, a man at the entrance to the town called out to him.

"Silversmith. Are you on your way home?"

Startled, Shinshichi peered at the figure through the starlight. He was hardened by full armor and armed with a spear. Shinshichi sensed he knew this man from somewhere.

3

"I am Kato Hachiyata, a vassal of the Lord of Itami Hyogo."

"Ah, good evening sir."

"You are very late in returning home. Where were you?"

Shinshichi choked up, but as a worldly man, he skillfully deflected.

"You say late, but I was ordered to repair a small armor brace. The work slowly ate up more and more time. These days, there's a shortage of craftsmen."

"What are you talking about, Shinshichi? No one around here has broken armor."

Kato Hachiyata moved his bearlike face buried under a beard closer and opened his mouth wide and laughed.

He switched the spear in his right hand to his left.

"Hey," he called one more time as he thumped Shinshichi's shoulders.

"Well, are you going back to Koyadera Temple again? … Don't try to hide it, I know. Don't worry, I am the security watch tonight. The squad leader is on patrol. Ha, ha, ha."

"… Sir?"

"What?"

"Why are you telling me to go back to Koyadera Temple?"

"You don't know? You're a dull fellow. I will ask about a discussion you'd like to have."

"Huh? Well, …"

Shinshichi trembled. The armored hand of Hachiyata still on his shoulder weighed heavy like a rock.

CHAPTER THIRTY-FIVE
THE LADY-IN-WAITING

1

SHINSHICHI DID NOT return to Koyadera Temple but was pulled by Kato Hachiyata to the shade of nearby trees. Hachiyata said, "Sit down on this tree stump," and sat himself down on the grass.

The soldier had a good-natured disposition by day and was always joking, but that night, he looked frightening. The look on his face made Shinshichi's skin crawl. He even readied his mind to be courageous.

"Shinshichi, the truth is this talk is a little strange. It's about what you believe your young sister-in-law from Shikama thinks. If the match is good, do you think she'd marry?"

What was he thinking? Hachiyata's words came out of nowhere. Being caught off guard put Shinshichi at a loss and wary of his companion's heart.

"My lord Itami Hyogo-no-kami-sama is already old, has palsy, and absolutely cannot perform a military role. Wataru-sama, the second son, is protecting the castle's northern rear gate. This lord seems to have caught sight of Kiku. When in town, he noticed Kiku with a maid carrying the shopping and walking with a white umbrella.... Since

180

then, he decided she will be his wife. He will have no other."

"What …?"

Finally, Shinshichi managed to meekly reply. Hachiyata was earnest. Shinshichi believed he was telling the truth.

Hachiyata said, "… But why now? In this battlefield surrounded by Oda's forces, I told him this marriage will not move forward. But to the lord, somehow now is not now. He said to only make this promise to Shinshichi from him. What he said is odd. If Oda's forces come to attack Itami Castle and I die in battle, this promise fades to nothing from which it came, and Kiku may marry into whatever family she wishes.… He said a promise until that day is acceptable."

"Ha, ha, haa … is that so?" asked Shinshichi and nodded. Appropriate to his profession, he understood the temperament of today's young warriors. When making love or ordering a full set of good armor, their view of life of "tomorrow, life is unknown" is always in their dreams. Moreover, the unknown life of tomorrow strengthened the feeling of living better today. Naturally, these warriors were cautious figures who somehow embraced death right before future dreams born from their desires.

"Shinshichi, you probably think this talk is ridiculous. You may be thinking about the difference in status. No, a more difficult problem is an impossible discussion between the son of Itami Hyogo-no-kami, a relative of Araki Murashige, and your younger sister given your deep connections to the Kuroda clan, these so-called opposing forces. This is likely an extreme act of the heart."

Shinshichi paled again. He was well acquainted with the internal situation. However, as he listened to the details relayed by Hachiyata, Shinshichi's terror and suspicion transformed into an entirely different notion. Kato Hachiyata was an unexpected shadow sympathizer of the alliance of Kuroda warriors.

2

Itami Hyogo-no-kami headed a powerful clan native to and having a deep history in this neighboring district.

Now, however, that power was gone. Their position changed after the restoration of Lord Araki Settsu-no-kami Murashige. As a part of the Itami clan, they were placed at the periphery of the clan and only carried the name. Even when their troops were under command, they were forgotten at the end of the column. Consequently, despite being in Itami, their hearts were still with the Oda clan. Above all, the sons of Hyogo-no-kami took this opportunity to plot the restoration of their family's fortunes. They covertly observed Kuroda Kanbei being held prisoner in the castle and the actions of the warriors in the death-defying rescue squad from the Kuroda clan that infiltrated the castle town. Their objective was to guide and assist them if given an opportunity. Then based on that deed, return to Lord Oda and together restore their family fortune as they long desired.

Before anything else, Itami Wataru, the second son of the Itami clan, took the vassal Kato Hachiyata into his confidence about another matter. This secret was Kiku. The feelings of this young warrior were conveyed with a pure heart through Hachiyata. While he left a deep impression, the belief that tomorrow may never come was elegant and simple. Because he may die on the battlefield, he said she was bound to the promise until that day.

"Please consent, Shinshichi. In turn, we will join forces. Our first revelation is the clan of Hyogo-no-kami will never submit to Araki Murashige in their hearts. I feel the day is near when the army of Lord Oda will approach the castle," said Hachiyata.

In response, Shinshichi gave a shout of joy and had no reason to refuse. He thought the devotion of the comrades dropped this man from Heaven to Earth and wanted to pray for divine support. However, one problem remained, what did Kiku think?

That was Shinshichi's sole concern. However, if the wish of the thirteen courageous comrades to save Kanbei from death is achieved through this, he thought his sister-in-law's answer would not be a problem. He surmised this young warrior equally loved Oda's forces and was a sympathizer. Shinshichi said, "Hachiyata-sama, this is how it will be. I'll leave what to say to you."

He adjusted his sitting posture on the ground and used both hands to bow to Kato Hachiyata who tapped his back again.

"Very well. I also saved face. Sufficient force will be provided to you.… Good night. We will deliberate another time," said Hachiyata and left.

A few days later, a messenger sent by Hachiyata came again. This time, Shinshichi was guided to an old estate of a samurai named Kouji of Itami. Hachiyata's lord Itami Wataru was already in his living space and waiting for him.

Wataru and Shinshichi rendezvoused there several more times. As expected, he relayed the content of those meetings to the members of the lord's rescue squad.

3

The thirteen men from the Kuroda clan unexpectedly found sympathizers in the castle. This confirmed their belief, "Heaven will have mercy on us, and our true hearts will succeed."

From wandering in darkness resembling despair, the first point of hope was felt there.

Fortunately, Itami Wataru worked each night on the defense of the northern rear gate. And under his charge, on the last moonless night in June, the skilled spy and comrade Mihara Hayato scaled the castle wall, entered into the castle and reached the lord's prison near Lake Tenjin in the northern enclosure of the castle to establish communication between the inside and the outside.

However, this plan ended in a spectacular failure.

Despite the advantages offered by Itami Wataru, the protection of the castle gate was not his only move. For four to six hours, Itami Castle was in an emergency, and the guards were on high alert. Immediately discovered by a patrol, Mihara Hayato was visited by two or three sharpshooter's bullets but escaped injury. He could only take flight like a bird and return.

The rumor spoken in the castle was "Lately, enemy spies have discovered many unguarded gaps in the northern enclosure. Don't let your guard down." The defenses there were further strengthened.

They had no way to get close and no plan to contact the jailed Kanbei. Even for Itami Wataru, getting close to Kanbei was impossible under the vigilance of the castle guards.

In the end, a desperate measure was born. Kiku would enter the castle. This action was accomplished soon after being considered.

"The maids who serve inside the castle feared the coming war and left the castle under the pretense of being ill or having a sick parent. The problem is all of them returned home and never came back. More than that, the shortage of women to serve was a problem for the lady-in-waiting."

This is what Wataru heard from senior vassals and jumped at this chance to recommend Kiku.

Kiku entered the castle as a person with a connection to the Itami clan. Starting with Araki Murashige, no one in the castle was suspicious. She was perfect. On the day she went to the castle, she was first interviewed in a room in the castle's west wing by the woman she would begin to serve that day. The woman was called the lady-in-waiting. Kiku thought she was an unrivaled beauty and the most beautiful woman she had seen in the world until that moment.

Needless to say, this woman was a concubine of Araki Murashige.

CHAPTER THIRTY-SIX
THE VOICES OF FIREFLIES

1

KIKU WAS IN harmony with the spirit of the lady-in-waiting. As the days passed, she began to speak with familiarity to Kiku. Whenever she was near, for some reason, the lady-in-waiting was inclined to question her about personal matters.

"Where are you from?" asked the lady-in-waiting.

"Well, … I'm from around here," said Kiku.

"Oh, the capital?"

"No. I'm from Naniwa."

"In Osaka."

"Uh-huh…. Yes."

She prepared herself for questions from the lady-in-waiting. But whenever she answered, she fretted and always became confused. At times, the lady-in-waiting deliberately made fun of her for not being worldly and unaccustomed to service as if she viewed these qualities as good.

"You are related to the Itami clan. Is that so?"

"Yes."

"Oh, in this house, you will work in the dormitory of Itami Wataru's bride."

"Oh, there …"

She blushed for no reason. She had no room for mistakes when asked a question she never imagined. Kiku did not know how to relax even a little.

But as the days passed, she became comfortable and remembered to ask a question before being questioned. When the talk seemed headed toward tedium, before she could be questioned, she asked the lady-in-waiting assorted questions.

When she did, the lady-in-waiting gave candid answers. She spoke to Kiku but to none of the other maids.

As a result, Kiku understood that as a concubine of Araki Murashige, the lady-in-waiting had been surrounded by fine clothes and tended to in the west wing, but was not the daughter from a distinguished family or a famous man.

The lady-in-waiting believed she was looking at a prostitute from the harbor who was brought back by Murashige from the area of Muronotsu he passed through on his way home from his visit to the encampment in Chugoku. From time to time, traces of her Chugoku accent slipped out. She often amused herself by playing with unexpected words of the lower classes.

"People are crammed into this castle. Right?"

Kiku became accustomed to hearing these words dropped with a sigh sometimes by the lady-in-waiting and knitted her beautiful eyebrows.

"It may be better if the enemy comes soon and the castle falls. If that happens, you will probably return … to Muronotsu."

The lady-in-waiting let those daring words slip out. She didn't always lower her voice. Her attitude was it would be fine for this to reach the ears of Murashige.

2

Muronotsu was close to Shikama, Kiku's home was also in Harima. She feared the Chugoku-raised lady-in-waiting would notice the Chugoku dialect she was unable to purge from her speech.

As expected, from then on, whenever anything related to speech was mentioned, the lady-in-waiting said, "Kiku, you've probably been in the Harima area."

"… Yes, yes."

"Where?"

"I have relatives in Shikama."

"Is that so?"

The lady-in-waiting laughed from the corners of her cool eyes. While nodding, she mumbled, "… I thought so."

At those times, Kiku's face blanched, but after that, the lady-in-waiting no longer doubted her.

Summer reached its height. The lady-in-waiting was cross. She did not seem to like summer in the lord's residence where her pristine hairstyle was spoiled. Her sole enjoyment was to wait for dusk, have the bamboo blinds on the veranda rolled up, and sit on the veranda in anticipation of the evening breeze.

"After the watering, fireflies will fly around, and it somehow gets cooler. Kiku, go and catch fireflies."

"Fireflies?"

"Chugoku has many fireflies, but you knew that. They are near water. If you go to water, they will be there. Catch a lot of them and put them in the firefly cage."

"Water…. A place with water…. Where is a place like that?"

"Go north along the garden. Pass behind the tower and look around Lake Tenjin."

"What? Lake Tenjin?"

"Are you afraid?" asked the amused lady-in-waiting.

"No, I'm not afraid."

Hugging the firefly cage, Kiku searched under the starlight in the direction she was told for the road. While inside the castle grounds, there were hills, forests, and shallow valleys as she approached the rear gate. Walking at night, especially in the mountains, was a little different.

3

"They're here. They're here. They're really here."

A horde formed from countless fireflies. Beautiful phosphorescent trails were drawn in the dark place as they flew and crossed paths. At the dangerous place at the water's edge, the fireflies flew high like a ball.

The damp ground made her pinch her nose. The darkness was unbelievable. She had a vague idea of the location of the lake's edge. The wisteria vines spread from the wisteria trellis as they pleased. Here and there, towering trees covered the sky again and again.

But she wasn't thinking about anything frightening or ominous, nothing at all. Only the words from her brother-in-law Shinshichi before she entered this castle called to her heart.

She thought, "This is surely the lake. It must be around here."

She did not chase the fireflies; they came to her, swarming near her sleeves and breast. She bent slightly to catch and place them in the cage.

"... Ah, there's a window."

She made sure her eyes were adapted to the darkness of that place. Directly on the other side of the lake, a building resembling an armory with walls of sixty-feet-tall pillars stood at the water's edge. She was able to make out one window. However, that window was so high she could never reach it.

More than that, she would have trouble getting beneath the window because it was on the lake.

"He must be in there ..."

Kiku truly believed this, and tears filled her eyes. The family lineage between that man and her was a relationship of a master to a servant. There was also a gap in social standing. However, each time the young lord of Himeyama lashed his horse and rode to Shikama, he never failed to visit her home; adored her father, his Uncle Yojiemon; and treated his young daughter like a friend. He always said, "Coming here cheers me up."

When the day ended and he said, "I should head back to Himeyama," and brought his horse to the back door of the house, the young girl Kiku never gushed with tears by herself. But the young maiden was unaware of the source of those feelings.

As the years passed, he disappeared from Himeyama. She often heard news of him from her father. The rumor whispered was his pretty young wife and son lived in the castle.

Since that time, the young woman fought against remembering her troubled spirit of her youth that resembled the flickering of the fireflies. Without noticing, she was living with her elderly father and her marriageable age had passed. Last year when she learned of this man's misfortune, she unexpectedly became anxious.

She could not express her feelings to her father Yojiemon. Fortunately, before they left, she appealed to Kinugasa Kyuzaemon and Mori Tahei from the shadows, and they added their power as his comrades. Working together, they fervently asked him to grant her wish and allow her to enter Itami Castle.

Even without power, she happened upon a turn of fate or heaven's pity and came to the vicinity of the jail where she believed Kanbei was being held. Kiku looked at the dark ancient lake a short distance from her eyes. While examining the fortified building, she didn't have the smallest notion of this situation being bad given this opportunity and divine aid. She did not believe in the impossible, only the possible. She forgot about the evening dew wetting her waistband and short sleeves leaning into the grass like a flower.

Eventually, she slowly rose.

4

Mud had naturally accumulated to a width of just one to two feet at the boundary of the earthen base of the building and the lake water. Ditch reeds and weeds grew thick there and formed a strip of shore along the base of the wall. She positioned herself close to the building and little by little inched sideways.

As she moved until nearly at the center of the lake, occasionally, broad areas with a wide accumulation of earth appeared. At those places, she paused to look around.

The window was nearby. She looked up high to see it on the outside. A wisteria vine of a wisteria trellis climbed into that place

"If the wisteria vine slips in ..." she earnestly thought like a young dreamy girl. She got as close as she could under the window, cupped her hands around her mouth, and eagerly called out, "Kanbei-sama. Kanbei-sama."

Noisy winds skimmed the top of the trellis. She tirelessly called at intervals.

"... Kanbei-sama. Are you there?"

5

Kuroda Kanbei lifted his head.

With fiery eyes, he glared around the inside of his cell.

The ceiling was high. The width and depth of the interior were wide. The rectangle was dark, and the floor was made of planks. Nothing had changed, even a little, when he opened one eye.

The only change he saw was the summer weather.

Summer came and the outbreak of eczema on his skin worsened. The roots of his hair swelled, too. He had to pass that time inside his cell. Aside from short walks, he could do nothing other than wait.

"Am I dreaming? ... Is it my nerves?"

KURODA JOSUI

His fatigue led him to rest his head on the thin
bedding and pillow.

He wasn't trying to listen to the barely audible wind
through the wisteria flowers from the lone bright window
but sat up with a start.

"I thought it was my nerves but ... but I think I heard
a mysterious voice."

He teetered as he sat up but did not stand. The
muscles shrunken by the swelling throughout his body had
robbed his healthy body of the strength to stand and walk.

"This is not a dream."

He crawled over the expansive floor like a baby
suffering from a stomach illness.

He cautiously turned around to look at the sturdy
lattice to his side. The soldier guard always stationed at the
periphery had changed.

He could see the faraway red torches on iron legs. No
one was there. Kanbei looked carefully then began
crawling again to a spot below the window.

He placed his ear and body close to the plank wall
and calmed himself for a few moments. Without a doubt,
he heard a human voice. Was he hearing his name being
called?

The blood pulsing through his body he had forgotten
long ago seemed to boil over. He was being called. Two
men named Kanbei certainly did not live in this area.

"Wha ... What? Who are you?"

He wanted to give a full-throated reply. Needless to
say, that desire posed too great a danger.

He hesitated. He did not move or speak.

His arm stretched up like a dead tree. His hand
grasped the tip of the wisteria vine that crawled in through
the window and yanked it down.

The wisteria branch he was staring at in the high
window shook. To prove the wind was not moving the
branch, he gave it a long pull then jerked it for a short
time.

EIJI YOSHIKAWA

After that, the voice calling from outside was charged with unusual emotion. He heard it more clearly than earlier.

"Are you Kanbei-sama? Is the person inside Kanbei-sama of Himeji? ... Please show your face or some part of your body, Kanbei-sama."

The voice resembling a shout filled in the gaps in the night breeze. Kanbei threw back his head in surprise.

"... What? That's a woman's voice. I'm sure that's a woman."

No one came to mind. "Of course, this is not a dream," he thought but remained unsure.

CHAPTER THIRTY-SEVEN
THE WISTERIA BRANCH

1

THE WISTERIA BRANCH on the window ledge shook. That was his answer.

Kiku's blood heated further when her presence was acknowledged by the jailed man.

"Kanbei-sama, Kanbei-sama. Soon a group of Himeji vassals will plan your rescue. Until then, whatever you do, don't lose hope or patience."

She gasped out words with this meaning and looked up at the shaking vine.

She doubted the imprisoned Kanbei could make out her words but couldn't stop shouting.

Then she spun around. Nearly at her feet, the lake water made a faint splash like a frog jumping in.

"...?"

She clung there with both hands and turned only her face to look over her shoulder. The lake's surface was unperturbed. Small ripples only passed over the wavelets stirred by the evening breeze.

"... Kanbei-sama, if I see them, is there anything you want me to tell them? Tell me what you want me to say."

Splash. This time the sound was louder. The direction

was different, and water hit the side of her face.

Kiku casually turned her eyes to the shore across the lake. Her pale face and shoulders lost all color at that moment and she shivered. She glanced at her feet like she was about to run off.

2

She wondered what to do. She could not quickly flee this place.

A castle soldier on watch came unobserved to the opposite shore of the lake. His eyes seemed to be watching her actions from a distance in the shade of a tree.

"What are you doing over there? You are definitely after Kanbei. Hey, hey, get that reed boat. Push the pole and bring that woman here," ordered the soldier who looked like the commanding officer. Two soldiers quickly thrust the poles of the small rotted tree boat and crossed over to her. Kiku cowered as she watched them approach. They pushed off the boat with ease and over to the officer.

"Do you work in the west wing? The north wing?" he asked with severe eyes. She knew there was no escape.

When she said, "I serve the lady-in-waiting," the officer grabbed her wrist with disgust.

"All right. Walk," he ordered.

The other soldier grabbed her other arm. She was sandwiched between two soldiers in full armor and hauled off in a way her feet never touched the ground.

The officer was a commander called Gondou Ijuro. Every man inside and outside who guarded the armory prison was under his command. Given his responsibility, he took a grave view of the woman's actions.

Kiku was marched off to the castle keep. That evening, however, Araki Murashige, the lord of the castle, was with samurai in what looked like a banquet in the west wing. Ijuro clicked his tongue and immediately changed direction and went to them.

"Excuse me, but the lady-in-waiting is a disgrace. It's

outrageous to forgive that woman."

He went around to the front of the garden of the west wing, passed the attendant to request an audience with Murashige. The attendant asked what was his business, but Ijuro refused to tell him.

"If I cannot see the lord, I cannot say."

The attendant reluctantly yielded. Murashige was enjoying the cool air with the lady-in-waiting. The vassals in the castle keep did not appear excessively suspicious during the banquet. He saw a single small drum abandoned in the room as an object of no interest.

The lady-in-waiting and Murashige were in this room but facing different directions. They looked out at the garden with separate hearts.

"What? Ijuro wants to see me. Why would he come here?"

Murashige looked disgusted. But when the attendant whispered something, Murashige's eyes became severe.

"Drag her there," he said pointing to the front of the large stepping stone.

Gondou Ijuro's figure immediately appeared. Kiku was pulled to the front of the garden and prostrated herself.

Murashige stared at Kiku's shadow from the veranda. His dreadful eyes brought to mind the valor heard of in the world as Settsu-no-kami Murashige.... After a short pause, he groaned, "Uh, who is this woman?"

He glanced at the profile of the lady-in-waiting beside him. He looked at her and Kiku as if comparing them.

However, the lady-in-waiting was indifferent. She flashed a sidelong glance at Kiku. She seemed to instantly understand Murashige's feelings but only stared at the flickering stars in the night sky over the eaves.

3

Gondou Ijuro excitedly explained the situation. Naturally, this matter reverberated greatly with the lady-in-waiting before his eyes. In this time of war, he was making a tragic plea from his heart as a loyal vassal to protect the castle. He felt compelled to fearlessly oppose and dissuade the lord.

Settsu-no-kami Murashige was not so foolish a ruler to be angered by the words of this faithful vassal. He drank in enough of Ijuro's feeling reflected in his glimmering eyes and listened to his detailed report.

Then he quietly turned to face the lady-in-waiting.

"Lady, were you listening?"

"Yes, I heard."

"Didn't this Kiku recently become a servant of yours?"

"Lord, you are well informed."

"... Oh well, I asked as a precaution. Half of the responsibility is yours."

"Why is that?"

"Why didn't I know this mysterious woman was placed here until today?"

"What is mysterious about her?"

"You heard Ijuro's words."

"Perhaps, Ijuro is entirely mistaken?"

"What are you saying?" said Settsu-no-kami who was usually gentle toward women but now flushed with anger.

He asked, "How is Ijuro wrong? He saw everything with his own eyes."

"No, no," she said, still looking undefeated. Using that unique quality of women, she never wavered in her argument.

"Kiku is my servant. I should be better acquainted with Kiku's nature than anyone else. Also, isn't a relative of the Itami family part of the lord's family? This maid is that. Ijiro's elegance by uttering words like 'a mysterious woman' or 'a despicable being' display great contempt for her and, in the very least, toward a servant of the lord."

She took him to task with the swiftness of setting a fire.

"I instructed Kiku to go to Lake Tenjin tonight. Kiku did not go on her own accord. To Kiku, this could truly be called a calamity. I told her to gather many fireflies and release them in this garden."

"You say that but …" interrupted Ijuro whose face unexpectedly showed fear. The lady-in-waiting said with a chill, "What is this? Do not speak to me. Control yourself."

She cut him off as he began and faced Murashige to glibly continue to deny the facts.

"You've said that half of the responsibility is mine. If so, then half of the blame should lie with the lord. Why was that mysterious woman placed in this residence with me who entered this castle to serve? Will I, as you always say, be returned or not be returned to Muronotsu? … That is your decision, Lord."

"Ijuro, Ijuro," said Murashige. He almost immediately began to discredit the importance of the commanding officer.

"Go for now. We will discuss this later. No, don't worry, this will be settled after Kiku's identity has been satisfactorily investigated. Please go."

Ijuro looked up with his forlorn eyes at the lord's face. He suppressed his urge to speak out. However, until he rose, the lady-in-waiting never stopped denying his accusation.

She said, "After leaving here, you should go again to the lake and investigate. I had Kiku carry my beautiful lacquered firefly cage. She must have dropped it somewhere.… How sad, a truly heartbreaking false accusation has been made against me …"

Ijuro did not look offended when he bowed as a military man and promptly withdrew.

Of course, the ensuing conversation was only between the lady-in-waiting and Murashige. Her tone changed somewhat when the two were alone.

"I also carry blame. I left the castle with Kiku. Please banish both Kiku and me. Otherwise, the two of us will

197

not receive the same punishment," she said sternly.

Settsu-no-kami Murashige looked embarrassed by this woman. His indulgence was impossible to hide given his reputation of having the warrior's flaw of being brave but lacking peace in the inner sanctum of his home.

"That's fine. That is not the problem. Ijuro did not come with willful malice. If it's a mistake, a mistake is permitted. There should be no disruptions inside or outside Itami Castle. If the vassals thought so, wouldn't they be conscientious about insignificant matters, too? I will leave Kiku to you. From now on, she will not leave the west wing."

Murashige eventually reassured her and looked relieved. On the other hand, his words only distracted her but, in the end, he understood the lady-in-waiting's mood.

In no time, this matter leaked from the mouth of one vassal to the next. The indignant Gondou Ijuro left the castle soon after. Murashige was enraged and cursed his disloyalty, but much of the clan remained silent.

From this time on, Itami Castle was filled with sloth. Signs appeared to reveal the emergence of disruptions to the fighting spirit.

The work at Azuchi was to sniff the air in the castle and the circumstances in the castle town were promptly reflected in the air. These secrets were frequently passed to Nobunaga.

CHAPTER THIRTY-EIGHT
MALAISE

1

THE ACTUAL WAR situation was not known in the inner circle of only women, but the fate of Itami Castle began to decline several months earlier. After summer began, the feeling was the fall of that castle would hit the bottom today or tomorrow.

The true situation was evident by climbing the highest tower of the castle and taking a panoramic look at the castle town. Still springtime, the enemy camp was not visible by shielding one's eyes or by the naked eye. From the end of spring, the encirclement gradually tightened to move the enemy's banner insignia to various desired locations. In the beginning, squads of Oda's army found in every direction had linked up and were in contact with the town of Itami.

In the camp protecting the exterior of the castle, around the beginning of August, troops under the command of Araki who had been fighting the enemy's advance guard left the trenches and began a full retreat to inside the castle walls. The soldiers and horses in Oda's army entered the town of Itami. For a time, the town came to a standstill.

"You are not the enemy. You have no reason to rebel with Murashige. Work. Work. Make your livings as usual," was the proclamation of Oda's army to the townspeople. However, out of fear, they did not return to their work.

Some of them were pressed into service to dig a long, meandering trench around Itami Castle. Fences and stockades were built two or three deep along the trench. The abundant manpower worked like bees under a blazing sun.

When finished, although horrible, the officers and men in Itami Castle would become caged birds. First, a flurry of arrows and a barrage of rifle bullets tried to inflict damage. The arrows and bullets were used up, and Oda's forces realized few remained. However, the strategy of Oda's forces seemed to be to go easy to avoid harming allies as much as possible and wait for the disintegration.

The commander-in-chief of the advance was Nobunaga's heir, Nobutada. He was aided by generals like Hori Kyutaro Hidemasa and Takigawa Sakon Kazumasu.

2

"They will come. They will certainly come around now. They absolutely will come. They will come."

When the castle commanders gathered to convene an emergency war council, the words of the commander Araki Murashige were extreme. More than conviction, his words were loaded with agitation.

"During the spring, when the great naval force of the Mouri clan came to assist with ships lined up from stem to stern, a written oath was given to me. While we were late in the preparation of armaments, they have no reason to go to the trouble of breaking the treaty and do nothing but leave us to our fate. I will believe in the Mouri until the end. A huge army coming to our aid is determined to land on the shores of Nishinomiya as soon as possible. Each of you must stay strong."

Murashige's words were for the followers who were

called on at the start of the fighting. These words were true at the end of the year, this spring, and even in the summer.

Nevertheless, over six months have passed, and the huge armies of Mouri Terumoto, Kikkawa, and Kobayakawa, the second front with warships, had not come.

Many of the castle commanders finally began to question the sincerity of the Mouri clan but said nothing to Lord Murashige.

The despondent Murashige thought, It's a shame. Those who had to be relied on were relied on.... Weren't Takayama Ukon and Nakagawa Kiyohide as reliable as my own two arms? But I was deceived and watched Takayama and Nakagawa change sides and quickly surrender at the gate of Oda's camp.

Despite this belief, surprisingly, Murashige did not voice his current lack of hope in the Mouri as August began.

On the contrary, this time he began to curse the immorality and betrayal of Mouri Terumoto. During the war council on September 1, he said things like, "Another tack must be employed to encourage prompt support from the Mouri clan. Letters will be written one after the other, and secret envoys will be dispatched. I will go and take Kikkawa and Kobayakawa to task."

Even after hearing his words, the commanders were not cheered. First, they wondered if there was enough time. Murashige hoped to meet with representatives of the Mouri. They understood the difficulty in achieving that objective.

However, bravery is bravery, and the prudent and straightforward Murashige seemed to believe in that possibility. From this perspective or at this juncture, a thorough examination of his leadership may have been appropriate.

After that time, he seriously considered slipping away from the castle. He decided to forget the castle and his positions as the lord who should be in the castle and the ringleader of the rebellion. He would sneak away alone and go down for now to the allied Hanakuma Castle in Settsu. Without a word of warning to the senior vassals in the clan or the key castle commanders, he began preparations on the evening of the following day, September 2.

3

Murashige unexpectedly appeared in the west wing to issue an order.

"Lady, prepare immediately."

The lady-in-waiting looked aghast and surveyed him from his feet to his head. Murashige was outfitted like a rank-and-file soldier off to a hunt in the open fields.

"Where are you going? Dressed like that ..." asked the lady-in-waiting and cast a cold look. Her insight and wisdom made the average woman look ignorant in every way. She assessed any situation in an instant.

"Anywhere is fine. As quick as you can, fasten your skirt and come with me."

"No."

"Why not?"

"I cannot go to some unknown destination."

"You never stop talking about wanting to leave the castle. Am I right?"

"You are leaving the castle."

"I'm leaving the castle. Going outside the castle walls."

"Well, isn't that a bit strange?"

"Why?"

"You are the lord of the castle. What will become of the many people in the clan?"

"Women know nothing. For your peace of mind, listen to me. As a war tactic, it's best for me to leave."

"Where will you go?"

"To Hanakuma Castle."

"Therefore, you intend for me to be shut up in

202

Hanakuma, too. In that case, it's all the same to me so I'll stay here."

"No, you will travel as far as Hyogo and return home. You will board a boat there."

"Is that so? Remember, to lie is the shame of a samurai."

"All right. You will go home. Hurry, get ready."

"Kiku. Kiku," she called to the maids' quarters.

Kiku did not answer; another maid came. Where was she? The maid reported that no one had seen Kiku that evening.

"Has the lord hidden her? If she is not brought along, I cannot go either."

The lady-in-waiting stared with shrewd eyes at Murashige's face. He was flustered and deceived by his complexion while shaking his head.

"Kiku already went. She was added to a group of senior vassals."

"That is a lie, isn't it?"

She did not believe him at all. But in a heartbeat, she accepted Murashige's awkward words as the truth. During that time, the first watch of the evening passed. A cluster of human figures lingered covertly in the darkness of the garden and urged Murashige to stand.

The followers on that night numbered just six or seven. When they came to him, they were unable to voice any complaints or grievances because they saw his tragic expression and his eyes filled with bloodthirstiness. The lady-in-waiting was quite petulant toward Murashige, but when surrounded by these warrior clan vassals, she trembled as she walked and buried the profile of her face as white as a moonflower deep in her veil.

4

"I said the lord is not here."

"What? Not here. Where?"

"In this castle."

"That's stupid."

"No, it's true. Last evening, he snuck out through the rear gate and moved to Hanakuma Castle."

"Is that true?"

"I just heard this from the senior retainer Ikeda Izumi."

"What?!"

Several samurai spat on the ground and barged into the room where the senior retainers were gathered. The elders Araki Kyuzaemon and Ikeda Izumi had been reluctantly left behind for reasons explained by Murashige and were trying to calm the agitated officers and men. Their voices grew hoarse and they wiped away sweat while trying to persuade them that this desperate measure was for the allies. If by chance, the lord reaches Hanakuma Castle. He will board a boat, go by sea, and safely infiltrate the domain of the Mouri clan and double back, without a doubt, they will be rescued by the great naval forces of Kikkawa and Kobayakawa. The forces may be on the way as they move toward Settsu by sea. When they arrive, the siege by Oda's army outside the castle will crumble within half a day, and their forces will scatter. Bring on the battle. This is another pause. A few more days will be endured. This castle will be abandoned. The yearlong siege and the actions of the samurai will return to foam.

"But what will happen? Denouncing the lord is not the way of a vassal. Witnessing this adversity and avoiding the fight can be likened to cowardice. There is only death."

Eventually, the vassals calmed down. But their internal agitation was impossible to stop. From that time, the fighting spirit in the castle resembled the leaves of a tall tree falling away in late autumn. Deserters scattered one after the other. Rumors slipped in from outside the castle like cold winds.

"Certain men are already conspiring with members of the Oda clan."

"Ukita Naoie of Bizen, who was on Mouri's side, is

threatening the border with the Mouri through collusion with the Oda clan, and reinforcements won't go to Kyoto."

From the beginning, the commanders in the castle warned that these words were rumors or dire news seeping in from the enemy side but gradually came to understand these voices as being closer to the truth.

First, Araki Murashige was reported to have gone down to Hanakuma Castle but didn't go that far and entered Amagasaki Castle where he stayed. The attitudes of some including the remaining commanders in Itami changed drastically.

One commander called Nakanishi Shinhachiro had a complete change of mind. With Nakanishi at the center, the leader of the Itami Hyogo force and his second son Itami Wataru who had given up on Murashige contacted Gondou Ijuro and concocted some plan.

"We'll take the initiative and attack them head-on with a squad of those whose minds have changed."

This scene was repeated. Naturally, a malaise took hold of all of Itami, and rapid disintegration soon followed.

5

In Itami Castle abandoned by the Mouri, those who must not be relied on were relied on. The spirits of the officers and soldiers cast off by the castle lord Murashige were fractured and scattered. Their weakness only worsened.

The senior retainer Araki Kyuzaemon stepped forward to be the military envoy to Oda and to present the following proposal.

"Our wives and children will be presented as hostages. Then we retainers will pass through to Amagasaki. In short, we will meet with the lord, Settsu-no-kami Murashige, and meticulously present our view to surrender this castle without bloodshed and both Amagasaki and Hanakuma castles. If Settsu-no-kami does not accept, both Amagasaki and Hanakuma will fall with us at the vanguard and surrender to the Oda clan. In the event, Lord Settsu-no-kami gains sudden enlightenment and readily surrenders, we will respectfully request only that our lives be spared."

Oda's army agreed. Araki Kyuzaemon and a few companions traveled to Amagasaki. But what was the result? Days passed, but Oda's army received no response. And the officers and soldiers in all the remaining castles received no reports. Oda Nobutada said to Takigawa Kazumasu, a tenacious and resourceful general, "What should be the plan? The inordinate engineering works dug around the exterior of the castle may be suspended. Kazumasu, enact your earlier plan immediately,"

Nobutada was a young general with an overwhelming defeated spirit. Nobutada's impatience with Kazumasu's strategy, like he feared taking risks, was understandable.

"All right? The moment has come."

Some time ago, Kazumasu described a plan to Nakanishi Shinhachiro to win over allies and was confident in its success. He contacted him in secret and arranged a date for the meeting. He encouraged him with "Fan the flames of betrayal!"

The confederates of Shinhachiro waited for decisive actions. Why? They changed their minds and had a hunch that their allies in the castle were indignant and under pressure by the danger of not knowing when an attack would come.

The secret command from Takigawa Kazumasu was to come on the evening of October 18, but they could not possibly wait until then. The situation was perilous. At last, two days earlier on the evening of October 16, with no time to make advance arrangements and without warning, flames were fanned from a corner in the castle.

"We have two days."

The steadfast forces of Oda outside the castle were rattled. Naturally, the confusion was more intense inside Itami Castle.

"Just as I thought, the one who changed his mind has taken off his mask."

"You rat! Did you make the first move?"

In the cauldron of one castle, the disaster of two supporters striking at the same time and falling together was played out under the flames. This fate was predicted. Sword versus sword was devastating.

Under the cover of night and against strong winds, flames engulfed the castle. The firelight and dreadful sounds inched closer and encircled Kuroda Kanbei trapped in this jail since the previous year.

CHAPTER THIRTY-NINE
A MAN'S LAMENT

1

SEVERAL DAYS EARLIER, a motley group of around ten men who appeared dressed as priests, soldiers, townsmen, doctors, and puppeteers furtively approached Koyadera Temple in the Koya district and lodged together in one section.

Their objective was to rescue their lord. Obviously, they were the soldiers of Himeji who had been wandering near Itami since spring.

Initially, there were thirteen. But Mori Yosobei fell ill along the way and had to return home. And very recently, Miyata Jihei and Ogawa Yosoemon split off as a team. They hurried to Chugoku with the promising news that the successful rescue of Kanbei-sama was just days away. One went to Hideyoshi's location; the other entered Himeji Castle for a meeting.

The squad gathered at Koyadera Temple to wait. They were well aware of the secret plan for renegades in Itami Castle to start fires inside on the eighteenth to lure in Oda's army.

Detailed accounts of their information were passed through the silversmith Shinshichi and Kato Hachiyata.

"At what time and on what day? Who is protecting the west gate? Who is at the north gate?"

Almost everything was learned directly. Of course, the imprisoned lord being in good health was also discovered.

However, nothing at all was known about one item. There had been no news about Shinshichi's sister-in-law Kiku. No evidence was found of her accompanying Murashige and the lady-in-waiting to Amagasaki Castle. She had not been seen in the castle.

"It may all end in a wretched discovery" was the hushed talk among the comrades. Because they could not bear making Shinshichi miserable, nothing was said around him. However, Shinshichi had resigned himself to that ending.

On the evening of October 16, Shinshichi happened to drop by to inspire the group. He said, "The plan is set for midnight on the eighteenth, the men under Nakanishi Shinhachiro in the castle will surrender the castle and invite in Oda's forces. A comprehensive secret plan will be signed between the two. On the anticipated day and for two more days, despite the difficulty, please stay here so the enemy is not alerted."

After calling attention again to this critical aspect, he returned to town. He came sometime between seven and nine in the evening, the time of the dog.

2

It was the time when one wondered whether an hour had come and gone. Shinshichi, who should have already returned home and asleep, knocked on the main gate of the temple again in a frantic voice and shouted, "Something's happened."

Mori Tahei and Goto Emon had probably been asleep.

"Is that Shinshichi?" they said and timidly emerged from the temple kitchen and went out to the gate.

Kuriyama Zensuke had jogged out one step ahead of them. He opened the gate and seemed to hear Shinshichi say, "Something's happened."

When he realized the pair followed him, Zensuke was calm but spoke with intensity.

"Get everyone ready now and gather here."

The weapons had already been brought into the temple. The men immediately came running, donned their armor, and grabbed hold of preferred weapons like long-handled spears.

Zensuke, Tahei, and Emon slipped past them, ducked inside the temple, armed themselves, and re-emerged.

However, the group still had no idea what had happened.

"Is everyone ready?"

After scanning the number assembled, Kuriyama Zensuke rapidly but clearly said, "I don't know what's going on, but the betrayal in the castle synchronized to midnight of the day after tomorrow was the sudden outbreak of fires that just happened. Since Oda's army did not anticipate this, Shinshichi is now flying through the air to reach them in a panic over this unforeseen event. And not one soldier has set out for the castle. We did not request the power of Oda's forces from the beginning. Our only aim was to save the life of our imprisoned lord. Over time or in the confusion of the moment, Kanbei-sama's life is further endangered as long as he's imprisoned by Araki Murashige's clan. From now on, we've got to be fast. Our mutual actions were arranged beforehand. But before our eyes, our allies will be surrounded by many enemies. Before the lord's safety can be confirmed, we cannot meet again. Be careful. No mistakes."

All ten figures behaved as soldiers. The shadows of the group danced excitedly and raced each other like night crows down the long roads between the rice fields of the Koya district.

When they went around the shadows of the forest,

the hills straight ahead and the castle came into view. The red fire lights on the road dyed the October night sky and pierced the Milky Way.

The roaring sounds of trumpet shells and bells and drums were heard on all sides outside the castle. The spirit of the beginning of an all-out attack was felt. But Oda's army could not yet see the shadows of the soldiers below the castle walls.

Unlike the movements of many soldiers and horses, the death-defying squad of ten Kuroda soldiers was swift. They broke the stockade on all sides of the hill and raced up to the rear gate. They saw no enemy who could block their way. Only sparks and smoke blew down from everywhere.

Once they reached the bottom of the ditch, they scaled the castle wall. Of course, this required complicated maneuvers. If the warriors inside from above the castle walls came to resist, in the end, they would be unable to easily keep their grip. They were defenseless. As if to say "Climb up here," thick ropes hung from two places. Of course, they were provided by sympathizers in the castle like Itami Wataru or Kato Hachiyata.

The ten divided into two groups and raced each other to the top. Shinshichi followed them. When he leaped over the castle wall, the ten men had not been able to huddle. The hot winds and the sparks wildly blew sideways. Indistinguishable desperate fights broke out all around between enemies and allies. The most ferocious flames were the large flames burning and rising to the third level of the tower. Flames were also visible in the northern quarter near the west wing. The crackling sounds burst forth and began to transform into a bright red pillar.

"Where is the armory jail?"

"Where is Kanbei-sama?"

The men dove under the fire and scrambled to find Kanbei.

3

Was there a lower place or an enclosure like an underground room that escaped being shrouded in black smoke? Instead, fierce flames rushed down from the center level of the tower and spread.

Kanbei sat in his cell. The flames swiftly reached the rough lattice. Black soot blew over the wide floor and collected near his knees. But there was nothing he could do. He sat in vain with his back against the wall in the northernmost corner.

In contrast to the flames, this wall was cold like a stone wall. Drops of fresh water seeped in. The sun never hit this wall at any time during the year.

The building was considered unsuitable as an armory because of the high dampness and was left unused for years until it became Kanbei's prison. His entire body was afflicted with miserable eczema. He was so weak he struggled to rise after waking.

"Has the day come at last? My body will burn up, and death is my unavoidable fate. I never expected Araki Murashige to witness my last days. The gloom in my heart feels like a burning sensation.... How panicked that idiot must be."

He couldn't help laughing. He was resigned to his own death and did not rise even for physiological reasons on the border between life and death. Sparks singed his knees. Their heat forced him to sweep them away. As he swept his hand, he waited for all four walls and the ceiling of his jail to soon erupt in flames.

He only thought about the commander Araki Murashige in this castle. He believed the attack by Oda's forces had nothing to do with rescuing him. But somewhere in his mind hung a dim ray of hope. It was the woman's voice that called him while shaking the wisteria vine outside the high window about one hundred days ago.

"… Whose voice was that? I haven't heard it since," recalled Kanbei.

When he looked up at the window, the wisteria flowers were beginning to drop off like they were being seared by a bright red autumn wind.

4

That evening, fires flared up in two or three places. At the same time, this sparked terrifying fierce, fights between allies in the castle. In the quarter where Araki Murashige's family and women lived, barefoot and wearing only the clothes on their backs, they crowded together to escape in an avalanche through the castle gate.

The besieged faction and the colluding faction took no notice of the women but were grateful for their escape and did not meet their terrified eyes in the castle. However, when the women flooded toward the castle gate, "Go back! Go back!"

A squad of heavily armored warriors pushed back the wailing women. The squad leader yelled from behind to the soldiers in front, "There may be cowards in disguise mixed in with the women and trying to escape."

Naturally, the enemy forces pressed closer. They may have been the soldiers under the command of one of Oda's generals, but all the eyes could see was a wave of black armor, spears, and bannermen.

"Okay, go. Okay, go. You go too."

One by one, the women's necks and black hair were inspected before they were shoved out the castle gate. During that time, the large gate opened. The commanders and soldiers competing with each other in bravery came face-to-face with eyes ready to dash outside and rushed inside like an angry wave.

The women were sent flying or trampled. Like flowers blown in a violent rainstorm, they huddled at the edge of a side gate. They shuddered together throwing away their sensations of life. Their bodies were inspected in succession and sent out of the castle.

One of them was Kiku. Shortly before the day Murashige left the castle accompanied by the lady-in-waiting, she was confined to a room in the lady-in-waiting's apartment. Murashige's family followed the orders left by Murashige and went to him without releasing her. She was unable to pass on a warning. She fought earlier to flee the castle.

If she stayed with the group, she would easily slip out the castle gate. However, when Kiku saw a gap in the people surrounding her, she instantly fled the group at full speed back to where she started. The entire castle seemed to be consumed by flames. Here and there crazed figures dove into the bloody battle where fierce warriors fought; leaders killed and were killed; war cries were exchanged; and fire dropped onto fire.

"… Oh. That low, sunken lake is at the bottom of this hilly road."

Eventually, she found the road she remembered passing through only once. It was a narrow road to Lake Tenjin where she had been sent by the lady-in-waiting to catch fireflies.

5

The squad was out of their element with prior knowledge learned from a drawing and the very different sensations felt when actually stepping on the ground. That was so in ordinary times, but inside a castle transformed into this bloody battlefield, the buildings and trees to be used as landmarks were enveloped by fire and smoke. And the enclosure was wider than imagined.

"Where is it? The prison."

"Where is Kanbei-sama?"

Kuroda's soldiers running around sighed deeply from the dilemma of finding him. Worn out by their nonstop action, their spirits were finally drained.

Exhausted as they were, they fought to maintain their

presence of mind on a goal that is easily lost. The flames they saw throughout the entire castle alarmed them. Fire has no mercy on time. Without making a false step and taking great pains to search there, they realized they were too late but did not stop rushing around.

"Kyuzaemon, do you know anything?"

Kuriyama Zensuke and Mori Tahei bumped into him near the base of the tower. Kinugasa Kyuzaemon in a parched voice asked, "Still nothing.... You?"

"No, nothing's been found yet."

"Have you seen a lake anywhere? A lake with a wisteria trellis."

"I focused too long on that lake and delayed investigating the other lakes in the enclosure. This area seems to be the northern enclosure. There's the tower."

"I will search the lake. I know nothing about the buildings."

He ran down through a pine forest. The larch trees and the bushes were incinerated.

After taking a lively stumble, Kuriyama Zensuke turned to look at what snagged his foot.

"Eeyah, that looks like a woman."

Choked by smoke, a woman had lost consciousness and fell over.

"It's Kiku," shouted Tahei and Kyuzaemon who stopped and stood before stumbling over her.

"What? It's Kiku," one said and lifted her and shouted into her ear. When she came around, she flew off like an arrow without looking at the faces around her.

She ran out to a lake. When they saw the lake water and a wide wisteria trellis, Kuriyama Zensuke and Mori Tahei ran after her.

"Ah, it's here," they shouted all at once.

As they looked, she was already submerged at the shore to her hips. A spray arose like from the dragon's daughter as she sloshed forward toward the base of the prison building.

215

"Kanbei-sama …"

She grabbed the wisteria tree and frantically climbed high up. Kinugawa Kyuzaemon followed her. Eventually, she grabbed onto the window of the jail and peeked in. She could make nothing out in the already reddened and darkened interior.

Kuriyama Zensuke and Mori Tahei entered through another entrance and came out in front of the thick lattice that partitioned the large floor of the jail. Four or five soldiers, who seemed to be from the Araki clan, appeared and made no attempt to block them but scattered. The two searched around outside the cell and discovered a rectangular piece of old wood about eighteen feet long in a corner. They picked it up and pointed its tip, like a bell hammer, and thrust it a number of times into the grating.

A section collapsed. After a few more blows, they burst through and let out full-throated shouts.

"Lord! We have come!"

"We are Himeji vassals. Lord! Lord …"

They looked around with eyes ablaze. Kanbei's figure was not easily discerned.

Kanbei was all right. That cold wall on the north side released steam in the hot air and smoke. He sat with his back to the wall with his legs crossed like a dead tree.

This time, he saw the unexpected figures of his vassals before his eyes. He choked up, moved by their loyalty, but his voice resonated in their ears although he seemed stunned. He had trouble believing his eyes.

"Ah. There."

"Oh … oh."

Finally, unusual voices were heard as if people were embracing and wailing. The two ran to the lord and helped him to his feet. They were shocked by the lightness of his body. The high window above them was smashed, and Kinugasa Kyuzaemon jumped down.

CHAPTER FORTY
THE DOOR PANEL

1

"**WALK. I WILL** walk by myself.... Let go," said Kanbei and rose using mysterious energy that could not be called actions of the flesh.

However, he took a few steps, staggered, and fell over. His legs and arms looked like bamboo poles with high joints.

"Ah! Be careful."

Kuriyama Zensuke turned around and leaned forward to offer his back.

"Lord, please let me carry you. I will run without stopping to the castle. Please hold on."

Kanbei's scrawny arms circled Zensuke's chest to clasp his hands together. He was light like a bundle of dried stalks. Zensuke looked back at his comrades Tahei and Kyuzaemon and said, "Now, we run. I ask that you don't lose sight of the lord and protect him from the front and back."

The black smoke made it too dark to see in the jail. Flames already blocked the area of the broken lattice. Mori Tahei smashed the area again with the same rectangular piece of wood.

Kuriyama Zensuke energetically ran past him through ghastly sounds and eddies of sparks. From behind, Kinugasa Kyuzaemon stood in the hot air and, in a searching voice, said, "Kiku. I don't see Kiku. Kiku."

Zensuke also stopped. He looked at Kyuzaemon, whose eyes were bloodshot, and anxiously shouted, "Isn't she outside? Below the window?"

From a distance, Kyuzaemon said, "I'll take care of the lord. Zensuke, Tahei, go ahead. Don't worry, I'll look for Kiku."

"We're off."

Zensuke and Tahei ran off. The tower had burned to the ground. Waves of fire kept coming. Throughout the castle, the spears and the long swords of enemies and allies glimmered. The final depiction of wild scuffles and strikes in battle formation between squads of warriors was the ghastly piles of bodies and the rivers of blood.

2

The distance between the castle keep and the front gate was long. Unaware of this, Zensuke and Tahei turned the wrong way. Although they passed through the inner gate, they could not find the final castle gate. Pursued by fire and blocked by soldiers, they were unable to run as they wanted.

"Halt! You're with Oda!"

A group of soldiers blocked their path with a line of bare swords. They were Araki forces crazed by death, and blood dyed their faces and entire bodies. In particular, several men ran behind them and stared at Kuriyama Zensuke's back.

"He's probably carrying Kuroda Kanbei who was in the jail. Maybe, I should take him," said one man and grabbed Kanbei's ankle, but he pulled back with all his might.

Zensuke waved his long sword and struck down the enemy behind him with a one-handed blow. The soldier screamed and his blood splashed into Zensuke's face. The enemy hit the ground as Kanbei fell off Zensuke's back and tumbled to the ground.

"Lord. Lord. Zensuke, help the lord," shouted his comrade Mori Tahei who was encircled by the enemy. His figure was invisible, engulfed by an unknown number of enemies. He fought bravely but worried only about Lord Kanbei.

At that moment, however, Zensuke seemed to be hearing the voices of forgotten sworn friends. Those were the faces of Fujita Jinbei, Goto Emon, Nagata Sansuke, and others.

"Is Zensuke here?"

"I'm here, Tahei."

Zensuke yelled to encourage his comrade-in-arms as he enthusiastically plunged into the Araki forces.

Spears flew. Battle swords were fractured. Men bit each other and brawled.

The Araki forces and Murashige's vassals stood firm against the siege. They were men who didn't discard the righteousness of "standing with the castle," that is, the best strong men.

Even with added supporters, he still did not yield. A ferocious fight was provoked by the souvenir of Kuroda Kanbei's head would be a flower to adorn one's last moment.

However, mortal combat lasted an instant. The number of Araki's men was instantly slashed. Itami Wataru among the conspirators near the castle gate happened by with a group of foot soldiers. The tide turned. Araki's warriors began to be beaten by an overwhelming number of soldiers.

Within the bloody battle, the abandoned Kanbei lying on the ground picked up a spear dropped nearby and used it as a cane to stand. His mind was not set on fleeing but on fighting. He pointed the spear tip at a staggering figure who looked like an enemy and had begun walking toward him.

He walked ten or twenty steps then fell hard again.
This time he did not rise. Blood gushed from his left knee.
Now flipped on his back like a turtle, Kanbei brandished
his working leg and the spear gripped by both hands.

3

The cold night air roused him from a brief blackout.
Having come to his senses, Kanbei vacantly moved his
eyes to the sky. The long time spent in jail endured only by
his determination may have made his way of life a habit in
him. He followed the fate he yielded to angry waves within
raging waves. How did he display hope and avoid being
pulled into the demon called nothingness? His spirit did
not lose sight of the spark of life where he pinned his
hope. He trained himself to overcome that horrible life
and his hopes until he became a man with undisturbed
clarity about his final moment and came to view the
universe and his mind and body as one.

"I ... will be reborn in the world."

Deep in his vacant eyes, Kanbei believed this to be
true.

He could see a sky full of beautiful stars. It was
autumn, and the Milky Way hung high in the night sky.

"What a vast sky."

Like a newborn, he looked with wonder at the beauty
of this world. Unstoppable tears flowed and tickled his
ears. Even with this perception, where was the proof he
was alive? Gratitude was a new source warming his tear
ducts.

He eventually realized, "... Am I riding on a door
panel?"

His body frequently shook, and he was hearing
squeaking and creaking sounds.

"Yes, I'm riding on a stretcher and being carried
somewhere. Where are they taking me?"

Although he should have been embracing anguish

and doubt, he was not. If his heart were questioned, only gratitude would be the answer. Like an ancient sage, his spirit resembled the sky, and his body felt like a favored child of the universe.

CHAPTER FORTY-ONE
THE RIPPLING HEADS
OF RICE PLANTS

1

"... **OH, ARE YOU** awake? Lord? Lord."

People approached the sides of his stretcher and moved their faces close. Kanbei shifted his gaze. The familiar faces belonged to his retainers Kuriyama Zensuke and Mori Tahei.

"Uh-huh ..."

Kanbei sucked in his snot. He knew he wanted to wipe his runny nose but was unable to move his hands.

Zensuke made the soldiers carrying the door-panel stretcher stop for a short time to ask the accompanying soldiers in front and back, "Does anyone have nose tissue?"

One soldier gave him a folded tissue. Zensuke softened it then wiped the lord's nose. Kanbei blew out what was deep in his nose like a child.

"You're probably in pain, but please endure a little longer until we reach troop headquarters," said a general he did not recognize from behind.

"While passing through the camp, vassals like

Takigawa Kazumasu and Iida Chitayu will guard you,"
answered Mori Tahei to give the lord peace of mind.

While lying face up on the door panel, Kanbei in a
terribly hoarse, thin voice only said, "Chitayu. Tired."

Perhaps out of awe, the retainer Kazumasu abruptly
stood up behind what he thought to be a seriously ill man
on the stretcher then nervously fell to his knees.

He repeated, "I am grateful to accompany you to
camp to meet Lord Nobunaga. If you wish, I will wait for
Nobunaga's orders. Because we will pass through the
encampments of allies, there won't be any danger. I will
escort you to just outside Itami Castle. We will reach Ikeda
by dawn. A doctor will be brought along. Feel free to ask
him anything."

2

After being shaken constantly, the sleepy Kanbei opened
his eyes. The doctor accompanying him had given him a
hot remedy twice to drink.

The medicine was delicious. When his tongue
discovered sweetness and bitterness, he also remembered
the pain in his body. His left knee, in particular, ached.
When he lowered his eyes to peek over his chest, his knees
were wrapped in surprisingly thick bandages. Whenever he
moved them, he felt he needed the strength to hold up the
root of a large tree.

"The troop headquarters in Ikeda is about a half mile
away."

Even after being told this, Kanbei drew a picture of
Nobunaga in his mind. He knew well what Nobunaga
thought of him until today and how Nobunaga viewed his
unforeseen misfortune.

He should not have heard anything about this from
anyone on the outside, but he clearly heard about one
thing despite learning about nothing else.

He was told the following words by Araki Murashige
soon after he was thrown in prison until he left.

"You appear to be loyal to Nobunaga but he's not buying your sort of loyalty. Rather he glares at a cunning man rich in wily schemes. The proof is in what Nobunaga thought upon hearing you entered Itami and did not return. Are you being cursed as a traitor, a schemer, or an ingrate? Do you know that Nobunaga became incensed like a raging fire and ordered Hideyoshi in Chugoku to attack and crush your father Souen living in Himeji and eradicate your family?"

Murashige planted the spirit of a grudge against Nobunaga in Kanbei's heart. Needless to say, Murashige worked hard to use Kanbei as an invaluable man in his own headquarters.

Because Kanbei was able to perceive that much of his true intentions, naturally, his only response was a smile. Somehow, he heard the facts that Nobunaga misunderstood him and without reflection became enraged; sent an envoy to Hideyoshi; and ordered Takenaka Hanbei to kill his son Matsuchiyo, who had been handed over as a hostage and whose head was seen in Azuchi. That news brought on a misery like the hair on his entire body stood up as the human feelings of a shallow man who still hardly understood his heart as a father.

"Since Gifu, I moved his heart during the several audiences I had with him and spoke from my heart, and he discharged the entire difficult situation of Lord Kodera's clan. Beginning with my father, I gambled the fate of my entire family and even handed over my son and heir Matsuchiyo as the hostage he demanded.... Even today, does he think of me as a man ignorant of the code of the samurai and without shame? My biggest regret is being viewed as a deceitful warrior."

While in jail, he chewed at his short sleeves. His blood boiled, and his flesh ached. For several nights, he resented the unbounded cruelty of Nobunaga, the general who knew nothing about the wretched warrior.

He did not lose himself in resentment but was

content. He seized on one view of life and death. If his previous rage and resentment were no more than weeds in his spirit and he didn't eradicate them with cheerful feelings, he would never reach that stage.

"To overcome the theft of my spirit, my time in the dark, cold prison was a dojo, a gift sent from heaven," he thought, "That was possible only in that place."

Long after, Kanbei himself sometimes recalled that time. Lessons for the body in the easy times of peace were taken in by a self-centered ordinary mind.

That aside, Kanbei was on his way to an audience before Nobunaga. At the pace of the servants burdened by the stretcher matching the gait of the soldiers accompanying them in front and behind, Nobunaga's face came closer to the side of his door-panel stretcher.

Kanbei thought, "This is my chance."

He may have heard various facts from Araki Murashige, but in the end, he was unable to conceal his regret in having to appear before Nobunaga in this condition.

He courageously pointed to the west and clearly yelled, "To Chugoku." Two times in his life, he may have sworn that he never wanted to see Nobunaga's face.

However, at the first break of dawn that morning, those feelings no longer seethed. He gazed from the stretcher at the ground in the dim autumn morning.

"Ah, this year, the fall harvest is good."

He recalled the happiness of seeing the droopy ears in the rice paddy at the roadside teahouse, stared at the dew on the grains glittering in the morning sun, and was struck by the vastness of the benefits of Heaven and Earth; his heart felt full.

Now in his head, Nobunaga's figure seemed no different than the droopy ears of a stalk of rice. In particular, it was clear that the greatest things are in this universe. When his emotions shifted to the mistakes committed by Nobunaga, he understood too well that the spirit of a vassal was nothing more than an ear on a rice plant.

CHAPTER FORTY-TWO
FINE WEATHER AT CAMP

1

AT HEADQUARTERS, NOBUNAGA barely slept the previous night. He knew the fall of Itami Castle was inevitable, and the outlook was the advance of his allies to absolute superiority. He determined the next command or strategy from information trickling in and kept an eye on the surrendering enemy generals. Bonfires burned in the camp throughout the night.

Around daybreak, Nobunaga heard this report:

Itami Castle is in ruins. Complete annihilation of stragglers. Under Nobutada-sama and Nobuzumi-sama, allied forces have entered the castle.

For the first time, he dozed off for a short time using his hands as a pillow.

Thus, he rose with the morning sun and walked through the camp filled with soldiers and horses. His habit for many years was to rise early. No matter how late he went to bed, the time he rose never changed.

The camp was centered on the expansive residence of a wealthy clan in Ikeda and the nearby cultivated fields. Nobunaga stood under a persimmon tree and woke to branches heavy with red fruit gleaming in the morning sun. From the distant gate with the large roofed, mud wall, the cavalry officer Yuasa Jinsuke galloped in. He kneeled to the distant figure of Nobunaga and said, "We have just returned with Kuroda Kanbei who was imprisoned in Itami Castle and rescued by allies. He is now guarded by the clan of Lord Takigawa. Where shall we take him?"

"What? Kanbei ... That Kuroda Kanbei was rescued from a prison?"

"Yessir. He's nearly dead and lying on a door panel. We also brought the doctor provided by the kindness of Lord Takigawa and a party of Kuroda samurai."

"Hmmm.... He's been jailed in Itami Castle until today?"

"Without a doubt. Since October of last year, he's been imprisoned in the castle for an entire year and, I believe, subjected to much cruelty."

"If that's true ... it's unlikely he has any knowledge about the situation in the castle."

A long sigh of shame accompanied each word spoken by Nobunaga. Deep regret filled his dismay. He was dazed for a short time and looked like he forgot to answer the man before him.

The only attendant Maeda Matashiro quietly entered from the side like he was trying to save the lord from his embarrassment. He said, "In any case, I will go and check on Kanbei's condition. I think that would be proper."

"Hmmm. Yes. Yes," said Nobunaga.

"However, Kanbei will be first if the group desires an audience ..." said Matashiro.

"Originally, he was going to meet with me. If he did not betray the Oda clan or concoct some scheme with Murashige and reached the extreme of wretchedness, it's not a matter of meeting or not meeting him, but of what is the best way to comfort him? I am at a loss. You should go quickly," said Nobunaga.

"Yessir," said Maeda Matashiro and ran off with Yuasa Jinsuke.

2

This morning amid the excitement of the winning forces, no one was thinking about the wounded on the front line and the sick enemy soldiers, but Kanbei entered this camp lying on his side on the door panel and protected by the Takigawa vassals and the doctor. Many soldiers and officers saw this, and all strained their eyes and gossiped.

"What's going on? Who's that?"

Word spread that he was Kuroda Kanbei of Himeji who entered Itami Castle last October, and no one knew whether he was dead or alive.

"Eh! That guy?"

Everyone was shocked by the complete change in his appearance. At the same time, some said, "He looks like he's alive."

The cacophony of rumors heard in the world around the time of his misfortune was recalled as if a recent event. They were misled by the detailed accounts and swiftly corrected in their minds the mistaken beliefs encircling Kanbei until that day.

Notably, what immediately came to everyone's thoughts was the problem of Matsuchiyo, Kanbei's son and heir. The boy had been entrusted to the Oda clan as a hostage. Last year, however, Nobunaga ordered his execution during a fit of suspicion and anger directed at Kanbei. His head was displayed at Azuchi by the hand of Takenaka Shigeharu. By early spring, the story was well known throughout the land and still fresh in anyone's mind.

"If Kanbei had proof and knew his child had been beheaded, what is going on in his father's heart?… On the other hand, the man whose single-minded devotion kept him loyal may not bear a grudge against the Oda clan."

People were struck by Kanbei's loyalty and escape from danger to return home alive. Thus, this danger was groundless. The meeting this morning between the man on the door panel who entered through the barracks gate and Nobunaga was imagined, and a queer tension was added.

The door panel stretcher bearing the sick man was carried in by the escorts and set down in the shadow of the broad side gate to wait for Nobunaga's orders.

"Oh,… so this is Kanbei?" asked Maeda Matashiro looking at the man on the door panel. His legs ran to that point and froze. He could say no more, only tears streamed down his face.

When he finally bent down on his knees beside the door panel, he glanced at Kanbei and, trying his best not to reveal his sorrow in his voice, said, "Do you remember me? I am Maeda Matashiro. Toshiie. Lord Kanbei, do you understand?"

Sometimes Kanbei looked like he wanted a sound sleep, but when he recognized Matashiro's voice, he turned his eyes up and nodded with a smile. Matashiro's eyes burned when he saw Kanbei's face. He did not grieve at the sight of Kanbei's disheveled hair and sunken cheeks. It was Kanbei's spirit that made him weep. A general in a military family appreciates the extraordinary loyalty in a military family from the marrow in his bones.

"This is fine.… Lord Kanbei, would you like your audience to be soon?"

Matashiro asked only this. Kanbei nodded again and softly said, "Whatever is best … I am anxious about being seen by the lord in this unkempt condition, but nothing can be done."

"What are you saying?" said Matashiro to console him and stood to listen to a message from Takigawa Kazumasu from one of his vassals. He heard a detailed description of the events leading to the lord's rescue from the direct retainers of Himeji, Mori Tahei and Kuriyama Zensuke, and was deeply impressed.

"Well, I understand your struggle. But for that alone, I feel the great joy of today.... Lord Kanbei, please come this way."

Maeda stood in front to lead him to one of the barracks in the garden. He would have liked the clan to take responsibility for Kanbei, but Kuroda Kanbei had the standing of an estranged vassal not yet forgiven by Nobunaga. This vassal received enough hatred to have the hostage killed. He knew Kanbei made a mistake. Until a pardon came from Nobunaga's mouth, he lay sleeping pathetically on the door panel.

3

Nobunaga returned to the living room. He sat with unusually sorrowful, tight lips. From time to time, the pages began to carry in breakfast preparations.

"Later. Get out," said Nobunaga while maintaining his meditative posture.

Nobunaga was a man who did not know regret. When he made up his mind, he was a man of character who did not have a dark mood that looked to the past and impeded progress. However, that morning, he knitted his eyebrows in a relentless, overwhelming shame. He admired the expression on the face with the cheeks of a mouth filled with a bitter taste.

First, his insight about the man had been wrong. The immense trust in Nobunaga as a general diminished greatly among his entire army. He has judged many people but did not conclude he misjudged this man.

Second, he had the hostage Matsuchiyo killed. He suspected Kanbei was an estranged rebel and allowed his fleeting emotions to decide. His shame was deep, and as a lord, his feelings did not match his face.

Despite this reflection, Nobunaga was seized by that introspection. He was not a man to delay meeting Kanbei and contemplate self-serving vindication. Nobunaga's spirit was always invigorated by the prospect of overcoming all obstacles before his eyes. Nobunaga was least interested in past events that weren't obstacles.

Ah, he looks weak. What is that look on his face? He probably hates me.

When this thought rumbled Nobunaga's heart, his bewildered frown was completely erased. Thoughts raced through his mind as he sat. He was human. Nobunaga made mistakes and errors. He was not a god. He was not a god but would perform the great task of unifying the country. If he blundered, he would only be stopped as a man unfit for this task. But Kanbei may come to trust him again just as heaven allows for small missteps.

In any case, compared to the task at hand and his ambition, trifling bitter thoughts ended up intentionally as a trivial matter that would not remain at the roots of his teeth. Eventually, his will and his body woke, he stood and muttered to himself, "Well, ... I wonder if he'll see me?" and walked in long strides out to the wide, open veranda under the full bright autumn sun.

How was his year in the Itami jail? Was he rescued from the battlefield? How was his health? He seemed to have forgotten everything he heard from Maeda Matashiro who had explained detailed answers to these questions.

He saw Matashiro's figure coming from far away and stopped walking like he remembered. Nobunaga nodded many times as he listened again to Matashiro's explanation.

"Is he seriously ill? ... Where did he pass through?"

"I escorted him behind the curtains on the east side."

Nobunaga went alone. Last evening, he sat in the general's seat in a meeting to hear about the war situation and meet with the commanders. The embers of bonfires scattered around the curtains.

Nobunaga entered the enclosure. Many men were prostrate on the ground about ten steps before him. The closest one who caught his eye was the door panel on the ground and the body lying flat on it.

"..."

When he saw Kanbei, Nobunaga did not sit on his campstool but froze in place.

4

"Tahei … Is he here?" asked Kanbei in a small voice from his door panel bed. He only saw the men prostrate around him.

Mori Tahei right beside Kanbei gently lifted his head. He whispered, "To pay respect to Nobunaga-sama, sit on this stool beside you."

Kanbei began to deftly move his body. However, as usual, his left leg did not move well. Tahei gauged his lord's feelings. He believed the wound on the lord's left leg gave him sharp pains and feared he'd be overcome with emotion upon hearing about Nobunaga being present. Kanbei told Tahei to forget about him and to have Nobunaga's face come close to his.

In a soft voice barely audible to Nobunaga, Kanbei asked, "… How are you?" and entwined his thin arms around Tahei's shoulders like a wisteria vine. Then he ordered, "Lift me up and set me on the stool.… And hold me from behind so I don't topple over."

Nobunaga sat on a stool then spoke.

"Kanbei, stay as you are, there's no need to stand. Please stay there."

However, Kanbei persisted despite being reassured by the men surrounding him. Finally, Tahei and Zensuke very slowly embraced him from the left and right. When he moved, this morning too, a great deal of blood from both knees gushed from his thick bandages. That quantity of blood coming from anywhere in this body resembling a dead tree was a surprise.

Kanbei sat facing Nobunaga and looked up at him from two hollow eyes. At the same time, he used both hands and bent down from his chest.

"I didn't think I would live to see you. Remarkably, I see that you have not changed.… I couldn't be happier.…

From my slight wisdom gained over the last year, I sought my own hardships and troubled others for a long time. Please forgive me."

Before Kanbei finished speaking, Nobunaga left his seat, walked to him, and got down on one knee before him.

He extended a hand to pat Kanbei's pointy shoulder bone.

"Kanbei. Today, I have no words. I was angry with you. I probably valued your genius too much. I suspected you fabricated a pretext and entered Itami Castle to assist Araki. Later, it was unclear whether you were in Itami or not, but my suspicion was not erased.... Until last evening ..."

"Everyone is exhausted by the calamity brought about by my thoughtlessness. I have no excuse."

"No, I want to apologize. Please allow me, Kanbei."

"That's ridiculous."

"Allow me, Kanbei."

"You've said enough. I don't know what to do."

"I made the mistake this time. A sage like you may have flaws in your wisdom, too. This January, I ordered the death of the hostage, your son Matsuchiyo.... Do you despise me?"

"I hold no grudge of any sort."

"It's wretched. And he was your heir."

"I recall the misery of wanting to take the place of my son as a parent ... but in this strange world ..."

"Do you think it is the fault of the world?"

"No, I do not."

"You don't think it's my fault or the world's, so whose fault is it?"

"I am not thinking about fault. I was one pebble gathered for the great task of unification of the country. No consolation is better than the honor of being noticed occasionally."

Maeda Matashiro waiting beside the campstool was

called by Yuasa Jinsuke and went outside the curtain. This morning on this eventful day, another surprise visitor for Nobunaga and for Kanbei appeared at the camp gate to seek a go-between without hitching his horse.

CHAPTER FORTY-THREE
HAIR LEFT ON THE GROUND

1

THE FRAIL-LOOKING GENERAL behaving unlike a soldier had a slim build and a fair complexion.

The handsome, young warrior with round eyes and dimples was around thirteen or fourteen years old. He wore full armor befitting his looks.

These two dismounted their horses at the camp gate. Three or four vassals accompanied them on foot. The horses were immediately passed to the hands of the attendants. The thin warrior was the young warrior's chaperone.

He said, "I wish to see Lord Nobunaga," to the commanding officer at the guardhouse then added, "I am Takenaka Shigeharu. I was granted leave from the Chugoku camp to recuperate and was confined for a long time in Bodaisan Castle of the Mori or in Nanzen-ji Temple and became very familiar with medicines. Because my health has been restored somewhat, on my way to report again to the battlefield in Chugoku, I've stopped by to pay my respects and to celebrate the fall of Itami Castle."

The commanding officer went into the camp to

report his return to Ujiie Sakyonosuke and Yuasa Jinsuke. They were acquaintances of Hanbei Shigeharu.

"Hey, why are you here today?" greeted Sakyonosuke with eyes widened by the surprise of this visit.

A doubtful Jinsuke asked, "Who is this child with you? I know he is not one of your children."

Shigeharu casually said, "You know him. He is Matsuchiyo, the Kuroda heir, entrusted to me by Nobunaga-sama. This healthy young man will be shown to his father Kanbei and meet the lord. Yesterday evening in Nanzen-ji Temple, we heard the flames rising in full force at Itami Castle and lashed our horses to hurry here."

The surprise of the questioners was laughable, but they had accepted the idea that Matsuchiyo had already departed this world. Given this unforeseen event, they embraced considerable anxiety and hesitation before showing them in to Nobunaga. They believed they asked about the circumstances over and over, but soon they seemed to hear what Takenaka came to tell them. A page Mori Ran came running from the distant barracks and said, "Lord Yuasa, Lord Ujiie show Lord Takenaka in.… What'd he say? The lord is busy, so please bring him right away."

"In that case …"

Yuasa and Ujiie following Ran escorted Hanbei Shigeharu and Matsuchiyo and timidly entered the barracks.

In fact, Kanbei Yoshitaka, still lying on the door panel, supported his body to sit up as if he had made a promise. What happened when Kanbei laid eyes on Shigeharu and Matsuchiyo's figures? Rather than penning a clumsy description, it is probably best to leave this to the imaginations of the world's parents. The truth may be more deeply felt in this way.

2

Kanbei was not a direct vassal of Nobunaga, but Hanbei

Shigeharu was a direct vassal of the Oda clan.

Kanbei followed his example and quietly sat facing Nobunaga. Hanbei apologized for neglecting work on the battle formation due to illness and celebrated the health of Nobunaga and the victory at Itami. The tone of his voice did not have the sense of urgency of a crisis. Until asked by Lord Nobunaga about the youth Matsuchiyo waiting on the side, no one broached this matter.

Nobunaga could no longer stand it and asked, "Shigeharu. Who is the child beside you?"

Hanbei's still face filled with a smile like he dropped pebbles into pond water for the first time. He said, "Have you forgotten him? Last year, this is the hostage from the Kuroda clan who my lord ordered me to take charge of and raise in Azuchi Castle. This is Matsuchiyo."

"Is this the Matsuchiyo from a short time ago? I see him, but ... didn't Matsuchiyo depart from this world? I definitely ordered Matsuchiyo's head to be cut off. I believe that was last summer."

"It is as you say."

"Then you respected my order and cut off his head soon after and presented it at Azuchi. What happened?"

"The severed head was false from the beginning."

"What? The head was a fake."

"Yes, I am prepared to take the blame. With all due respect, I deceived my lord."

"Hmm, ... is that so?"

A groan escaped Nobunaga, and he looked again at Matsuchiyo's figure. The contrast between Hanbei Shigeharu and Nobunaga was like fire and water. The eyes of the side vassals watching the unfolding of this event with bated breath met by chance on Nobunaga's face and lips.

A frown that would upset those gathered did not appear on Nobunaga's face. Instead, his face filled with a joy unable to conceal his calm interior and looked absolutely carefree. A gentle look never seen before vividly altered his eyes.

"… Is that so? That's what happened?" was all he knew to say. On the other hand, if he looked at the father Kanbei, he thought his loss for words out of shock was reasonable. The surprised Kanbei looked at his son who should have been dead and unexpectedly saw a child growing up and healthy. He was unable to become another man filled with the worldly passion of parental love. The body lying face down on the door panel writhed and racked with enough pain to stifle tears and a runny nose.

"… So what is my punishment?" Hanbei Shigeharu timidly made his plea to Nobunaga, "I perverted your command and took responsibility. That is worth the death penalty. The sacred teachings of Buddha must not be disturbed. Today, I've come to you only to ask for your verdict of a sentence of death."

All of a sudden, Kanbei unknowingly wriggled his unmoving body like he was weeping or shouting from the door panel.

"You're a blessing. Hanbei. I have no words for your act of friendship. Until I die, I will not forget your kindness.… Your precious life cannot be exchanged for the life of my son."

Kanbei looked at Matsuchiyo and beckoned him with his hand.

"Matsu, come here."

"Yes, Father."

Matsuchiyo approached his father's side. He looked at his father's transformed appearance and couldn't hold back his tears. With both hands on his face, he cried bitter tears.

"That is no way for a samurai's son to behave."

Kanbei comforted him with his mild chiding.

"Who is your greatest benefactor, second only to your parents?"

"Takenaka Hanbei-sama."

"That is true. In that case, you will listen to reason. Is it acceptable for your greatest benefactor, who saved your life, to die? Before Lord Hanbei is given death by the lord's rebuke, you will take that short sword from your obi sash and cut your own stomach and die. Your father will watch. You are your father's son. You will die so that the world will not laugh at you."

"Yes, Father," answered the youth with his eyes rounded. The strength to not cry filled his face. He took out the short sword and began to loosen his obi sash.

At that moment, Nobunaga suddenly walked toward him and slapped the youth's shoulders two or three times. For the father Kanbei and Takenaka Hanbei to understand his words, he said, "Young man. Enough. You are fine. There's no need to die. Everything occurred because of my mistake. Forgive my error. I once heard an old story from China."

Nobunaga returned to his stool and closed his eyes to the attendants on his left and right then spoke.

"There was a warlord Cao Cao of Wei. Once during a march to Bokuho, Cao Cao took pity on the farmers and issued an edict not to cut the wheat. However, Cao Cao's horse jumped and destroyed a wheat field. Cao Cao enforced his own law that he broke. He directed his soldier to cut his hair and leave it on the ground.... Shigeharu, when did you tell me that story?"

"Did I tell you?"

"My hair will be cut and left on the ground. I did not learn the customs of China, but I feel that I am the one to blame. Shigeharu, go to Chugoku immediately and assist Hideyoshi. For now, it's best for Kanbei to go to the nearby Arima Hot Springs to recuperate."

Nobunaga again called from his stool, "Matsu, come here."

While patting his head, he said, "You're a fine boy.... You have this fine father and this fine teacher. You are a lucky fellow. Surely, your future military service will be distinguished. Go with Shigeharu to Chugoku. I will celebrate your first campaign."

Nobunaga took out his short sword and placed it in Matsuchiyo's hands.

3

A military palanquin arrived at the Ikenobo lodge in Arima.

The proprietor of Ikenobo, Saki Tsuemon, gave instructions to the employees and guided the gravely ill man to an inner room away from the public eye. With one mind, the members of the household cared for him with hospitality and kindness.

For the first time in a year, Kanbei descended into hot water.

His body of only skin and bones was supported by the hands of a maid and one of the inn's manservants as if he were breakable and gently slipped into the tub.

Kanbei used the edge of the tub as a pillow. However, his body didn't seem to float.

"… Aah."

For the first time, he felt relief in his body. He thought, I am alive, and said, "This is a mystery … a mystery."

Looking back as if everything were new, he considered it all to be a miracle. Matsuchiyo was alive. He thought about that more than being alive himself. It was a miracle beyond miracles.

"Everything came about because of Hanbei Shigeharu's friendship."

When he felt that, he had to sense the favor of Hideyoshi, the man at his back. Thus, he became conscious of the meaning of the universe.

"If I take a broad view, I only think of the one who lent life to me, the one who saved one child, and the great one who is unseen. I'm alive. What command will heaven send to this body?"

Eventually, his thoughts ended there. There was no trivial love or hate or current displeasure in his situation.

He quickly returned to health; only his aches were not answered by heaven's will.

"Recovery is impossible if too much time is spent in the hot springs. That's enough for today," said the proprietor Saki Tsuemon and ordered the servants to move Kanbei's body. They scooped him up like a load into a bamboo basket.

That day, the muck did not drop off. His yearlong growth of hair was like a woman's, rarely combed, and only tied with a string.

Wearing clothes free of lice and lying on soft bedding, his body felt like it was floating in space.

Kuriyama Zensuke and Mori Tahei visited after night fell to report on the war situation in Itami. This time, without letting the enemy take a breath, Oda's army launched secondary full-scale attacks on Amagasaki and Hanakuma, two castles of Araki Murashige with reserve power.

"Lord Takenaka brought along Matsuchiyo-sama to inform Nobunaga-sama of having the time to go to Harima. The child often looked like he wanted to be by his father's side. However, his enthusiasm for his first battle was remarkable, and he excitedly accompanied Lord Takenaka."

Kanbei listened with delight to this news told beside his pillow but may have been drained by the long bath.

"I'd like a little nap," he said and shut his eyes.

He fell asleep.

He wondered how much time passed when he woke with a start, but only a soft firelight was beside his pillow. He didn't hear the footsteps of the inn workers or see the figures of Tahei and Zensuke on night watch. He only heard the sound of wind flowing through the pine trees outside the window.

I'm thirsty, he thought, but no one was around. He looked up and around the pillow and tensed at the sight of a mysterious person.

"Who? ... Who's there?" he called out without thinking. A young woman stood still across from him at the back wall in a dim corner of the room not reached by light.

When he roared, "Who's there?" the woman seemed upset. Her bright eyes looked up towards Kanbei, and she clasped her hands together.

She answered in a near whisper, "It's me, Kiku ..."

CHAPTER FORTY-FOUR
HEART

1

"**WHAT? KIKU?** ..." said a doubtful Kanbei, his eyes wide open, "Are you the daughter of Yojiemon from Shikama? You're that Kiku?"

He said this several times like he was dreaming. She answered and he impatiently asked more questions.

"When I was imprisoned in Itami Castle, were you that woman who called my name from outside the high window where that wisteria vine crept in? The time was the beginning of summer when the wisteria vine was young."

Kiku nodded, then her tears spilled onto her knees when her heart reawakened to her painful thoughts of that time.

"What were you doing at Itami Castle?" Kanbei asked like he was trying to unravel a nagging puzzle and forgot the pain of his body in his sickbed. The sliding door opened. Kuriyama Zensuke appeared and said, "Are you awake?" He carried in a tray holding a medicinal extraction.

"Zensuke? Water. First, bring me water," said Kanbei.
Kiku jumped up and said, "I'll get it."

Then Zensuke whispered, "Lord, you probably surprised her."

"I didn't expect her. Why did Yojiemon's daughter come here?"

"On the night Itami Castle fell, after the lord escaped, Kinugasa Kyuzaemon stayed back alone to search for and eventually found Kiku who had fallen into the ancient lake behind the jail and saved her at the last moment."

"Oh, … that night at that time?"

"Kiku braved flames and smoke to guide us to the lord. If Kiku had not been there, I don't know how the master and his servants would ever be reunited."

"What I don't understand is why was Kiku in Itami Castle? I just asked her but …"

"To the thirteen men who left Himeji with the pledge to rescue the lord even if they died trying, Kiku was added as a member of the rescue squad ready to face death."

"With that weak body …"

"Because her father Yojiemon is old, she came in his place and was trusted as a comrade. The silversmith Shinshichi in Itami was also a dutiful sibling. He spoke with the rebels in the castle, and she entered service to constantly search in secret to find out whether the lord was alive."

Kanbei was hearing this for the first time. He said nothing like his spirit was numbed by a strange excitement. The master and servant heard quiet footsteps walking down the hall. Kiku came with the desired vessel of water.

Kanbei drank the water from the bowl in the woman's hand, then lay his head down again on his pillow and shut his eyes.

"Everyone should sleep."

The visitors went to Mori Tahei and Kinugasa Kyuzaemon in the adjacent room. Kanbei eventually extinguished the bedside lamp.

2

After ten days passed, Kanbei was able to move by himself from his room to the bathtub.

"I want to go to Chugoku. I want to capture Miki Castle as soon as possible."

"When you get a little stronger," the vassals often said to placate him. It was out of his control.

Nobunaga inquired about Kanbei several times during his recuperation. Each time an envoy met with Kanbei, he brought many gifts and spoke gracious words "You've healed well. After you've recovered completely, it would be best if you return to Himeji and rest for a time."

Kanbei stated his hope to Nobunaga's intermediary, "Today, Miki Castle is under a long siege by Lord Hashiba. The hard fight of the siege army was extraordinary. After my recovery from illness, I ask your permission to resume my duties in the armies participating on the Chugoku battlefield, preferably as in the past."

Of course, there was no objection to that duty, but Nobunaga repeatedly inquired about him so he would not overexert.

"I'm fine now. I can ride a horse. Tomorrow, I will leave this inn," Kanbei insisted on the twentieth day. The vassals informed the inn's proprietor and asked him to hire a horse.

Mori Tahei and Kuriyama Zensuke had misgivings not only because of the lord's health but also the dangers of the journey home.

Itami had fallen, but Amagasaki Castle, the current location of Araki Murashige, was surrounded by Oda's forces, and Hanakuma Castle in Hyogo still had not fallen. Naturally, dangers were expected along the roads.

If the excuse to stop was the danger, Kanbei's disposition did not know how to stop. Even today, without saying a word, he methodically explored the situation through his comrades and looked for the best roads to travel.

They reported, "A safe route to enter Hyogo is difficult."

People from that region said, "The safest way is crossing the sea by boat. Leaving from Osaka is dangerous because of the conspiracy at Hongan-ji Temple. A fishing boat must be hired near Mikage and quietly depart."

However, judging by the rumors leaking in from that region, the dangers were extreme by any route other than the sea.

The reason is, currently, Hashiba's forces were fixated on Miki Castle; and Oda's main force encircled Araki Murashige. The surprised Mouri did not stand by and watch. Relying on their naval strength in Seto that should be regarded as unrivaled, at that moment, off the Chugoku coast, which originally extended from Osaka to Geishu, large and small military ships of their navy were surveyed, as if by their owners, without missing one ship.

"If there's a chance encounter, we will easily be slashed and killed. The lord's body still has not fully recovered. He will have difficulty making it through enemy territory with an injured leg…. Where could he pass? What's the safest route?"

This problem tormented Tahei and Zensuke until the evening before they departed the hot springs inn.

However, the silversmith Shinshichi had not visited for a while but suddenly arrived at the inn on the morning of the departure carrying an unexpected, brilliant idea as a souvenir.

It was a note from the Konoe clan. The good relationship between Akashi Masakaze, Kanbei's grandfather, and the head of the Konoe clan came to an end in the last few years. This connection was not a shallow relationship but one through the art of tanka poetry. Shinshichi had done occasional work for the Konoe clan. When the Itami siege was broken, he proceeded to Kyoto with a comrade named Goto Emon and to request a letter from the court written with the purpose of appealing Kanbei's position, being entrusted with the business of the Konoe clan, and permitting various actors to go west.

3

Kanbei was able to walk without a cane. His injured leg was wounded, and he walked with a pronounced limp.

"This will not heal in my lifetime."

That morning, Kanbei was seen off by the proprietor Saki Tsuemon and many others and walked out to the edge of the eaves of the hot-spring inn. He muttered that everyone seemed to be fixated on his leg.

The hired horse was led to him.

Kanbei hooked his hand onto the saddle but could not mount. Finally, with the help of others, he settled on the saddle.

"It's inconvenient when a warrior cannot mount a horse alone. In the future, I'll have to practice riding more frequently," said Kanbei and laughed from stop his horse.

The gathering of inn people looked up at him, and he lowered his head under the eaves.

"You have been very kind to me for so long."

Kanbei made his horse advance. In addition to the difficulty in mounting, he seemed unable to insert his foot into one stirrup while riding.

Kuriyama Zensuke approached the side of Kanbei's horse and softly urged, "Lord, Lord. Please say a few words."

Kanbei looked at his encouraging eyes. As he left Ikenobo, Kiku was loitering at the nearby crossroads of the hot springs town to see him off. Beside her stood her brother-in-law, the silversmith Shinshichi. When the pair saw Kanbei looking at them, they lowered their hands to their knees to silently express the significance of the farewell.

Kanbei guided his horse to stand before the two. The

woman remained in a bow and did not raise her head.
Kanbei's eyes focused on her like he was waiting for her to
lift her head.

"Kiku."

"… Yes."

"When will you return home to Shikama?"

"…"

Why did Kiku blush bright red? He could not see her
eyes, but she seemed to be crying. Tears rolled down to
the tips of her toes.

Kanbei did not understand the meaning of those
tears. He thought they were merely the sadness of parting.
Her melancholy was comforted by lightheartedness as in
the past.

"It may be difficult for a while, but if Miki Castle falls
and the battle ends, I will probably visit Yojiemon's
home…. But until then, you should return to Shikama …"

Now, tears ran swiftly down her cheeks. Unable to
watch, Shinshichi hurried to take her place.

"Lord, Kiku will not return to Shikama."

"Oh. Is there somewhere else?"

"I don't know where she will live but her marriage has
been arranged and she will marry."

"What? She will marry into another family? … Well,
she is of marriageable age."

Kanbei was enveloped by sadness. He frequently
looked at her. He often smelled the single branch of
chrysanthemum flowers she placed in a Tamba vase in his
room during his convalescence until yesterday. Leaving the
branch in a back room, this morning had an ephemeral
feeling. Sensitive blood coursed wildly throughout his
entire body.

But nonchalant to the end, he said, "Well,
congratulations. What family will she marrying into?"

"Originally, it was the Araki clan, but due to this war,
she will marry a relative, a man named Itami Wataru, the
son of the leader of the Itami Hyogo force who joined

Oda's forces," said Shinshichi with great difficulty as her brother-in-law. If this place were not public like the crossroads of the hot spring town, Kiku might have broken down in tears. Hidden behind her brother-in-law, she covered her face with her sleeve.

"Um, marrying the son of the general of the Itami Hyogo forces who surrendered is a strange connection. No, he's a surrendered general and will stand with Lord Oda. I am also a man under his command. Give him my congratulations," said Kanbei.

"Thank you," she said.

"Kiku, I will never forget for the rest of my life the long time spent in the castle. Marry and be a good wife."

Kiku didn't answer. She was hidden behind Shinshichi. However, the moment Kanbei's horse moved, she slid her sleeve to glance eagerly at the man on the horse. Kanbei turned around and looked back at her mournful eyes. He gently slapped the whip on the horse's belly in opposition to his heart being pulled from behind.

Tahei, Kyuzaemon, and Zensuke were also in a hurry, spoke only parting words, then galloped off matching his horse's pace.

4

The roads to Hyogo and Harima were passed with ease. The fear exceeded the danger. The safe-conduct pass from the Konoe clan was the talisman. This was taken out and presented only once at the gate for the Minatogawa River near Hanakuma Castle.

"Beginning with seeing my retired father, wife, and son at the front of Himeji, my homecoming will be filled with joy. I don't know how many days I have to wait."

Kanbei's chatting with Zensuke and Tahei came to sound like this. The expression on his face said he wanted this meeting to happen as soon as possible.

"Anyway, the man who should not have returned alive will return alive looking like this."

They conversed happily but eventually came to the area of the Kakogawa River where they abruptly changed direction.

Kanbei said, "Only Zensuke needs to come with me. Kyuzaemon and Tahei, go ahead and tell the people in Himeji that I'm safe. If Miki Castle has fallen, one of you come back."

This was the only message sent to his home along the way. He headed to the backcountry in northern Harima where Hideyoshi's siege army was positioned.

As they neared the mountains, the autumn colors deepened and reminded them of the season. The bad roads along the way had deeply-cut ruts hollowed out by carts and horses transporting military supplies. Seeing the signs of destroyed stockades and trenches at their destination, as well as, the broken swords and rusted metal helmet visors dropped on the grass, they believed a protracted, fierce battle had been fought in the area.

Later, Hideyoshi's army attacked with force and advanced to positions far in front of troop headquarters on Mount Hirai while Kanbei was there and continued to challenge Miki Castle that hadn't fallen. Hideyoshi's camp was being moved to high ground a distance so short if they shouted the enemy would understand.

"Yoshitaka has returned," said Kanbei.

"Ah, Kanbei?" asked Hideyoshi.

"I'm sorry for the worry I caused?"

"Actually, I worried for a while, but … it's all right now."

No words can describe the depths of the emotions of Hideyoshi and Kanbei when reunited after more than a year. The pair did not need many words to communicate. The article of *Mashakuki* [An Interpretation of Demons] that mentioned the situation in reality at that time provides a better description of the circumstances. The elegant appearances of the faces of these two great men were described perfectly.

Chikuzen-no-kami (Hideyoshi) met Yoshitaka (Kanbei), made his move, and slapped his forehead. The meeting in this world was a joyous occasion. In the beginning, he would sacrifice his life and go to the enemy's castle. He thanked the world and felt he should return its kindness. Chikuzen crying before and after should be remembered. Yoshitaka also welled up with tears.

Kanbei was comforted. Through Nobunaga's gracious words, through the branch of flowers placed by Kiku, through Hideyoshi's tears, he could forget everything in the mind of one man to another poured into his hands. He forgot the more than a year of terrible suffering and his body crippled for life.

"Anything for this man ..." Kanbei thought with conviction.

CHAPTER FORTY-FIVE
A BEAUTY FACES DEATH

1

"**KURODA KANBEI'S IN** excellent health."

"Kanbei has returned to camp after the battle without a scratch."

These words were communicated from dugout to dugout of the allies. This might have been related to the renewed fighting spirit of the allies who showed fatigue from the long siege of the enemy's impregnable castle. His return alone had meaning. Whether notified or not, Takenaka Hanbei, who earlier went to Chugoku with Matsuchiyo, came to Hideyoshi's camp.

"It has truly been a long time. Indeed, seeing him safe today is like a twisted rope of fortune and misfortune. No one understands the unexpected moments of life."

As usual, Hideyoshi said little and betrayed no expression. It meant more to him than the mental reality of enjoying the rebirth of a friend.

Hideyoshi held a small banquet that evening.

"Nothing has come into this camp, but if sake jars are scant, we will drink in the sentiment. It's been a while since we've had a private party ..."

The master and his two followers sat in a triangle and

talked late into the night.

Autumn was cold in the mountains. Kanbei was prudent and did not drink much. Hanbei barely touched his cup. Kanbei thought it was the fault of the moonlight reflected off the canopies in the camp, but the anxious look on Hanbei Shigeharu's white face prompted Kanbei to ask, "You were ill for a while, are you better? Today only my health is being celebrated, but ..."

"No, no, I'm the same as usual ..." said Hanbei while looking over his lean frame and smiling with sadness.

"In the end, this sickly body is incurable. The doctors have given up in despair. However, even if I live for one hundred years, I will meet hard-to-meet famous leaders. With only longevity, I will have hard-to-find good friends. Furthermore, I live in unique times and have already lived to the age of thirty-six, so I have no reason to feel dissatisfied with heaven."

Even that night, Hanbei's body was feverish and he shivered at times.

He came to terms with his body during his convalescence and returned again to this battlefield without curing his illness. He realized his illness was incurable and death was not far away. He was born to be a military commander and lamented dying on a tatami mat. Accompanied by Matsuchiyo, he went to Chugoku and took the opportunity to return to Hideyoshi's side.

Hideyoshi supposed he was a little healthier than before and was very concerned, but found Hanbei noble given his clear resignation to life and death. Hideyoshi's words were unable to move his resolved front.

2

It was late autumn. News came of a sudden worsening of Hanbei Shigeharu's illness. His camp curtains fluttered in the chilly night winds. In the hospital in Marukigumi that evening, Hideyoshi sat at his bedside where Kanbei had been since the previous night nursing Hanbei in every way.

"I think the time for goodbye has come. Good health to you Lord and to you Kanbei," said Hanbei to the men at his bedside as he became aware of his last moments. Hideyoshi drew closer to embrace him.

"The work in Chugoku is unfinished, so your leaving feels like losing light on a moonless night. I relied on you as a teacher and asked you to be my right-hand man. Are you going to leave first? You have a hard heart, Shigeharu.... Shigeharu," lamented Hideyoshi. Many direct vassals were in the adjacent room, but he did not stop his unseen regret and grieving.

Hanbei called over his younger brother Takenaka Shigekade and his page to gently raise his body. To Hideyoshi, he humbly thanked him for his favor for half a lifetime then in his usual tone said, "A man's death is like a being of the treetops returning to the ground. The dying man is said to be cruel and those left behind, compassionate. If viewed from the position of an older man of prominence, it is merely a commonplace, natural occurrence. The tears of regret now from a man like our lord are not from an ordinary lord. Especially, the great task of Lord Nobunaga is unfinished. All of your futures will probably be extraordinary. This will not end in grousing and complaining.... And after I die, Kanbei Yoshitaka will be here. To me, Yoshitaka is a friend, a samurai who truly knows what it means to be a samurai. Leave all future plans to him. You can depend on him.... By today, I've shared most of the helpful bits learned by this unworthy pupil and know I have your kind understanding...."

When Hanbei finished speaking, he looked philosophically at the night scene outside.

"Ah, the moon is bright and the wind is cool.... This world is truly a beautiful place. What will a moonlit night look like on the journey ahead?" he muttered and was gently laid on his back again. The prayer beads and sacred robe arranged while alive in the armor box were searched for and placed at his side. He closed his eyes for a while but eventually looked through narrowed eyes around the area. The word "Goodbye" seemed to slip from his lips. His pulse had already ceased. Kanbei called to him, Hideyoshi called to him, but he never answered again.

"It's a shame Matsuchiyo didn't make it in time," Kanbei repeated over and over. A messenger had been sent to Himeji right after Shigeharu fell seriously ill with the message:

> *Your important benefactor is seriously ill. Come quickly to care for him.*

Matsuchiyo arrived late that night. Mori Tahei, Goto Emon, and the others jumped on their horses to rush here but did not arrive in time to see him alive. The youth mourned Shigeharu's death as the former teacher who was by his side for ten years.

No, the death of this young, great military tactician brought sorrow to the entire advancing force.

Shigeharu was laid to rest by the whole army with the following words.

> *The dignity of this man is now gone from this camp. All the officers and men are at peace.*

His delicate body was too weak to withstand heavy armor. Paired with Kanbei Yoshitaka, they were called the peerless twins of Hideyoshi. Shigeharu was asked to carry the sack of ingenuity.

The whole army said, "I can't believe it. He was just thirty-six years old."

His untimely death was mourned, even by the rank and file.

3

At the beginning of December, the war situation on the Settsu front took a sudden turn for the worse. As expected, the superior Oda forces swept away the Araki and their accomplices. During this time, Itami still held up. Araki's senior vassals emerged from the castle and promised Oda's army that they would persuade Murashige to surrender Amagasaki and Hanakuma. Because Murashige didn't listen, he could not be stopped by the allies and plunged into Oda's forces, but in the end, he escaped.

Later, when Itami fell, Murashige knew "this place is also dangerous" and moved to Amagasaki. Finally, the hot pursuit by the enemy closed in and again he absconded from the castle, fled by boat from the shore of Hyogo over the sea, joined the navy of the Mouri clan, and begged for safe harbor.

The world smiled.

Did Murashige believe in assistance from and pledges by the Mouri and turned on Nobunaga? Although the three castles at Itami, Amagasaki, and Hanakuma were attacked and fell, he put his trust in a disloyal country that had yet to come to his aid. Still not having come to his senses, he fled to beg for protection. In the end, he was at a shameful extreme.

Around December 19 of that year, however, the world saw the last days of a vile military family. On that occasion, Murashige and his clan entrusted their wives and children, the old and young, and the woman servants to the hands of Oda's forces.

At Nanamatsu in Amagasaki, Nobunaga had the pathetic people killed without mercy. The bereaved families of the traitors served as an example to cowardly warriors. It was a savage punishment. Using fire, spears, and firearms, more than five hundred men and women were executed on all the street corners. The people shuddered at Nobunaga's ferocity. Everyone shielded their eyes, at least, to the brutality on Nobunaga's face.

However, no one placed any blame on Nobunaga. Naturally, Araki Murashige and his accomplices were reviled for being cowardly men. They were unfavorably rumored to be a disgrace to military commanders.

An honorable woman in her last moments was reputed to be the opposite of a cowardly bunch of men and women. That day, she would become one of the people killed on a corner in Nanamatsu. Despite being dropped from and dragged by a cart, she unabashedly wore a colorful, short-sleeved kimono over her burial clothes. When her execution came, "Please wait a moment," she said in a cool voice to those nearby, fixed her obi sash, and put up her hair. She gently signaled, "If you please," and achieved final moments not reached by men.

A rumor began like "That woman was probably the lady-in-waiting in Itami Castle."

A few moments after her death, two accompanying nuns received her head and kimono.

"Maybe she was the younger sister of the lady-in-waiting?"

"Was she a wife in a samurai family from somewhere?"

People actively searched for her identity, but no one knew.

They found out much later. A newcomer to the troops under the command of Oda Nobuzumi knew her. She was the wife of Itami Wataru. Her name was Kiku.

4

"Lord, what are you thinking?" asked Kanbei.

"Kanbei? Clumsy thinking resembles resting. I was absentminded until I saw an enemy castle that would not fall when attacked," said Hideyoshi.

"Recently, you sometimes radiate displeasure in silence and look up with no energy."

"Do I look that listless? ... It's impossible," muttered Hideyoshi and quickly turned his face and laughed like he was recalling his cheerfulness.

"What is impossible? What?"

"As I expected, I suddenly feel empty, I'm finding it hard to forget Hanbei Shigeharu's face. It seems like a complaint, but I grieve over the loss of Shigeharu's intelligence."

"Well, that is a worldly passion."

"Absolutely, I have that worldly passion."

"No, you say that but are you commanding me, who has no plan, to devise a good plan?"

"Ha, ha, ha. If you try, I will not interfere."

The two roared with laughter. In reality, after the loss of Hanbei Shigeharu, Hideyoshi was forlorn for a time. Whenever the opportunity arose, he talked of memories of Hanbei. It was so often, it almost became unmanly. Not to mention, Hideyoshi even said this one time, "Seeing Hanbei's death was a great sorrow to me, more than the death of the great strategist Zhunge Liang in Shu Han."

After hearing this, Kanbei was envious of his dead friend. While struck by the affection of Hideyoshi, who adored a good vassal, he wondered how great was his confidence in Shigeharu.

Kanbei made a secret vow "For a lord with one leg and discouraged, from now on, I must be both legs."

He was so galvanized he could not speak.

Now is now.

Hideyoshi's silence toward him was no doubt the iron wall of the enemy before their eyes. He urged him with, "Kanbei, do you have a device to break down the walls?"

Hideyoshi was an impatient man. Kanbei observed a reason for his impatience two or three days ago.

Several days earlier, the reason came from Nobunaga in the following notification to inquire about the war situation.

> *All of Settsu is calm. The mop-up of the Araki allies is finished. At this time, what is the situation at Miki Castle in Chugoku that's been under a prolonged attack?*

Needless to say, Nobunaga's fretting became Hideyoshi's frustration.

For a long time, Kanbei racked his brains over this matter even in his dreams. Finally, he hit on a plan and began working on it two days ago. He found the first step and came to confer with Hideyoshi.

"You must have heard that Goto Motokuni who was the court adviser in the enemy Miki Castle is in this residence," said Kanbei.

"What? Goto Motokuni is a senior vassal of Lord Bessho Kosaburo," said Hideyoshi.

"He came last night."

"Where?"

"To my camp. He slipped away from the castle."

"What? Goto came to surrender?"

"Yes, he did. He is not a coward like Araki and his accomplices."

"Well, why did he come?"

"The truth is Komori Yosozaemon and I dispatched a letter tied to an arrow to seek a meeting because the adviser Goto is in the second seat. Through his guidance, our secret meeting produced results. Late last night, his son, who will turn eight this year, came for a visit carried by the vassals."

"They carried the child?"

"Yes, a child of Motokuni was entrusted to me, the enemy. Motokuni returned to the castle again.... The residence. The fall of Miki Castle will happen in two or three days."

"Is that true?"

"Why would I lie?"

"Well, how can you be so sure?"

"There are no edible grasses or tree bark in the castle. And the corpses of horses and even the rats have all been eaten."

"Rice provisions began to run out several months

ago. The spirit of the castle soldiers is high. If struck by the resolve to die, until the castle is taken, the ability to easily harm an ally is inexcusable.... Is that being considered?"

"I cannot stand being the target of a last-ditch attack. And I've been racking my brains to prevent that."

"Well, you think like me. What shall we do?"

"This evening, I will go to the castle and meet with Captain Bessho Kosaburo and members of his clan for a serious negotiation. First, Araki will be defeated. Won't Mouri discard Araki and leave him to his fate? Clearly, I will explicitly warn him about his interests and successes and failures in order to persuade him."

"Well, what should be the argument to an enemy who has struggled for two whole years?"

"Is there anything that makes you uneasy?"

"Yes, there is."

"What?"

"A wise man is a slave to his intelligence. I think it would be good not to repeat the mistakes of Itami Castle."

"Ha, ha, ha. I, more than anyone, have learned that from experience. This time, I don't have that fear. The senior retainers, the adviser Goto and Komori Yosozaemon already agree with my opinion and through a small number of sacrifices, his wish is to save the officers and soldiers in all the castles."

Kanbei's words brimmed with confidence.

CHAPTER FORTY-SIX
THE MAN WITHOUT A CASTLE

1

THE NEXT DAY, Kanbei headed to the enemy Miki Castle as a military envoy.

Because his leg wound had not healed, he walked with a limp — this became chronic and crippled him for life. He ordered Kuriyama Zensuke to have a military palanquin built to take him to Keibin. He rode it that day as the envoy to the enemy.

He introduced many of his own inventions into his palanquin. A conventional palanquin was heavy and lacked maneuverability. He was unable to meet the enemy and move in the palanquins he used recently. He proposed a new style of palanquin that was a mix of a military palanquin and an ordinary one.

The weight of the palanquin was lightened by using bamboo as much as possible. The roof was removed, and only a deep boat-style seat remained. It also rode high on the shoulders like a *mikoshi* shrine. Two poles were carried by six men. The front pole was shouldered by two men and the back pole by four. In this configuration, the bearers could easily move forward and backward, and Kanbei riding while seated could use his spear or sword.

The main objective in a difficult situation was to allow him
to charge into a melee and freely cross swords with the
enemy.

"What do you think, Tahei?"

As he swayed on top along the way, Kanbei looked
back at Mori and Kuriyama who followed behind.

"Through the ages, this sort of vehicle was used by
military commanders in battle. I just may be a pioneer."

"That is not so. It's almost certainly not so. I heard
that long ago, a military force came into difficulty against
the ferocity of Taira no Masakado as he led the Tengyo
rebellion. They carried out a wooden statue of his uncle on
a palanquin to the front. Masakado threatened to shoot his
uncle with an arrow and chased them to attack."

"But I am a living man. A wooden statue is not a
precedent."

"Zhuge Liang was said to always command the entire
military while carrying a feather fan. He rode on a four-
wheeled vehicle and passed swiftly through the battlefield."

"Liang? Of course. But this palanquin fits a warrior in
our country more than Liang's four-wheeled vehicle. I'd
like to dash one time into a melee."

"Will this happen today?"

"No, not today. I learned a lesson at Itami. I will not
proceed with a clumsy plan a second time."

Before facing Miki Castle, Kanbei spoke with
conviction about the success of this mission. The objective
of his mission was to save the lives of the several thousand
men now on the verge of starvation in all of the castles
and to force the men responsible for the siege to cut their
stomachs.

That night, Kanbei met with Bessho Kosaburo, the
lord of Miki Castle. They met in a room of the castle
stronghold lit only by moonlight.

The castle lord Kosaburo was just twenty-six years
old but a young general who spoke frankly to Kanbei.

"There is no lamplight because we've eaten the candle

wax. Rats make no noise in the castle because we've eaten every last one."

After recounting various matters, Kosaburo made an indifferent pledge.

"In the original handling by Chikuzen-no-kami, while a pledge was made at one time to the Oda clan, we were confined here for two years rolling over in our sleep toward the Mouri. Naturally, the men to blame, beginning with me, will cut our stomachs. However, handing over the surrendered men to officers and men outside of the clan will add to their shame, they may believe living is useless, and our committing seppuku will be meaningless. Besides sparing the lives of those in the castle, if these points are handled with the compassion and the etiquette of a military family, I will bow down to your proposal."

"The magnanimous Chikuzen-no-kami-sama has reflected on those issues, but I will tell you my plan," said Kanbei.

Next, Kanbei met with other clan members and senior retainers. Goto Motokuni and Komori Yosozaemon spoke their minds and participated in the deliberations that proceeded smoothly.

After that day, three or four more meetings were held. The defense and offense of two long years were repeated. Unspeakably desperate battles were endured, then finally, the end of enemy and ally was negotiated.

2

The resolution took more than a year. Seppuku of the lord of the castle, Bessho Kosaburo, and the surrender of the castle was decided to take place on January 17.

The day before, Hideyoshi donated three barrels of sake and abundant food to the castle.

Kosaburo rejoiced, and a messenger came the next morning with this salutation.

During the banquet you kindly held last night, the wives and children, brothers, senior retainers, and

*their court ladies lined up before the lord. Everyone
had an enjoyable time and chatted about memories
from this life. Your parting on the following day was
announced, and everyone was reluctant to leave. Be
sure you commit seppuku as promised between three
to five this afternoon, the time of the monkey.*

The corpses were to be examined by Hideyoshi's agent.

The interior of the castle was cleaned by a multitude of hands until not a speck of dust remained. As the hour neared, the lord of the castle Kosaburo, his wife, and even their suckling baby were dressed in ritual white kimonos for death. His younger brother Hikonosuke and others in the family sat in the row of seats of death in the hall.

One of them was Bessho Yoshisuke as the man who initiated the events that led to today's fate in Miki Castle, but he soon disappeared.

Kosaburo was about to speak but first said, "I do not see my uncle."

The people about to die waited anxiously and wondered what happened to him, but Yoshisuke never returned.

Kosaburo told himself that his uncle was responsible as the most influential man in the clan to urge opposition to Oda's forces and brought on today's ruin through his friendly relations with the Mouri. Despite his misgivings, Kosaburo was unable to consider his despicable behavior at that moment.

In this misery, he thought that was possible. In a short time, a noisy group of indignant vassals came, fell to their knees in the large hall, and held back their tears. The severed head of Yoshisuke was set down, and the group apologized to Kosaburo.

"After seeing the incomprehensible situation this morning, as expected, Lord Yoshisuke thought to save his own life or set fire to the tower. Agitated by so much cowardice, we took this head with our hands. Please accept this apology and allow us to commit seppuku in your service."

Some men stifled tears, and others yanked open their kimonos to kill themselves with their swords.

"Wait! I will not allow you to selfishly kill yourselves," Kosaburo scolded.

"Why is my clan willing to cut open their stomachs today? Thank you for that slight boost of joy for me. Regrettably, my uncle's behavior smeared mud on the name of the Bessho clan. If Heaven sees this, Heaven will commit suicide, too. If Earth knows this, Earth will anger. The killing by your hands was not on my behalf. What you say is a flaw that should be called a crime."

Kosaburo stood as he spoke, walked out to the wide veranda, and, without a word, lowered his head to the officers and men prostrate in the garden and lamenting the separation.

"Everyone's efforts in the besieged castle for the past two years were unprecedented. We ate the roots of plants, licked the bones of field mice and dead horses, and fought. Now, that is all in the past and is certainly the glory of a military family. As the captain of the castle, please forgive my incompetence and deserting your ambitions. After our deaths, the warriors will save each other and seek their own futures. Sadly, the disgrace of my uncle Yoshisuke will remain to some degree.... Today our bodies will learn a good lesson. Fidelity to one's principles once a vow is made cannot be changed. I misread the trends over time. My destruction is due to my lack of foresight because of my youth. I am a fine example."

When he finished, Kosabura returned to his seat, immediately picked up his short sword, and cleanly slashed open his abdomen.

One after the other, his wife, their child, and his brother Hikonosuke prostrated themselves in deep red blood. Miyake Bizen, a member of the clan; Goto Motokuni, the senior retainer and adviser; and Komori

Yosozaemon martyred themselves, too.

> *Now, no one bears a grudge. My life is exchanged for*
> *the lives of many.*

These were the final words of Kosabura Nagaharu.

The death poem chanted by his still young wife expressed her joy at dying with her husband and leaving a world in which the husband or the wife usually dies and leaves the other alone.

The prepared mind of this woman was an example of forbearance to men. Bessho Yoshisuke's wife was one person who exhibited bravery at this time. Without fussing or causing a disturbance, she understood the disgraceful deathbed of her husband. After the death of Kosaburo was confirmed to his wife, their three young children, two boys and a girl, approached her on their knees, shut their eyes, and placed a sword in their mother's hand. Later, she spontaneously extended her throat to take her own life. The tanka poem on *tazuka* paper beside her read:

> *My body goes to Heaven*
> *And to my children*
> *Lost on the way to the next world*

3

That same day, Hideyoshi entrusted a sealed letter to an express messenger on horseback. This urgent message informed Nobunaga of the fall of Miki Castle.

Earlier, songs of triumph poured from Azuchi when the subjugation of Araki was achieved. The situation is described in *The Records of Nobunaga*.

> *The heads of three Bessho will be presented at*
> *Azuchi. All the enemy's possessions are now yours.*
> *Your influence has expanded beyond comprehension.*
> *Together with Chikuzen's prepared mind, a major*
> *enemy was destroyed. The honor of the bow and*
> *arrow could not surpass his bravery and strategy.*

But the eyes of the world never viewed Nobunaga's success over Araki Murashige and Hideyoshi's accomplishment at Miki Castle to be at the same level.

"After Nobunaga attacked them, the situation became bleak with the withering of the plants. But after Chikuzen-no-kami attacked and defeated them, what remained resembled the buds of trees and grasses emerging from the cold ground. What could possibly be the difference?"

This vague impression persisted with the public, but where was the root of these views?

That is to say, compared with generals like Shibata Katsuie, Niwa Nagahide, and Takigawa Kazumasu, Hideyoshi's status was still slightly inferior. However, since this military achievement, senior retainers made modest re-evaluations of him.

"Chikuzen is also a shrewd man."

At least, similar men who pointed at him and called him wily felt ashamed and gradually decreased in number.

"I want to show all of this to Hanbei Shigeharu!" Hideyoshi shouted on the day he entered Miki Castle for an inspection.

Kanbei also remembered him. He remembered the departed in his heart and proclaimed the day's event to his soul.

"This stronghold did not easily fall, so I've decided to make this my castle base to look out on and rule Chugoku," said Hideyoshi.

"No, you cannot," said Kanbei.

"I cannot?"

"If you do, you may say it's unrivaled as a fortress, but is unsuitable for transport, surrounded by mountains, and not a land for governing."

"You are right. It makes no sense for me to live here."

"Himeji Castle satisfies all of the conditions for a lord's castle."

"But doesn't your family live there?"

"No, have you forgotten? The first time I went to Gifu, Himeji was the foothold of the Chugoku strategy. I always intended to give it to you and promised to do so before Lord Nobunaga."

"Give it to me? Hmm,… Himeji?"

"Mail over the sea routes is good. Mount Shosha and Mount Masui stand behind the castle. A river runs through the castle town, and the highways … Excuse me."

"Kanbei, you have pride in your country."

"No, my pride is elsewhere."

"What? It is …"

"My noble father. My good wife. Loyal vassals. The family tradition places them together as one. Although our dwelling will move, our family tradition will not vanish. I believe the small place where my father Souen, wife, and child will stay is fine."

"Thank you. Go quickly to Himeji and build a new building for me in the enclosure."

"Until then, will you remain here?"

"Right after the plastered walls are painted, I will move from here to Himeji. Can it be finished by March this spring? I have little patience. Please hurry."

"Well, it will be finished quickly."

Several days later, Kanbei left for Himeji. Accompanied by a dozen attendants, they brought along a horse for him to ride and his usual military palanquin on the trip.

Kanbei was returning home after a long absence. Matsuchiyo returned previously. He was returning home for the first time since the Itami mishap.

Whether he rode the horse or rode in the military palanquin, an orphan sat in front of his knees. The boy was nine years old.

One night last year before the fall of Miki Castle, Goto Motokuni, the Bessho adviser, entrusted Kanbei with his son, the child of an enemy general.

"I would not trust the future of this child to no man

but you. When Miki Castle falls, each person will die along with the castle and bear the pain of bringing along innocent children to the other world where there may be evil passions and laughter. I'd like you to place him at the end of your retainers and raise him to manhood."

"Son, why do your eyes looked glazed? Are you sad?"

"Oh," the young Matahei shook his head and brusquely said, "It's nothing."

The eyes of the boy, who was rather quiet for a child, did not look lonesome.

"You can think of me as your father. The late Motokuni asked that I become your father. Do you think of me as your father?"

"Um," said Matahei while nodding.

"You don't think so?"

"Yes," he said while nodding and squirming. The boy at Kanbei's knees looked tense.

"If you go to Himeji, there are people who will become your friends," said Kanbei, but the boy did not cheer up. Kanbei understood his heart. He will be entrusted to Mori Tahei and Kuriyama Zensuke, added to the line, and made to walk on his own. He'll soon liven up and start jumping around and playing pranks with the horse's tail.

"Ha, ha, ha. Of course, a boy isn't raised in a military palanquin."

Kanbei felt even better. This orphan will be raised in the traditions of the Kuroda family. After he becomes a man, he will become a man known to the world as Goto Matahei Mototsugu. But at that time, hints of this budding sprout were not visible to anyone.

CHAPTER FORTY-SEVEN
ONE ZORI SANDAL
AND ONE GETA SANDAL

1

KNOWING HE WAS coming home, his wife, son, and vassals lined up at the gate to Himeyama to wait for him.

Kanbei's entourage arrived. His son started smiling when his father's face came into view. His wife was moved to tears. The faces of the clan members burned with emotions.

"I'm back. It seems everyone has come out to greet me."

When his horse stopped, Kanbei threw his lively voice from above the group then stiffly set one leg and gently lowered himself to the ground.

"Oh, your leg?"

The vassals stared. Many were unaware of the injury he suffered while away.

At one time, his wife had given up and resigned herself to the belief that only hair and fingernails from his dead body would return. Her husband's left shoulder drooped noticeably, and he walked dragging a lame leg. But she only saw him as being safe.

"Matsuchiyo, go to your father and replace his cane with your hand."

She wanted to go to him but instead trusted and encouraged her son.

Matsuchiyo ran to him.

"Father, give me your hand ..."

Kanbei laughed loudly and looked around at his child, wife, and the others present.

"I'm fine. That's not necessary. Even now, I intend to rush into many battles for decades to come, I won't be led with my hand pulled by a child. My walk is unsteady. My posture is bad, but that doesn't make me a bystander. Don't worry because it's all right to walk with a huge droop of my shoulder and to disregard my appearance."

Kanbei turned to the group of attendants behind him and said, "What do you think Matahei? Where's Matahei?"

"Yes!" answered Matahei encouraged by the others and speedily came forward.

Kanbei rested one hand on his son's head and the other on Matsuchiyo's head, and turned to his wife.

"This child is the son of an enemy general I picked up in the battlefield at Miki. He is not the child of a cowardly general. He is blessed with good blood and will become a fine samurai in the future. He's a little too young to be one of Matsuchiyo's friends, but he'll mature."

When they went inside the castle, Kanbei asked, "And my father?"

A slight illness kept him in bed since yesterday and he was waiting there. When Kanbei heard this, he said, "Is that so?" Without changing out of his traveling clothes, he hurried to Souen in the castle keep.

2

The grand renovation of Himeji Castle began early in February, a few days after Kanbei's return.

Hideyoshi dispatched Asano Yahei to be the magistrate. Many people came to assist.

The castle on Himeyama was originally built as the home for Kuroda Souen. As the family fortunes grew, people were drawn there from his hometown, and the castle became the only stronghold of the clan. Studies of castle construction of that era show its sole merit was not the possibility of renovation but the need to rebuild the entire castle.

The previous castle was demolished. The line of the new stone wall was built high and was beautiful. The sounds of chisels and echoes of axes at the location of the castle tower being built to the scaffolding of the tower announced to this country the coming dawn of a new age.

However, building is building, and war is war. Between the two, the ensuing Chugoku strategy centered around Hideyoshi did not rest for a moment.

In February, Kanbei conferred with Hideyoshi, sent a messenger to the Kojima area, met with Ukita Naoie in Okayama, and planned and built several fortresses. He fortified the border and described the powerful Takabata clan in Kojima as an ally then returned home.

When he returned, he inspected the construction and left again. Accompanying Hideyoshi's army, he attacked Miki Michiaki of Aga Castle and subdued Uno Masanori of Mount Chozui and Uno Sukekiyo of Yamazaki Castle.

June began with a pause in these mop-up campaigns. The provinces of Harima and Tajima were subdued.

Himeji Castle was nearly finished. Hideyoshi left his younger brother Hashiba Hidenaga at Miki Castle and moved the entire army of men and horses. After that, the new castle in Himeji became his base.

Kanbei's father Souen was an early settler on this mountain and recalled heartfelt memories. He lived in one of the old buildings until their last days there. Finally, Hideyoshi moved in. Kanbei, his wife, and his children moved to Gochaku Castle.

Gochaku Castle had been vacant since spring. Therefore, Kodera Masamoto, the lord of the Kuroda clan who lived there after Lord Akamatsu, and the elders all pleaded with their lord, "The age has come to this." They did their best not to misdirect their lord's house based on their experiences. Nevertheless, they betrayed Kanbei for Araki Murashige and acted in concert with Murashige. Once again, they changed loyalties and rebelled against Nobunaga. Their rash and disgraceful behavior was exposed to the world.

But Murashige was ruined in an instant. Miki Castle fell. And he suddenly became aware of the crisis at hand and heard about Kanbei's return to Himeyama. Kodera Masamoto had neither any real power nor conviction from the beginning. This alarmed his senior retainers who came this far through deception or tricks and opportunism. The pitiful lord is the lord, and they are who they are. Within one night, they all abandoned Gochaku and fled to his preferred destination.

"It's painful to move into the castle of the former lord who fled …" said Souen with distaste. Kanbei convinced him to grin and bear it for a short time so he moved there out of necessity.

Around the beginning of July, Hideyoshi bid farewell to the new castle and advanced his forces to move the front to the border between Inaba and Houki. Until the end, Hideyoshi was aggressive day and night. His non-stop activity and brain always marched ahead of the times.

It was September when this phase came to an end and Hideyoshi returned to Himeji. Amid the fragrance of trees, he sat in his new, picturesque castle and said, "Where will your father and wife and children live?"

"You've given me Gochaku, so they will move there."

"Ah, that's so. I've heard Gochaku is an old, cramped, tiny castle. It's a shame to leave this fine land."

Hideyoshi attached an inventory to a letter of commendation and bestowed it on Kanbei. Hideyoshi made requests and sought permission from Nobunaga through this letter.

A letter bearing Nobunaga's signature gave him land for one million koku of rice in Harima. The inventory specified land divisions inside of Fukui, Ibo-gun; Iwami; and Ise-mura.

"I know quite a lot."

Kanbei was not humble. He delighted in the truth. He was added first in a line of daimyos.

He served the Kodera clan from the age of sixteen, and his first stipend was forty koku. In his twenties, he worked as an unusually young retainer but did not receive a high stipend of several hundred koku. Looking back, since his twenty-first year, his unswerving loyalty and mental anguish at that time came to an end in the words hardship and tough battles in addition to life and death. The alignment of his limbs on his body was peculiar. Future generations could easily view him as a lucky man who had the opportunity to meet officers and warriors in a country at war. However, even in that age, living and becoming a daimyo were hard. In any case, Kanbei delighted in his honesty. He would, no doubt, rush holding this inventory and commendation to Gochaku and his father. Just past thirty, he was feared throughout the military as a brave general with ingenious plans, but his sons still had an adept parent at home.

3

From winter of that year to January of the following year, Kanbei was not by his father's side in Himeji. He took rare, personal trips on foot.

Were they excursions to inspect government function or to investigate enemy movements? His travels didn't appear to be for only those reasons. All his thoughts were traced to "Where is the former lord Kodera Masamoto now?" and he searched various provinces.

After leaving Gochaku, the only rumor was Kodera Masamoto went into exile in Bingo. However, the human emotions at the places he wandered differed from those of the friend who thought Masamoto depended on him. He also left the few servants he took with him. News came that he fell ill in Tomotsu and died.

"Nonetheless, his young son Ujimoto and his wife are surely still here."

Kanbei returned home once to obtain Hideyoshi's understanding and headed to Tomotsu.

Despite going to Tomotsu, his residence was unknown. Although he came down in the world, the lord of a castle was thought to live with three or four footmen and servants. When Kanbei went to the residence he discovered a row house in a rundown alley. Ujimoto's work had completely changed into manual labor. Masamoto's wife was carrying Ujimoto's child on her back as she washed diapers.

"Kanbei? I don't want you to see me like this."

His sudden visit made Ujimoto and Masamoto's wife apologize like they wanted to jump in a hole and cry. Kanbei was truly disheartened. He took a false step, but their human figures and the family's fortune had plummeted. He was shocked by the mercilessness of society.

"In any case, come home with me. I don't want to worry about you coming to harm."

Kanbei instructed the vassal to prepare everything so that the wife of the former lord, the son he left behind, and his grandchild could return with him to Gochaku.

Kanbei made a third plea through Hideyoshi to Nobunaga.

"Please, calm your anger and permit the succession of the Kodera clan to be inherited by the son he left behind."

Still, Nobunaga did not give permission. Hideyoshi showed little enthusiasm only for this. The reason was he was in the midst of crushing large and small, formerly powerful families everywhere. The breakaway of Kodera Masamoto was particularly noxious. He thought it politically unpleasant to allow that clan name to be revived.

However, Kanbei thought of the favors done for him in the past and did not break from Ujimoto and his family. Kanbei split off a portion of the domain he received as his stipend. Later, Ujimoto's descendants were raised over successive generations as guests of the Kuroda clan. This practice began during Kanbei's generation and continued until the Meiji Restoration.

That year, Kanbei was given an additional one million koku of rice and attached to the castle in Yamazaki. Kanbei immediately made his father live there. Souen was delighted and sensed he would live there for the rest of his life.

And to memorialize this time, Kanbei established a new military standard and a fringed *matoi* standard as their clan's emblems. The symbol on the banner had been the *Eiraku-Tsuho* copper coin as a white pattern on a black background. The previous family crest was a mandarin orange, but Kanbei changed them to wisteria arranged in a whirl.

On the day of the Presentation of the Colors ceremony held before the altar in Yamazaki Castle, Hideyoshi made a point to come and give his congratulations.

"Brave and courageous. Kanbei is in the prime of his life as am I. This banner plunging one after the other into the enemy to divide the ranks will be a sight to see in Kanbei's generation."

At the feast held later, he asked skeptically, "A family crest is rarely changed, but you have changed the crest to a whirl of wisteria?"

Hearing this, Kanbei set down his cup and recounted his year of suffering in Itami Castle to Hideyoshi for the first time that evening. Then he turned to look at the retainers, seated among them were Mori Tahei and Kuriyama Zensuke.

He answered, "So that I never forget their loyalty, my profound desire is to instantly recall the jail window in

Itami when arrogance rises in my spirit because when my body is safe on shore, I stop praying. Every day, I lay down and looked at the wisteria flowers at the jail window. They left a deep impression on my spirit. You could say they were my teacher and an auspicious omen for my clan."

If his years are counted once again, in the ninth year of Tensho, Kanbei was thirty-six years old.

CREDITS

Japanese source text:
Aozora Bunko.
Yoshikawa, Eiji. 黒田如水 (*Kuroda Josui*), Shukan Asahi,
Asahi Shimbunsha, January to August 1943.
Accessed February 6, 2017.
https://www.aozora.gr.jp/cards/001562/card53195.html.

Cover image:
National Diet Library Digital Collections.
One Hundred Aspects of the Moon: Moon over Mount Inaba (月
百姿　稲葉山の月) by Yoshitoshi, published by
Akiyama Buemon, 1885.
Accessed November 18, 2018.
http://dl.ndl.go.jp/info:ndljp/pid/1306414.

Kuroda clan crest:
National Diet Library Digital Collections.
Kaneko, Gentaro. *The Biography of Kuroda Josui* (黒田如水
伝), Hakubunkan, 1916.
Accessed November 16, 2018.
http://dl.ndl.go.jp/info:ndljp/pid/1917589.

http://www.jpopbooks.com

ABOUT THE AUTHOR

Yoshikawa Eiji (August 11, 1892 - September 7, 1962)
was a Japanese novelist and master of the historical novel.
He was born Yoshikawa Hidetsugu in Yokohama, Japan.
His father Yoshikawa Naohiro was a former samurai in the
Odawara clan. After working at a variety of jobs, he gained
fame as a popular writer with the serial publication of the
novel *Naruto Hicho* [The Secret Record of Naruto] in *Osaka
Mainichi Shimbun* (August 11, 1926 - October 14, 1927). He
gained a wider following with *Miyamoto Musashi*, published
serially beginning in 1935. A prolific author, he received
the Order of Culture in 1960 and the third Mainichi
Geijutsu art prize in 1961. In his honor, The Yoshikawa
Eiji Prize for Literature was established in 1967 and The
Yoshikawa Eiji Prize for New Writers in 1980.

From the Japanese Wikipedia page for Eiji Yoshikawa
(https://ja.wikipedia.org/wiki/吉川英治) (Accessed
February 6, 2019)

http://www.jpopbooks.com